# Cliffhanger

Skirmish Cove Mysteries
Book One

*AWARD-WINNING AUTHOR*

# SUSAN PAGE DAVIS

Scrivenings
PRESS
Quench your thirst for story.
www.ScriveningsPress.com

Published by Scrivenings Press LLC
15 Lucky Lane
Morrilton, Arkansas 72110
https://ScriveningsPress.com

Printed in the United States of America

Paperback ISBN 978-1-64917-185-6

eBook ISBN 978-1-64917-186-3

Library of Congress Control Number: 2022930580

Editors: Elena Hill and Linda Fulkerson

Cover by www.bookmarketinggraphics.com.

*FIRST STORY - NOVEL INN*

*TO BLUFFS OVERLOOKING BEACH* ⇧

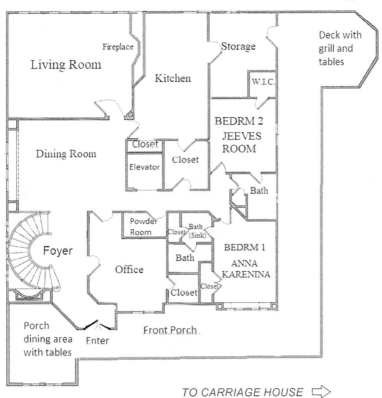

*TO CARRIAGE HOUSE* ⇨

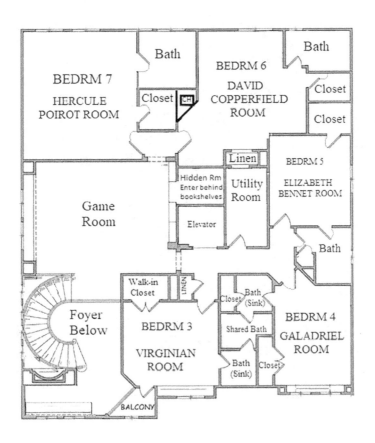

BEDRM 7
HERCULE POIROT ROOM

Bath

Closet

Bath

BEDRM 6
DAVID COPPERFIELD ROOM

Closet

Closet

Linen

Game Room

Hidden Rm
Enter behind bookshelves

Utility Room

BEDRM 5
ELIZABETH BENNET ROOM

Elevator

Bath

Walk-in Closet

LINEN

Foyer Below

BEDRM 3
VIRGINIAN ROOM

Closet

Bath (Sink)

Shared Bath

Bath (Sink)

Closet

BEDRM 4
GALADRIEL ROOM

BALCONY

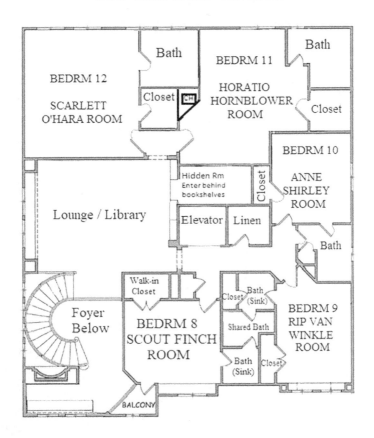

THIRD STORY STORY - NOVEL INN

BEDRM 12

SCARLETT
O'HARA ROOM

Bath

Closet

CH

BEDRM 11

HORATIO
HORNBLOWER
ROOM

Bath

Closet

BEDRM 10

ANNE
SHIRLEY
ROOM

Bath

Lounge / Library

Hidden Rm
Enter behind
bookshelves

Closet

Elevator

Linen

Walk-in
Closet

Foyer
Below

BEDRM 8
SCOUT FINCH
ROOM

Closet

Bath
(Sink)

Shared Bath

Bath
(Sink)

Closet

BEDRM 9
RIP VAN
WINKLE
ROOM

BALCONY

# PROLOGUE

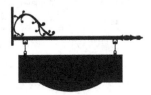

Danielle called up the stairs, "Bailey! Hurry up, we've got to leave."

Her sixteen-year-old daughter appeared in the upper hallway, pulling a wheeled suitcase slowly behind her.

"Get a move on," her mother said.

Bailey stopped at the top of the stairway, scowling as she pushed down the long handle on the luggage and picked it up by the top strap. "I'd be fine here by myself."

"We've had this conversation," Danielle replied. "It's not happening. Now, put your suitcase in the car."

Bailey's lips kept their sullen twist as she bumped the heavy bag down the flight, one step at a time. "I don't see why you have to go to Maine."

"That's where the reunion is."

"Why can't I at least go with you?"

"Oh, please. You'd hate spending an entire weekend with a bunch of women twenty years older than you."

Bailey didn't deny it.

"Come on." Danielle put on her sunglasses, slung her purse

over her shoulder, and grabbed the handle of her own luggage. She eagerly anticipated this trip. The Maine coast, old friends, relaxation. No worries.

"Hold on." Bailey stopped halfway down the stairs and leaned on the railing, exaggerating her breathing.

"Oh, stop it. You'll be fine at Aunt Natalie's."

"I don't even know where you're going."

If Danielle hadn't known better, she'd have thought her daughter was deliberately delaying their departure. She let out a big sigh. "It's a little town called Skirmish Cove, Maine. A hotel run by one of Emma Glidden's old teachers."

"Sounds boring."

"I knew you'd think so." Danielle threw open the door to the carport. "I'll unlock the trunk. You've got your phone. You can call me if there's an emergency, but I expect to have a carefree—" She froze with one foot on the top step.

Bailey reached the bottom of the stairs and came up behind her. "What's the matter?"

"The car. It's gone."

"Wha—" Bailey peered over her mother's shoulder.

Danielle stepped down into the carport and yanked off her sunglasses. Her pulse raced as she looked fruitlessly down the driveway. "I can't believe this."

"Maybe Dad moved it before he left," Bailey said.

"No, his truck was parked behind it." Danielle sighed. She should have gotten up when Paul did and seen him off for the fishing trip, but she just couldn't pry herself out of bed at 4 a.m. And besides, he'd told her not to bother. She'd slept until seven thirty. The car must have been there when he left or he would have woken her up.

She shook her head and pulled out her phone. She'd never called 911 in her life, but now seemed to be the time.

"Boxborough Police Department."

"Hello, this is Danielle Redding, and I'd like to report my car has been stolen. That's right. Can you send an officer to my house?" She rattled off the address while Bailey tugged at her arm. "What?" she snapped.

"How do you know it was stolen?" Bailey asked.

"That's the only possible explanation." The dispatcher spoke in Danielle's ear, and she turned her attention back to the phone. "Yes, thank you. I'll be here." She disconnected and searched her phone for the information she needed.

"I guess you can't go to Maine," Bailey said in a little-girl voice.

"Don't be silly. Of course I'm going."

Bailey gulped. "Should we call Dad and tell him to come home?"

"Are you joking? He's been looking forward to his fishing trip for months."

Bailey's hangdog look made her relent.

"Okay, I'll try him." She pulled up Paul's number on her favorites, but it rang six times then went to voicemail. "He's got to be out of the service area." Just what she'd expected. She renewed her online searching. "Aha!"

"What are you doing?" Bailey asked.

Danielle tapped an icon. "Calling that rental place out by the highway."

"R-rental?"

A brisk voice responded to her ring, and Danielle said, "Hello, I need a car for the weekend." She quickly gave the information the rental agent needed.

"Your car will be waiting, Mrs. Redding," the voice said.

"Thank you. It may be an hour or so. I have to deal with the police about my stolen vehicle."

She signed off and turned to her daughter. "Let's get the

luggage near the front door. We'll take a taxi to the rental place after we talk to the police."

"Mo-om."

"What?"

"*Please* don't make me go to Aunt Natalie's."

"Oh, sure, like I'd leave you here alone when a thief stole my car right out from under our noses during the night."

"I could stay at Caitlyn's. Her mom said I could."

"No, my sister is expecting you in Portsmouth." Danielle frowned at her daughter. "I don't know what's the matter with you. You *like* Aunt Natalie. She's probably got something fun planned for you this weekend."

Bailey scowled and jerked the handle of her suitcase around.

# 1

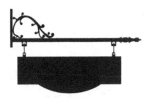

Jillian Tunney grabbed her clipboard and followed her sister out the door of the carriage house. A light breeze off the water ruffled her short hair. Walking the few yards to the Novel Inn, she pulled in a deep breath of sea air.

As they mounted the steps, she looked back and paused. Beyond their little house, she couldn't quite see their nearest neighbor's home. Only the top of his flagpole peeked over the trees.

"Kate," Jillian said.

Her sister reached the side door of the inn but turned back, her eyebrows arched.

Jillian pointed. "Zeb has raised a signal."

Kate came to stand beside her, staring past the snug carriage house. The bluff on which their home and the inn sat grew higher to the north, with the shoreline below more rugged and inhospitable. A hundred yards away, a rock-lined crevice sheltered a stream that tumbled down to meet the cove. On the other side, Zeb Wilding's squatty little house hugged the bluff like a cabin on the deck of a ship, a flagpole out front like a mast.

"What's it say?" Kate squinted at the distant banners fluttering in the breeze.

"Y-Z-J," Jillian said, reading the flags from top to bottom.

"You'd better go." Kate reached for her clipboard.

Jillian hurried along the path that had formed between the two houses when her parents owned the inn. Her father had built a bridge to span the stream, and her steps echoed as she strode over it.

It was probably nothing, but she didn't take their elderly friend's signals lightly. Zeb had been an officer in the Navy Signal Corps decades ago. Set in his ways, he refused to buy a computer and used his flagstaff to run up messages. The Y-Z flags announced that what followed was not a distress signal, but represented a plaintext message, in this case the letter *J*, for Jillian.

Zeb sat on his front deck, a compact, rounded form wearing a wool pea jacket against the early May sea air. She waved when she was still twenty yards away. He waved back and nudged a deck chair with his foot.

Jillian mounted the steps and sat down beside him. "Morning, Zeb."

"Morning, Jillian."

"I saw your Yankee-Zulu-Juliett." Not that many people could read the international flag signals Zeb habitually flew, but he'd given Jillian a list. They'd agreed a couple of weeks ago that this array meant he wanted to talk to her.

"What's up this morning?" she asked. "Everything all right?"

"I keep hearing on the news about those antique thieves."

"Yes, that's concerning." Jillian studied his face. "You're not afraid they'll break into your house, are you?"

"What? No. I don't have anything valuable."

She shrugged, knowing that wasn't completely true. Zeb had some fine specimens of old brass compasses, quadrants, and an astrolabe he'd collected because of his love of sailing ships.

"But you do," he said.

She laughed. "Oh, I suppose we have a few antiques, but most of the furniture in the inn is functional, not old and valuable."

"But you have a lot of artworks. Collectibles."

"We do. Memorabilia, I guess you could say. But most of it is modern stuff or reproductions."

Zeb grunted. "Still, someone who loved the Horatio Hornblower books, or Sherlock Holmes, they might want to steal what you've got."

"I suppose so, though we don't have a Sherlock Holmes room."

"You don't? Why not?"

She smiled. "That's not a bad idea, if we decide to change the décor in one of the rooms. Right now we have Hercule Poirot, though, and Rip Van Winkle."

"There, you see?"

Jillian nodded, thinking about early editions her parents had acquired of some of the books whose characters the Novel Inn rooms were named for, and the framed book illustrations that hung in a couple of the rooms. Those were worth something. "I suppose, to the right collector, some of it would be attractive."

"Of course it would. That's why people come and stay at your inn. They love it! And some might love it enough to filch it." Zeb made a displeased face.

"But it's not really the type of thing those thieves have targeted."

"Don't kid yourself. Those crooks will take whatever they think they can sell. And don't forget that poor woman in Bucksport. She came home early and interrupted a heist." Zeb nodded sagely. "Look what it got her. Dead, poor woman."

She studied him closely for a moment. "We're careful, Zeb. We very rarely leave the inn empty, and we keep someone at the front desk day and night." The hired night clerk was an expense she and Kate had debated doing away with, but they'd decided the risk was too great. "I really think we're safe. And we go over the rooms after every guest checks out, to make sure nothing's missing."

"Oh. Well, I guess you're doing all you can do. What about the carriage house, where you live?"

"There's nothing in there worth stealing, honestly."

He nodded grudgingly. "All right. Oh, I wondered if you could join me for supper tonight." Zeb's pink face was full of hope. His bald pate hid beneath an old yachting cap. Jillian was glad he kept his head covered, even this early in the day. His white hair had mostly abandoned ship years ago, leaving him susceptible to sunburn.

"I'm afraid not, Zeb. We have eight new guests coming in today, and we'll be nearly full this weekend."

"Wow, that's a lot."

"It's the fullest we've been since we reopened last month. But it is getting closer to Memorial Day." Every Mainer knew the tourist season ran from Memorial Day to Labor Day, with a surge of leaf peepers in the fall when the foliage colors peaked. "Maybe we can get together when things start to quiet down?"

"I guess." He was hiding his disappointment, Jillian could tell.

"Would you like to come over to the inn Sunday and have dinner with us after church?" she asked.

His expression brightened. "Aye, now that sounds acceptable."

Jillian laughed. "Good. I'll see you then, if not before." She stood. "Sorry to dash off, but Kate and I have eight rooms to get ready."

He saluted her gravely, and Jillian returned the gesture.

"Bon voyage," he said.

She hurried over the bridge, smiling.

Kate had relieved the night desk clerk, Don, and he waved to Jillian before he got in his car. Though the sisters had agonized over his salary, he was worth it.

"Dad always said someone had to be at the desk if there were guests," Kate had reminded her.

"I know, it's for their safety," Jillian had admitted. "And we don't want a late traveler to stop in and find no one on duty." So they paid Don to doze in a chair in the lobby five nights a week, and a college student on weekends. At least she and Kate were able to sleep soundly each night.

Kate stood behind the check-in desk in the small lobby, consulting the computer. "No one came in during the night, and all is calm, but Room 7 is checking out early."

"Ready to go to work?" Jillian asked.

"I'd rather be walking the beach, but yeah. We've got a lot to do."

They prepared breakfast for the current guests—two couples and two singles—and set food out on the dining room buffet.

They had developed a system in the last month. Jillian cooked the scrambled eggs, bacon, and biscuits. Kate made sure the milk and juice cooler, coffeemaker, and hot water dispenser were full, along with the covered plastic bins of muffins, doughnuts, Danish pastries, and cereal. Then she checked the dishes and other supplies. Most of the racks and bins were already full enough for today's small contingent of breakfasters.

As Jillian carried the pan of hot eggs to the warming table, a couple entered the dining room.

"Hi," she called cheerfully. "Good timing. I'll be right out with the bacon and hot biscuits."

"You realize this weekend we have more rooms booked at one time than we have since we re-opened," Kate said as the sisters tiptoed up the stairs twenty minutes later. The early rising couple had checked out with disposable coffee cups in hand and lavish praise for the Novel Inn—especially the Hercule Poirot Room, where they'd stayed.

"I know," Jillian said. "We can handle it. I hope the guests all like us and tell all their friends." They went through the second-floor utility room to the main linen closet. While they were choosing the supplies they would need, the maid they hired as needed arrived.

"Oh, hi, Mindy," Kate said as the young woman walked past the washer and dryer to join them. Mindy was a single mom with two children in primary school, so the inn's hours suited her.

"Good morning. Looks like you two are hard at work."

"We've got eight new guests arriving this afternoon," Jillian said.

"How many?" Mindy's carefully shaded eyebrows shot up. She never came to work without full makeup.

"Eight singles," Jillian said.

"No couples?"

"No, they're all women. No one asked to be roommates, but if they change their minds when they get here, we can accommodate them."

"Is it some kind of retreat?" Mindy looked from one sister to the other.

Kate grinned. "They're cheerleaders."

"Former cheerleaders," Jillian corrected her. "They were a squad in high school, but that was almost twenty years ago. One of them is a former student of mine, and she told me about it when she made the reservation. She also said she wasn't sure who got along with whom nowadays, so she booked a room for each of them, and no one has complained yet."

"Great." Mindy pulled a bandanna from her pocket and tied it over her shoulder-length brown hair. "How many of the guests we already have are staying over?"

Kate looked up at the ceiling as though the old house had a chalkboard up there with the registry printed on it. "Mr. Philson is staying the weekend. He was eating breakfast when we came up, and he said he was going out after, so you can do up the Virginian Room anytime. The couple in 7 is gone already. Mr. Miller is checking out later, and the Littens are staying until tomorrow."

"Got it."

Jillian handed her a clean set of towels. "Go ahead with Mr. Philson's room. We'll start prepping the ones for the cheerleaders."

"Most of them should be all done up," Mindy said. She opened the louvered doors to the closet where they kept the cleaning cart and put the towels on it.

As she moved away, Jillian said to Kate, "She's right. The ones that haven't been used this week will just need a little dusting. Let's start with Liz Bennet and Galadriel."

"We'll have to give them two rooms with men's names, you know," Kate said. The twelve guest rooms were named for fictional characters, half male and half female. It seemed natural to put six of the arriving cheerleaders in the rooms named for feminine characters.

Jillian pursed her lips as they walked toward the hallway. "I'm thinking David Copperfield. No one's in there now, so it's clean. What about Rip Van Winkle, when Mr. Miller is gone?"

"I like the Hornblower room better. It's bigger, and it's got that wonderful ship's cabin décor, and the telescope for watching boats."

"The Littens are in there."

"Oh, that's right."

"I was thinking we should keep the Poirot Room free after Mindy cleans it, in case other guests come in." Jillian stopped before the door marked "Elizabeth Bennet" with a hand-painted, flower-strewn plaque.

"I guess that makes sense. If a couple came with a kid or two, we'd need a big room for them," Kate said. "Okay, Rip Van Winkle it is. Just remind the guest—no wakeup calls in that room."

Jillian laughed. She unlocked the door to Room 5, and they went in. The canopied bed and period furnishings could have come right out of a Regency Era country house. This was one room that had not been redecorated in the fifteen years her parents had owned the inn, and it was one of the most popular, even though it was one of their smaller rooms.

Crocheted gloves, dance cards, an old London map, and an unfurled fan made a collage in a large picture frame. A period corset and an Empire-waist dress hung on the wall as decorations, along with framed posters from two movie versions of *Pride and Prejudice.*

The bed was ready. Kate plied the dusting brush while Jillian went through a checklist they kept for each room. Towels, extra pillows, facial tissue, bath tissue, hair dryer, coffee maker, coffee, disposable cups, shampoo, and on down the column.

Then she checked that room's special list. They always

made sure all of the artworks and theme decorations were in place before a guest checked in, so that if something went missing they would know when it disappeared. Most small items were protected in display cases or secured to the walls in their frames.

Nothing had vanished since they'd inherited the Novel Inn from their parents. Her dad used to tell stories about items walking out the door with past guests. Over the years of her parents' ownership, there were a few embarrassing encounters with departing guests, and twice Dad called the police. As Zeb had implied, some folks just couldn't resist the special decorations.

Twice in the fifteen years they'd run the place, Jillian reflected. That wasn't so bad. She hoped she and Kate never had to ask a guest to open his suitcase before he walked away.

The Galadriel Room was far different from Elizabeth Bennet. Instead of Regency-era furnishings and crocheted doilies, it held a queen bed with a carved teak headboard and frothy hangings. Ethereal curtains hung at the windows. The framed prints were of scenes from the elven country in *The Lord of the Rings*.

The dresser's drawers had carved pixie faces on the front. On the desk sat an inkwell in the shape of a curved horn, held steady in a pewter base, and quills trimmed to be used as pens. A garden gazing ball stood on a heavy wrought iron stand in one corner. The round mirror's frame was a lacy gold creation. Looking into it, Jillian could almost imagine a scene from a faraway land showing up in the glass.

"I love this place," Kate said.

Jillian smiled. "I agree. This room is perfect."

"I meant the whole place. I've loved it since Mom and Dad bought it. I only ever got to live here summers, while I was in college, but I've always thought it was the coolest hotel in the world."

"I know what you mean."

Kate was only eighteen when their parents bought the Novel Inn, but Jillian had been married to Jack for several years by then.

"I'm glad we decided not to sell it." She wasn't sure what would have happened if Jack were still alive. He'd had a good job, and she doubted he'd have wanted to move down here. But now that she'd been alone four years, having her sister for a housemate and running the quirky inn seemed like a terrific idea—if they could make it pay.

She checked off each of the artworks and decorative items. "They let me sleep in the Scarlett O'Hara room once, and I loved every minute."

Kate came to stand beside her, the blue duster in her hand. "You know, I liked having my own apartment and being independent, but I liked coming back here even more. This place was such a wonderful gift from Mom and Dad. I'm just sorry we had to lose them to get it."

"Yeah." Jillian walked to the bathroom doorway and turned on the light. She made a quick visual inspection of the spotless fixtures and the supplies. Check.

She and Kate had agonized over what to do with the hotel after their parents' car accident in March. In the end, both gave up their jobs and homes to move back here. They now lived together in the old carriage house behind the inn, which their father had remodeled as private living quarters.

Their brother, Rick, was an equal heir and partner, but he wanted to keep his fulltime job as a police officer. He and his family lived about three miles away. He'd told his sisters he would be a silent partner and help out whenever he could. So far, so good.

"Do you miss teaching?" Kate asked.

"Yes." Jillian considered that for a moment. "I miss my students. I don't really miss the job. How about you? Do you miss the doctor's office?"

"Not a bit." Kate had manned the reception desk for a busy medical practice, with three physicians as her bosses. "Give me this place and the carriage house any day."

Somewhere within the house, a door closed.

"I'll get Copperfield next," Jillian said. "Run down and make sure everything's okay in the dining room."

———

"When Mr. Miller had breakfast, he said the wall holder for the hairdryer is loose," Kate told her sister later, when Jillian spelled her at the front desk.

"Mr. Miller used the hair dryer? I wouldn't have thought it with his short hair."

"Go figure."

"Okay," Jillian said. "I'll get up there with a screwdriver. We need to keep a toolbox with the basics up here instead of having to run down to the garage all the time."

"Dad used to have one in the storage room, but I think Rick appropriated it," Kate said.

"Wonderful." Jillian rolled her eyes toward the high ceiling. "Next time he drops by, I'll tell him we need it. But yeah, I'll fix that before I start my bookwork." She kept the financial records up to date for the inn. The sisters took turns at the lobby desk and divided other chores however it seemed most practical. "You know, I think we're going to see a bit of profit this month, even after we pay Mindy and the night clerks."

Kate grinned. "Terrific. Maybe next month we can start paying ourselves."

"Yeah. We need to talk about doing some ads or something. We got a notice from the state tourism board yesterday about putting the inn on their website. I think Mom and Dad did that every year."

Mr. Miller entered the lobby with luggage in tow, ready to check out, and Kate said. "Let's discuss that later."

The first of the cheerleaders arrived shortly after one o'clock. Kate was still at the front desk, but she called Jillian out from the office. Emma Glidden gave out a little squeal when she saw her former teacher.

"It's so good to see you again, Mrs. Tunney." She looked around with eager green eyes. "I love this place already."

"Thanks, but I think you're old enough to call me Jillian now." She stepped forward and gave Emma a little hug. "It's great to see you too. Thanks for thinking of us for your reunion."

"Oh, I'm so excited about it. And everyone thought it was a fantastic idea. I sent them the link for your website, and they all loved it." Emma sobered. "I know I'm early, but I couldn't help myself."

"You're fine," Jillian said. "This is my sister and co-owner, Kate Gage."

"Hi," Kate said. "Let me check you in, and Jillian can show you to your room." They had designated the third-floor Scarlett O'Hara Room, one of their largest and most glamorous units, for Emma. After all, she had brought them this onslaught of business.

While Jillian continued to chat with Emma, Kate ran her credit card and programmed a key card for Scarlett O'Hara, Room 12.

"Here you go." She handed the key to Emma. "Jillian will take you up in the elevator."

"Oh, wow. An elevator, in this old house?" Emma turned wide-eyed to Jillian.

"Yes, our parents had it put in about fifteen years ago," Jillian said. "It's a huge help, especially for the third-floor rooms and heavy luggage."

They wheeled Emma's bags around the corner, still laughing and chattering. Kate smiled and sat down on the stool they kept handy for whoever manned the desk. Jillian had taught Emma her first year as a teacher. At twenty-two, she wasn't all that much older than her high school students that year.

Emma had moved away after her freshman year, when she'd taken Jillian's English class. She spent her last three years of high school in Augusta, at Cony High. It was there she became a cheerleader and got to know the other members of the squad. Kate reflected that if all eight former cheerleaders were as enthusiastic as Emma, they might be in for a raucous weekend.

Two more women walked in the front door, and Kate stood and smiled.

"Welcome to the Novel Inn. I'm Kate. May I help you?"

By the time she had checked in Alicia Boyken and Patrice Flynn, Jillian had returned and was ready to help them move their luggage to the Elizabeth Bennet and Galadriel Rooms, on the second level.

"You have Wi-Fi, right?" Patrice asked as they turned the corner.

"We sure do," Jillian said heartily.

———

Danielle Redding jammed on the brakes and squinted at the GPS screen on her phone. Where on earth was this thing taking her? She ought to have been at the hotel by now. She pulled the phone from the cupholder and studied it for a moment.

"Better turn around. Just great!" She shook her head. "Shoulda made sure this car had a built-in GPS before I took it." Her whole day had been like this, from the moment she'd opened the door and realized her car had been stolen.

With a sigh, she inched down the road in the heavy shade, looking for a place to turn around. A small bridge with concrete sides appeared ahead. Not a good place to try to maneuver. She thought she caught a whiff of sea air, which was maddening—to be able to smell the ocean but not see it. She had to be close. Emma had said the hotel was right on the shore.

Past the bridge, she found a small, grassy lane leading off into what looked like a hayfield. She turned the unfamiliar car around laboriously, trying to watch both ways before backing out onto the road again. How did she get in such an isolated place, anyway?

Relieved to be safely on the pavement once again and headed back toward the last turn she'd taken—the *wrong* turn, she was sure—she settled into the seat and looked forward.

Something smashed into the windshield, jarring the whole vehicle and shattering the glass. She slammed forward, and whiteness enveloped her.

# 2

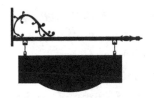

Seven of the cheerleaders arrived at the inn by four thirty, and a giddy catch-up session was under way in the first floor living room, where the large windows offered a breathtaking view of the bay. Kate had suggested they wait there for the last straggler—the former head cheerleader, Danielle Redding. The sisters agreed the living room was a better place for them to congregate than the second-floor game room, just outside quiet Mr. Philson's door, or the library one flight above.

Jillian came out of the office, where she had paid Mindy her hourly wages for the week.

"'Bye, Mindy," Kate called to the maid, just as the women in the living room broke into a lively cheer for the Cony High Rams. "Man, they're loud," she told Jillian in a stage whisper.

"You said it. They sound like a bunch of sixteen-year-olds."

"I guess that's what they want this weekend," Kate said with a shrug.

"Yeah, I get that feeling. It's a real getaway, from their jobs, families ... everything." Jillian peered through the dining room toward where the women were lining up in a formation they had used on the sidelines at high school football games. "They asked me to make them a reservation for dinner, so I set them up at Sheldon's Seafood."

"Good choice. It's close, and the food's great."

"Oh, by the way," Jillian said in a confidential tone, "Heather Saxon complained about the Anne Shirley Room."

Kate bristled. "Whatever for? That's a charming room!"

"Yeah, but she wanted something more glamorous that didn't have a children's book theme."

"Oh, good grief." Kate rolled her eyes.

"It's okay," Jillian said. "Emma's switching with her."

"What? You gave the complainer Scarlett O'Hara?" That didn't seem right.

"Emma offered. She was very gracious, and Heather jumped at it when she saw the room."

"I'll bet she did." Kate shook her head. "That was your perk for Emma."

"It's all right. Really. Emma, it turns out, has a thing for Green Gables, and she read the whole series when she was a kid. She loves the Anne Shirley room." Jillian walked over to the double front door and peered out. "No sign of the last one."

"Well, I'm holding the Anna Karenina room for her." The ground floor room would be easy to settle the latecomer into with her luggage. Kate looked at the clock. "It's after five. What time's the dinner reservation?"

"Six." Jillian frowned as another robust cheer broke out. "Who's sleeping right above Mr. Philson?"

Kate checked her roster. "Uh, that would be Bobbi Talbott, in Scout Finch."

"Right. Maybe we should ask her to please keep it down. You know Mr. Philson likes peace and quiet."

"Yeah, we should request that any midnight gab fests be

held toward the back of the house. I hope they'll respect the rule for quiet hours after ten o'clock."

Emma and Alicia Boyken, whose long, blond hair was intricately braided, came through the dining room toward them.

"We're a little concerned about Danielle," Emma said. "Alicia and I have both tried to call her and text her, but we haven't heard anything from her."

"She's probably just running late." Jillian gave them a brilliant smile. "Isn't she coming in from Massachusetts?"

"Yes, Boxborough," Emma said. "She moved down there a couple years after she got married. But still, she told us she'd be here before this."

Alicia pushed back a lock of hair. "Danielle was always resourceful. I'm surprised we haven't at least heard from her."

"Let's give her a little longer. Can we serve you ladies some iced tea while you wait for her?"

"That'd be great," Alicia replied.

———

A searing headache pounded Danielle's skull, and her cheeks stung. She put a hand to her temple and when she drew it away, she felt stickiness. Blood. It took her a minute to realize she was in the rental car.

With a ragged breath, she blinked and looked around. Everything looked odd. White powder. The steering wheel wasn't right. That was it, the airbag had deployed. She lifted her head and stared at the shattered windshield. What on earth had she run into? She could make out trees outside—maples, she thought, and a few pines. Movement in the rearview mirror caught her eye.

Someone pounded on her side window, and she jumped

away from it, sending a dart of pain through her head. A man was bending down and peering at her.

"Are you okay?" He yanked the door open. "You have your seatbelt on. Good. Can you unbuckle it?"

"What happened?" Danielle could barely hear herself, and her voice sounded strange.

"You hit a tree."

She frowned and looked at the windshield. A tree did that? Why wasn't the front of the car wrapped around it?

"Come on, let me help you." He reached over her, groping for the seatbelt release.

"I—" She sighed and let him find it then haul her out of the compartment. Weariness settled on her, and when he pulled her to her feet she nearly collapsed.

"Easy, now." He guided her a few shaky steps and opened the door on another vehicle. A pickup truck. White, like her rental car.

Danielle wasn't sure she could climb up into the cab, but he gave her a solid boost and then buckled her in.

"My purse," she said.

A moment later, he set her leather bag beside her right foot then went around the truck and vaulted into the driver's seat. He started the engine and headed off down the road. She tried to turn her head and look back at the car, but it hurt to do that, so she faced forward and concentrated on breathing.

After a few minutes, he turned onto another road. They were still in the country. Maine. She was in Maine, she was sure of that.

She tried to focus on the driver. "Who are you?"

The man glanced her way. "How you doing now?"

"Not good. I—I guess I crashed."

The fiftyish, brown-haired man threw her another quick look. "Yeah, you had an accident."

She closed her eyes. "Something hit me. My car, I mean." He didn't respond, and she blinked at him. "What's your name?"

"Uh, I'm Bob."

"Where are you taking me?"

"I'm taking you to the hospital in Bucksport. You look pretty shook up, so I thought you needed to see a doctor."

"Bucksport? No, I'm supposed to be in ... in ..." She frowned, and that hurt too. "Skirmish Cove, that's it. Are we near there?"

"Well, yeah." He pulled up at a stop sign and looked over at her. "There's no hospital, though. It's a little tiny town."

"Take me to the hotel."

"What hotel?"

"Uh ..." She leaned back against the headrest. "Am I bleeding?"

"A little, but I don't think it's bad. You hit your head, though. You ought to be looked at."

"Just take me to the hotel. I'm supposed to be there." Once she connected with the squad, they'd help her. Gingerly, she probed the sore spot on her temple. It didn't seem to be actively bleeding, just tacky. A Band-aid would fix that. But her head ached, and she felt a little woozy. Probably her blood sugar. "I need something to eat," she muttered.

"Huh?" He peered at her. "What did you say?"

"Oh, nothing, I just need something to eat. A candy bar —anything."

He frowned. "Let's get you to a doctor."

They were driving past picturesque homes now, on a very rural road—little saltboxes and Cape Cods.

"Aren't we in Skirmish Cove?"

"We were—well, we were near there. But I really think you need a doctor."

She frowned at him. If he was that sure she needed medical attention, why hadn't he called an ambulance? A wave of panic hit her. Where was her purse? She patted around herself on the seat frantically.

"What?"

She pulled in a shallow breath. "Where's my—Oh, there it is." Her leather bag was cuddled up to her foot on the floor, right where he'd put it. She bent to retrieve it. "I need to call —" She paused, groping for the name. "Emma. I should call Emma."

He kept driving.

Danielle unzipped the bag and rummaged in it, methodically at first, then in a frenzy. Her breath came faster, and her pulse raced.

"It's gone."

"What?"

"My phone."

"Are you sure?"

"Yes. Look, I don't care about hospitals. Take me to Skirmish Cove. I'm supposed to meet someone at a hotel there."

He hesitated, his foot hovering on the brake pedal. "I don't know ..."

"Please! Look, you know I was in a wreck. The driver's not supposed to leave the scene, are they?"

"But you were hurt."

"Take me back!" Her head swam.

He eyed her uneasily. "Okay, lady. Calm down."

She tried to catch a deep breath as he found a driveway and turned the car around.

"Do you have a cell phone?" she asked once they were pointed back the way they'd come. The trees alongside the road swirled.

"No, I ..."

She rolled her eyes and winced.

"What's the hotel's name?"

She swallowed hard. "I'm trying to remember."

"I don't live in Skirmish Cove, but I think there's a few. They get a lot of tourists this time of year."

Danielle's head hurt from her efforts at concentration. "Something Hotel. Or Motel. No, that's not right. I didn't make the reservation. My friend did. But it's some storybook hotel, something like that."

He shook his head. "Never heard of it. Look, I have a friend who lives a couple miles from here. Why don't I take you to his house, and he can help you out. He'll have a phone book and a computer. He can help you—"

"No." She definitely felt unsafe, with the stranger blithely trying to talk her into going to yet another strange man's house. "No, I need to find my friends right away."

He came to another stop sign, and off to the left sat a gas station. She could get out and walk over there—the owner could probably help her. She swiveled her head slowly. To the right she could see several more businesses—a seafood place, a grocery store, and—

"There's a motel down there."

He looked where she pointed. "You think that's the one you want?"

"I don't know. Just take me there, okay? If it's not the right one, I'll figure it out."

A minute later, he drove slowly into the motel's parking lot. It didn't look very inviting, though the neon sign said *Vacancy*. The red paint of the office building was peeling, and the line of one-story units looked bleak and definitely no-frills.

"You want me to go in with you?"

"No," she said quickly. "This is fine. Thank you very much."

"Oh, you're welcome. I wish I could've done more."

The look in his eyes as he said it made her shiver. She fumbled with the door handle and eased down onto the pavement. The pickup was higher than the vehicles she was used to. She staggered, nearly falling, but caught herself on the edge of the door.

"You sure you're okay?"

Danielle pulled in a breath and blinked a couple of times until the world stopped spinning.

"Yeah. Thanks." She remembered to grab her purse then shut the door and headed slowly for the office. When she reached the door, she turned and saw him still watching her. At once he put the truck in gear and drove to the exit, spraying a little gravel.

A white pickup, she told herself. What make? It was too late to tell as he pulled out and headed on down the road. She gave herself a mental kick, wishing she'd gotten more than his first name. A license plate number, for instance. Oh, well.

Her legs felt like rubber as she wrestled the door open and went inside. A heavyset young man rose from a stool behind the counter.

"Can I help you, ma'am?"

"I—yes. I—" A wave of dizziness hit her. Was it her blood sugar or the bang on the head?

"Are you okay?" he was staring at her head.

"Oh, yeah, just a little bump."

"Do you want a room?"

She grabbed the edge of the counter. "I need to sit down."

"Yes, ma'am. There's a chair right over there. I can check you in and take you right to the room, if you need to rest."

The searing pain in her head was nearly unbearable now. "Maybe that's best." She sidled over to a plastic chair and sank into it.

"Your name?"

"Danielle Redding."

"Do you have a credit card?"

"Uh, yes." She dug into her bag and pulled out her wallet. Trying to suppress a groan, she rose and walked stiffly to the counter. She opened the wallet and squinted at it. Which side were her credit cards on?

She realized the desk clerk was looking at her billfold, which held several hundred dollars in cash. She'd wanted to be prepared to spend a bit this weekend without the bother of credit card bills later.

"Uh, how about if I pay in cash?"

"Well, we're supposed to take a credit card, just for security. Do you have one?"

"Yes." She found them—a plastic sleeve with four cards—and eased out the one she used most.

After he'd run it through the scanner below the counter, he said, "Okay, Unit 14."

"Do you have vending machines?" she asked.

"Yes, right over there." He pointed to his right, and she followed his gaze. A small alcove held three upright machines.

"Thanks."

He returned her Visa and gave her a room key card. Danielle walked slowly to the vending machines and scanned them. Food. She needed something.

She picked a chocolate bar and a can of Pepsi. Was there anything with protein? She spotted a pack of cheese crackers with peanut butter and selected it. They all fell into the machines' trays, and she stuffed them into her roomy purse. Where could her phone be? Back in the wrecked rental car, no doubt, along with her suitcase and her glucose monitor.

She started to turn toward the desk again, to ask for help finding the other hotel's name and address. Without her smart phone, she didn't have Emma's number, or any of the cheering squad's. Her head pounded.

The clerk was watching her with an air of suspicion. He hadn't asked for her license plate number, or if she had luggage, for which she was glad. Best to get right to the room and get the glucose inside her. She'd grab a nap and then sort it out. She turned on wobbly legs toward the door.

———

The seven women stayed somewhat calm for an hour. Though they were subdued, Jillian felt a storm of emotion hovering, about to break. She was out of ideas when Emma approached, her brow furrowed. "Do you think we should go to the restaurant?"

"That's probably a good idea," Jillian said. "I'll call Sheldon's and tell them you're on your way. When Danielle gets here, we'll send her over."

Emma's brow cleared as she made the decision. "Okay, thanks. It's getting kind of tense in there, and I think everyone needs a distraction. But I admit, I'm worried about Danielle."

"When did you last hear from her?" Jillian asked.

"Alicia talked to her this morning. She said she was almost ready to leave Boxborough, and she'd be here in plenty of time. She was detouring to her sister's house in Portsmouth, but unless she stayed there several hours, I don't know why she's this late."

Jillian couldn't understand it either. Any competent driver leaving Boxborough, Massachusetts, before noon would have reached the destination by now. And if she'd been delayed, shouldn't Danielle have let her friends know?

Emma grimaced. "Alicia and I have both tried calling and

texting, but Danielle hasn't responded. That's not like her. I don't suppose there's anything you can do?"

"Well ..." Jillian glanced at Kate. "Our brother is a policeman. I could call him and ask if he's heard any accident reports or anything like that."

"Would you? I'd feel better." Emma's green eyes were practically pleading.

"Sure," Jillian said. "Why don't you all get your jackets and head out. You can walk to the restaurant easily. We'll give Rick a call."

Kate went with Emma to spread some calm and assure the women they would soon be reunited with Danielle. While they went to get their coats and purses, Jillian gave Rick a quick call and told him about their missing guest.

"Everyone's really worried about her. If you could just check on traffic reports, or whatever it is you do ..."

"Okay, I'll check reports for I95 and Route 3," her brother said.

As she thanked him and hung up, the cheerleaders entered the lobby with Kate, who gave them directions to the restaurant. They saw all seven out the door, and the inn seemed tranquil. Jillian went into the office and sat at her desk, and Kate came to the doorway.

"Did you get Rick?"

Jillian nodded. "He said he'll do some checking and let us know if he hears anything."

They didn't want to leave the front desk unattended in case Danielle arrived, so Kate fixed supper plates for them in the kitchen and carried them out to the lobby.

Jillian smiled ruefully when she saw the leftover spaghetti and garlic bread. "Thanks. We eat over here more than we do at our house."

"I don't mind." Kate pulled over a chair from beneath the

curved stairway and sat down with her plate. "I really thought she'd show by now."

Their other three guests were all in for the night, and quiet had settled over the inn when the cheerleaders returned around ten o'clock. They seemed in good spirits, and Jillian guessed some of that came from a couple of cocktails apiece.

"Any word from Danielle?" were Emma's first words as she came through the door.

"No. Sorry." Kate looked past her as the front door opened again. "Rick." She looked around, her gaze landing on her older sister.

Jillian's heart sank. Rick wouldn't have driven over if he had no news. She stepped forward and held up both hands.

"Ladies, this handsome gentleman in uniform is our brother, Rick Gage. I know you're all anxious about Danielle, so let's give him our attention. Rick, tell us what you know."

Rick drew in a deep breath. His face was somber, and Jillian didn't like that. He'd probably planned to talk to her and Kate privately, not face the cheering squad.

"I do have a little news," he said, looking around at the anxious faces. "I don't know yet whether it has anything to do with your friend or not, but a rental car was found abandoned on the outskirts of Skirmish Cove. The county sheriff's office is handling it. I'm headed over there now, and I'll call when I have anything one way or another. I don't want to upset anyone, but it's possible this car was rented to Danielle Redding."

# 3

Alicia gasped and stepped forward, pushing the others aside.

"Officer, Danielle told me she rented a car this morning." Her face was pale, and Jillian hurried to her side.

"Are you all right?" Jillian touched her coat sleeve gently.

"Yes, thank you." Alicia's contorted features said otherwise.

Rick took out his notepad and looked toward Jillian apologetically. "I only stopped in because you were on my way to the scene."

Jillian understood. He didn't want to be delayed here and probably wished he had simply phoned her, rather than coming here and upsetting all the guests. But then, he might not have gleaned this bit of information.

He shifted his gaze to Alicia, who was tall, blond, and had flawless skin. She would have made a perfect cheerleader back in the day, Jillian thought.

"Your name?" Rick asked.

"Alicia Boyken."

"Could you tell me exactly what she said, please?"

"She called me this morning, before she left Boxborough. She said she had to get a rental car, and then she was going to take her daughter someplace. Then she'd head up here. But she was sure she'd get here before five o'clock."

"And you haven't heard from her since?"

"No, none of us have, and we've tried."

Rick scribbled notes as she talked. "Do you know what company she rented the car from?"

"No. I don't think she'd set it up yet when I talked to her."

"What time was that?"

Alicia frowned, fingering the end of her golden braid. "Nine thirty? Ten, maybe."

"All right, thanks. Our department has traced the plate number, and it's my understanding that the car in question was rented in Massachusetts. But the officer on the scene hadn't found the driver or the rental agreement when he called it in. A resident reported the accident after she found the abandoned car, but there was no sign of the driver. Did Ms. Redding say why she had to get a rental?"

"No, I don't think she did," Alicia said. "I assumed her car was out of order."

"Okay. This is helpful. You'll be here all night, Ms. Boyken?" Rick asked.

"Yes. We all will be." Alicia waved vaguely at the other six women in her group. She gave Rick her cell phone number.

"Can anyone else add anything to that?" He looked around at all of them. "Anybody else talk to Ms. Redding today?"

Emma Glidden stepped forward. "Several of us sent her texts and tried to phone her, but she didn't answer any of them."

"All right, I'll get going."

Jillian nodded. "Thanks, Rick. We'll be waiting for news."

Kate, who still sat on the stool behind the desk, threw Rick a bleak look as he hurried out the door.

"I don't think I can sleep, not knowing what's happened to her," said a woman with long, frizzy brown hair.

Jillian forced a smile. "Maybe you ladies would like to move into the living room."

"Sure," Kate said. "We can bring you some coffee or—or—"

"Hot cider," Jillian said quickly.

"That sounds wonderful," said Gwen Vale, a woman with a slight build whose auburn hair helped Jillian remember that she was staying in the Copperfield room.

Kate helped her fix the hot drinks and carry trays to the living room. They had lit a fire in the fieldstone fireplace, and several of the women pulled their chairs close to the blaze, but the mood remained somber.

"I hope she's all right and doesn't have trouble with sugar," said Bobbi Talbot, the woman whose long hair bushed out around her shoulders. "You don't want to mess with that."

Jillian stopped in front of her with the coffee tray. "What do you mean?"

Bobbi reached for a mug of coffee and a sweetener packet. "Thanks. Alicia was just saying that Danielle has blood sugar troubles."

"That's right, she's a Type 1 diabetic." Worry lines creased Emma's forehead. "I'd forgotten that. She always took insulin and her monitor to the away games in case she had an incident."

"I remember that. She was always pricking her fingers," dark-haired Heather Saxon said. Jillian had pegged her as the group's troublemaker. She had complained about her room until Emma switched with her, and she seemed inclined to whine a little when the spotlight veered off her.

"Well, it's necessary," Alicia said. "Type 1 diabetes is when your body doesn't produce enough insulin, so Danielle used that monitor to tell her when blood sugar levels were too high."

"Do you know if she wore a medical alert bracelet or pendant?" Jillian asked.

"I'm not sure," Alicia said. Now she and Emma both looked worried.

"I just wish she'd get here so we can do all the things we had planned," Heather muttered.

Silence fell over the group. After a few seconds, Heather apparently noticed the strained quiet.

"Not that I want her to be sick," she said hastily. "I hope she's okay, and she gets here and has fun with us, that's all."

Jillian took a few steps to the next pair of seated women. "Would you like coffee or cider, Bobbi? Gwen?"

"Thanks." Bobbi took a coffee mug from her tray.

"I'll have the cider," Gwen said with a smile. "It's clever of you to learn all our names so fast, Jillian."

"She's a teacher. They're born with that talent," Emma said, and they all chuckled.

Patrice Flynn passed on a hot beverage and stood. "I'm going up to my room and call home. This whole thing makes me want to touch base with Ned and the kids."

"Me too." Rachel Barker, a beauty with a dark complexion and midnight eyes, pulled out her phone and got to her feet. She was the shortest of the cheerleaders, and earlier the others had teased her about always being the one at the top of the pyramid. "I'm going to call Tom."

"Are you coming back?" Heather asked.

"I don't think so. Good night."

The others called good night to Rachel and Patrice and sipped their drinks, talking in low tones. One by one, they trailed off to their rooms.

"Well, I guess we don't have to worry about them keeping the other guests awake," Kate said to Jillian as the last two went up the stairs.

"Yeah." Jillian let out a deep sigh. "I'm exhausted. And worried."

"Me too." Kate went over to the stool behind the front desk. "Why don't you go next door and get to bed? I'll wait for Andy."

Andy Cummings was their weekend night clerk. Jillian wished suddenly that Don was scheduled for tonight. At two hundred twenty-five pounds and six feet tall, Don looked solid and no-nonsense. Andy, on the other hand, was a long-haired twenty-year-old student, slender and bookish. Not that she expected any trouble, but Jillian felt uneasy with the turn events had taken.

"Okay. I'll check the downstairs windows and go out the back. Zeb mentioned those antique thefts this morning. We want to make sure we lock up tight every night."

She went through the dining room first, checking the slide lock on each window, then into the living room. Her phone rang, and she yanked it from her pocket. "Rick," she said after a glance at the screen. "What have you found out?"

"Hi, Jill. The rental car was involved in a one-car accident. It was severe enough to deploy the airbags, but the driver has apparently left the scene. The sheriff's department hasn't found him or her yet."

"You mean ..."

"Nobody's in the car or nearby. It's in an isolated spot, on Heston Mills Road. We're looking for the driver now."

Jillian swallowed hard. "Is it Danielle's rental?"

"I don't know for sure yet. We haven't been able to get through to the company."

"What would she be doing out there? It's not on her route from the highway to here."

"Don't know that either," Rick said. "The sheriff's sending more men out to search for the driver. We'll look along the road, but it's possible they were picked up by a passerby."

"Or carjacked by an axe murderer."

"Let's not get dramatic."

"Easy for you to say." Jillian drew in a breath. "Rick, I'm worried about Danielle. We all are."

"I know. We're trying to borrow a K-9 unit. We've got the name of the rental company that owns the car. This is between you and me, but they have a branch in Boxborough, where Danielle is from. I'm not sure this car was rented there, though. I tried to call them, but they don't open until eight in the morning, so I'll call them then."

"Don't they have a twenty-four-hour number?"

"We're working on that. So far we haven't reached anyone who can help us."

"Okay, did you find anything else?"

"I shouldn't discuss that, Jill."

"Oh, come on. We've got seven women going nuts on us here." Jillian believed in logic and reason, but she wasn't above a little exaggeration to get information out of her little brother.

Rick sighed. "You can't tell them I found a cell phone in the car."

"Is it Danielle's?"

"I don't know yet. We want to check for fingerprints before we do anything else."

"Okay, that's good." Jillian's mind raced. If Danielle had met with foul play, someone else might have touched her cell phone.

"After we do that, we'll see if we can unlock it and check the contacts and recent calls and texts."

"Oh, yeah." She hadn't thought about the phone having security measures. "What if you can't?"

"Then we can't. So this could take a while," Rick said. "We're having the car towed to the police garage."

"Not the county sheriff's?"

"We're closer, and they're happy to have us take this one, since it could involve a serious injury. I'll let you know what progress we make in the morning."

"Thanks."

"No prob."

"Oh, Rick, wait a minute!"

"What?" His impatient tone was obvious.

"One of the guests told us a few minutes ago that Danielle Redding is diabetic."

"So that would explain the glucose monitor and insulin supply we found in the suitcase."

"There was a suitcase?" Jillian almost yelled.

"Yeah. In the trunk. No luggage tag, though. Look, Jill, we don't know it was her, okay? You can't tell those women about it until we know something solid."

"All right. Thanks, Rick."

Jillian put her phone to sleep and went to the lobby to fill Kate in. To her surprise, she heard voices overhead when she passed through the dining room. Apparently some of the cheerleaders had stopped in the game room just above and were continuing their conversation there.

"I thought they were going to bed."

"I guess some of them changed their minds." Kate yawned and rested her elbow on the desk and her chin on her hand.

"Yeah. Well, Rick just called."

Kate's spine straightened. "What did he say?"

"They found a phone and a suitcase in the car, but they still don't know for sure if they're Danielle's."

"You're kidding. I wish I could see that suitcase."

"Me too." Jillian decided that promising not to tell the guests was not the same as promising not to tell her sister. "Get this—they found a glucose monitor in the suitcase."

Kate's mouth opened in a silent scream. She leaned forward and whispered, "You heard what they said. Danielle is a Type 1 diabetic."

"I told Rick."

"They've got to find that woman," Kate said.

"Well, he's aware now. But he said we can't tell the others until they know for sure it's her stuff."

"What do they want? It's got to be her."

"They're checking the phone for prints, and they may have to ask the phone company to help them unlock it."

"Oh, boy." Kate shook her head. "Well, on a lighter note, Dr. Englebrite called me today."

"Your old boss? What did he want?"

"He begged me to come back to work for him."

Jillian laughed. "I'll bet he can't find his stethoscope without you."

"He's not that bad. At least I didn't think he was. He said the last month has been chaos for him and his partners."

"Aw, come on. They haven't found a new receptionist yet?"

"Apparently not one they like," Kate said. "Don't worry. I have no desire to go back to the medical practice."

"Good to know." Jillian thought she might be able to sleep now.

Lights swept over the wall.

"That must be Andy," Kate said, walking to the door.

He came in a moment later. His hair was pulled back in a ponytail, almost as long as Alicia Boyken's French braid. He slapped a thick medieval poetry book down on the desk and smiled at Jillian.

"Hi, Mrs. T."

"Hi, Andy. I thought you were done for the semester."

"Summer class."

"Oh, okay. Looks interesting. Listen, we expect a late guest, so please be watching for her."

"It's a Mrs. Redding, and we've given her the Anna Karenina Room," Kate said. "That's so you don't have to take her luggage upstairs and disturb the rest of the guests."

"When's she coming?" Andy asked.

Kate made a face. "She was supposed to be here earlier, but she hasn't shown up yet."

"That's right," Jillian said. "We think she may have been involved in a fender-bender, but she could show up anytime. And if she does arrive, please call my cell. We're a little worried about her, and we want to know the minute she gets here."

"Will do." Andy took Kate's place behind the desk and sat on the stool.

"So, we have a lot of guests," Kate said with deceptive cheerfulness. "If anyone needs anything, it's up to you to see to it."

"Of course."

"Unless it's a major thing," Jillian said quickly. "Then you call us. You know the drill."

"Right."

It was only Andy's third weekend with the inn, and she still felt a little hesitant, leaving him in charge all night, especially with ten guests in the building and another expected.

A burst of laughter sounded from upstairs but was quickly quelled.

Jillian wondered if she ought to speak to the women, but she hated to do that. She was glad they weren't being maudlin with so little information, and she hated to play the bad guy.

Kate ducked into the office and came out with Jillian's

clipboard and her tote bag. As the volume of the voices overhead increased, the desk phone rang.

Andy pushed a button and picked it up. "Front desk, this is Andy. Uh-huh. Sure. We'll take care of it."

He hung up and shrugged. "The guy in Room 3 is complaining about the noise. Should I go tell them to keep it down?"

Jillian sighed. "I'll go. It's the cheerleading squad. I thought they'd quieted down for the night. Maybe they can move it into one of the back bedrooms if they still want to talk."

She handed Kate the clipboard and climbed the stairs. She had nearly reached the second floor landing when the conversation became clear.

"I'm sure Danielle will be all right," one of the women said.

"Yeah, she'll probably be here in the morning with a story to tell," said another.

Jillian took another step upward. She could see four of the women now, huddled in the comfortable chairs near the bookshelves.

"Well, she's ruining our weekend," Heather Saxon said. "It would serve Danielle right if something happened to her."

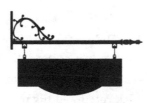

K ate stood at the inn's kitchen stove the next morning, turning bacon with a long-handled fork. The back door opened, and Rick walked in. He stopped almost immediately and sniffed the air with great drama.

"Ah! Coffee and bacon!"

Jillian, who was unpacking fresh muffins and doughnuts that had just been delivered, turned to look at him. "I guess we know who hasn't eaten breakfast yet."

"Have you been up all night?" Kate asked.

"Yeah."

"You look it."

"Sorry." Rick rubbed a hand over his stubbly chin. "Wow, looks like you're feeding an army." He reached out to filch a slice of bacon from the platter, but Kate swatted his hand.

"We are," she said. "If you want to eat here, wash your hands and sit down in the dining room."

"Okay, if I'm allowed."

"You're allowed, provided you tell us what you know about Danielle."

"I guess that's a fair trade."

Jillian turned from the counter with a steaming mug in her hands. "Here. Fresh coffee. I was going to wait to start the eggs when the first guest made an appearance, but for you, I'll make an exception."

"Great. Thanks." He took the coffee and set it on the drainboard while he washed his hands.

Jillian snapped her fingers. "Oh, I forgot to tell you—Zeb Wilding is a little concerned about the thefts in the area. I think I calmed him down, but when things aren't so crazy, maybe you can stop by and talk to him about it?"

"I'll do my best." Rick retrieved his mug and ambled to the dining room.

Kate shut off the burner and took the platter of bacon out to empty into a pan on the warming table. Rick had set down his coffee and taken a plate at the self-serve array. She frowned at the glazed doughnut he selected. "Trying to live up to your cop reputation? Homemade biscuits will be out of the oven in a few minutes."

"Good. I'll save this for dessert." He spooned a few fresh strawberries onto his plate.

Jillian appeared a few minutes later with the promised eggs, and Kate ferried out the biscuits and extra condiments. The sisters fixed plates for themselves and sat down with Rick.

"All right, give," Jillian said. "You look awful, by the way."

"You girls are tough at six thirty in the morning." Rick opened a butter pat and plopped it on half his first biscuit.

"It's closer to seven now," Kate said. She was four years Rick's junior, and they'd always wrangled. Jillian was usually more sympathetic toward him, but Kate always gave him grief to make up for some of his past teasing.

Jillian laid a hand on the sleeve of his uniform. "It's okay. In fact, we appreciate your diligence. Is the car Danielle's?"

"We think so, but we're still not a hundred percent sure. We haven't found the driver. The officers in the field are starting to wake up everyone who lives along Heston Mills Road to see if anyone can shed light on the accident. We hate to do it so early on a Saturday, but this person could need medical attention."

"How far away are the neighbors?" Kate asked.

"The nearest house is about a half mile from where we found the car." He shook his head. "The driver picked a pretty isolated spot to crash it." He frowned.

Jillian got up to refill his coffee. "You must have learned something new."

Rick looked at his watch. "I'll be calling the rental company in about an hour. We've been trying all night to reach Danielle Redding's husband, Paul, but we haven't had any luck. No one answers their home phone. We've asked the Boxborough police to go by there and see if anyone's in the house."

"That's a start," Kate said. "What are your plans for the search?"

"Now that it's light, we'll have more men join in with the door-to-door canvassing. If we don't find anything soon, we'll broadcast a call for volunteer searchers. We need numbers, so we can really comb through the woods. If the driver was disoriented and wandered off, she could be anywhere."

"There was nothing in the car with her name on it?" Kate couldn't keep the skepticism out of her tone.

"I don't think so. We've got an officer going over the contents of the suitcase again. Definitely a woman's things, but nothing seems to be marked. And there aren't any business cards or anything like that."

"That's a lesson for us all," Kate said. "Tag your luggage, at the very least."

"Didn't she have a purse?" Jillian asked.

Rick picked up a piece of crisp bacon with his fingers and broke it in half. "If she did, it went with her. All we found was the phone and the suitcase. If possible, I'd like to talk to her friends again after I call the car rental company."

"I think we could arrange that," Jillian said.

They continued to talk while they ate. Mr. Philson came in for breakfast, followed by Rachel Barker, an early bird among the cheerleaders.

"Excuse me," Jillian said. "I'll just make sure our guests have what they need."

"I think I'll call Diana. And I need to check in with the station. We had a call at 2 a.m., and we had to send Dave Hall, our rookie, to respond at the Sorenson house."

"Wait," Kate said. "You mean Ian Sorenson's mansion?"

"That's the one. Except the movie mogul got divorced last year, and his ex has the house now. She's only here about ten percent of the year, but she wants us to patrol the grounds for her."

"What? You let rich people order you around?"

"No, we told her to hire her own security guards, or at least to put in a top-of-the-line electronic security system. And the alarm went off early this morning. I want to check in and make sure Hall's okay and find out what was going on out there. All these antique thefts, you know."

"Oh, right. I suppose Mrs. Sorenson has some really expensive things in that great big house down the shore."

"I've never been inside, but you're probably right." Rick picked up his doughnut and went out on the porch.

Kate stood and cleared their dishes. She was glad he was at least letting his wife know he was all right and having breakfast at the inn. Rick usually worked the four-to-midnight shift, and Diana tended to worry when his job kept him away all night.

Kate was loading the dishwasher when he came into the kitchen at ten after eight.

"How's Diana?" she asked.

"She's good. Not ecstatic, but she's okay. By the way, I got hold of the car rental agent in Boxborough."

Kate paused with a handful of dirty silverware and looked up at him. "And?"

"And I'm ready to talk to your guests again. Are they all down here?"

"Mostly, I think. I saw Heather in a caftan and Gwen wearing her housecoat."

"I don't insist on formal dress," Rick assured her.

Jillian stuck her head in from the dining room, leaning on the door jamb. "Hey, Rick, the whole cheering squad is in the dining room, and the couple in the Hornblower Room hasn't come down yet. I thought this might be a good time for you to talk to the ladies."

"Great. Thanks."

Kate closed the dishwasher and followed him into the dining room.

"My brother is here to talk to you all," Jillian said in her classroom voice.

"Morning, Officer Gage," said Patrice with a flirtatious smile. She was a pretty woman with blond hair that Kate had decided wasn't natural like Alicia's, but Patrice had an outgoing personality and seemed to get along with all the others.

"Good morning." Rick kept his face sober.

Kate wondered if that was a common struggle for police officers. She knew Rick was happily married, but some women just went wild over a man in uniform. What was Patrice thinking, anyway, coming on to him when her friend was missing? And wasn't she the one with a husband and two kids at home? Some women's behavior baffled Kate.

Rick looked around the room and nodded. "I asked for you all to meet together so we could discuss your friend's case. I'm sorry if we got anyone up earlier than they wanted."

"We're all anxious to hear about Danielle," said Emma.

"Of course. And feel free to eat while we talk. The most important thing is, we haven't found her yet. However, a few minutes ago, I called the company that rented out the car we found." He paused and looked at their faces, some of them drawn with anxiety. "Yesterday morning, this car was rented to Danielle Redding in Boxborough, Massachusetts."

Several women caught their breath, and Alicia Boyken sobbed.

For the next few minutes, Rick laid out what he and his fellow officers had done during the night and what they hoped to accomplish that day. "When we're finished here, I'll call my chief. If no leads have turned up, he'll put out a call for volunteer searchers. We'll comb the woods and fields in the area where the rental car was found. I know it's not the way you planned to spend your weekend, but it might be a way you can help Ms. Redding."

Rachel, the quiet one who had come early to breakfast, raised a timid hand.

"Yes, ma'am?" Rick said.

"Have you checked hospitals?"

"Yes, we have. So far, we haven't found anyone who sought medical aid and had injuries consistent with this accident. Now, I'd like any of you who knew Danielle personally to tell me anything you can think of that might help us. Any contact you've had with her recently, for instance, or anything about her family and close friends. If you have any idea where we might find her husband, please say so."

"Danielle is diabetic," Emma said.

He nodded. "Thanks. Jillian told us that last night. Our officers know that if her blood sugar isn't regulated, she could develop serious symptoms—all the more reason we need to find her quickly. Now, what about family and friends?"

"We're all her friends," Alicia said. "We don't see her very often, but we all like her."

Gwen, with the auburn hair and pixie face, said, "Heather doesn't. She and Danielle never got along."

"That's just catty, Gwen," said another.

"Heather?" Rick asked, looking at her pointedly.

"Yeah. So, we're not best buds. So what? What does that have to do with her crashing her car and getting lost?" Heather shook her head, setting her shoulder-length chestnut waves tossing.

"So, what's up with you and Danielle?" Rick asked gently.

"Danielle got to be head cheerleader our senior year," Gwen replied.

Heather made a sour face at her.

"Well, somebody's got to do it, eh?" Rick asked with a faint smile.

His effort to lighten the mood worked on some of them, but Heather's expression remained hostile.

"Heather wanted it more than anything," Gwen said.

Bobbi spoke up. "It's true. They've squabbled for years. Heather never forgave Danielle for beating her out of being captain."

"They got in a hair-pulling fight once during a basketball game," Patrice said.

"And whenever I'm around Heather, she bad-mouths Danielle if she's not around," Alicia added.

Emma and some of the others looked troubled.

"Okay. Moving along," Rick said, but he scrawled a note in his pocket notebook. "Let's think about the present and Danielle's family. Did any of you meet her husband, Paul?"

"I was at their wedding," Emma said.

"Me too. I've met him several times," Alicia offered. "But I think they had a little tiff recently."

"What about?" Rick asked.

Alicia shrugged. "We met for lunch a couple of months ago when I was in Boston. Danielle didn't go into detail, but they were fighting over money."

"Probably Danielle was spending too much," Heather muttered.

Rick made notes. Jillian caught Kate's eye and lifted the coffee pot, her eyebrows quirked in question. Kate nodded. Topping off the coffee mugs might ease the tension.

"They have a teenaged daughter," Emma said.

Rick focused on her. "What's her name?"

Emma shook her head, but Alicia said, "Bailey. I met her once. She's cute. About fifteen or sixteen."

"Any other kids?" Rick asked.

"I don't think so," Alicia said.

"Didn't you tell me last night that she was going to take her daughter someplace for the weekend before she came here?" He looked straight into Alicia's eyes.

"Yeah. She didn't say where."

"Do you know the names of any of Bailey's friends?"

"No, sorry. Since they moved to Massachusetts, I haven't kept up on the family details."

"Okay." Rick closed his notebook. "I'm going to go back to the scene. If any of you think of anything else that might be helpful, please tell one of my sisters or call the Skirmish Cove police station. Thank you."

The women went back to eating and chattering. Kate walked with Rick to the door.

"When will you sleep?" she asked.

"I don't know. Thanks for breakfast."

"Anytime. I mean it."

He started to open the door, and she touched his arm. "Rick."

"Hmm?"

"Is there anything you're not telling us?"

He let out a deep sigh. "There was blood on the driver's airbag—what was left of the airbag. But that's off the record. Do *not* tell the cheerleaders."

Kate nodded gravely.

Rick's phone rang, and he pulled it out. "Officer Gage." He opened the door and walked out onto the front porch.

Kate stood in the open doorway and made no pretense of not listening.

"Yeah, thanks," Rick said. "What do you have?" After a pause he said, "We've established that she rented a car for her drive to Skirmish Cove." He gave the name of the rental agent he had spoken to and her phone number. "Have you been able to locate Ms. Redding's husband or daughter? Could you please keep trying? Ms. Redding may be seriously injured."

He closed the connection and looked at Kate. "That was the desk sergeant at Boxborough P.D. He said Ms. Redding reported her car stolen yesterday morning."

"You're kidding," Kate said.

"Nope. That's why she needed the rental, I guess."

"Wow."

Rick ran a hand over his whiskery chin. "I'd better get going."

Kate watched him drive away. In a bigger town, he'd have

been sent home at the end of his shift. Rick was one of the heroes, as far as she was concerned.

She went back inside. Jillian was keeping up cheerful chitchat with the women, and Mr. and Mrs. Litten had come into the dining room.

Kate walked across the room, giving an upbeat comment to a couple of those she passed. At the kitchen door, she turned and signaled to Jillian. Her sister joined her in seconds, and Kate shut the door.

"They found out why Danielle rented that car," Kate said in hushed tones. "Her own car was stolen."

"When?" Jillian asked.

"Yesterday morning, or during the night before, maybe. I'm not sure."

"Okay, well I told the cheering squad they can turn on the TV in the game room upstairs or the library on the third floor, so they can catch the local news together. When the call goes out for searchers, several of them want to go and help."

"I think that's great," Kate said. "I want to go too."

Jillian nodded. "I'll stay. Mindy's coming in to do the rooms, but we need someone on the front desk or in the office."

"Agreed," Kate said. "Thanks for letting me go."

She slipped out through the storage room and ran over to the carriage house to put on jeans and hiking boots. When she returned to the inn, Jillian was coming down the stairs into the lobby.

"Hey," Jillian said. "The chief just made the announcement. All volunteers report to the Charter farm on Heston Mills Road. The cheerleaders are getting ready. They'll carpool."

"Okay, then I'll take off," Kate said. "I hope she wasn't out there all night."

"It was chilly last night," Jillian agreed. "There's one more thing." She looked over her shoulder, and Kate gathered that this bit of news was for her ears only. "Rick just gave me a heads-up. The police got into Danielle's phone. They saw her calls from Alicia and Emma, and all their panicky texts. But a few days ago, she also did some texting back and forth with someone named Mickey."

"Mickey? Is that a guy?"

"They think so. She wanted to set up a meeting with him over here. Apparently he lives in or near Skirmish Cove."

They went to the lobby to speak to each of the cheerleaders as they went out the door.

Emma and Alicia came down first. "I sure hope they find her soon," Emma said.

"If she stayed in that area, I'm sure they will," Jillian said. "This is probably the most helpful thing you can do right now."

Alicia frowned. "I keep trying to remember anything about Bailey and her friends. Your brother seemed to think that could be important."

"I suppose it might be," Jillian said. "The police haven't been able to locate either Bailey or her father, and for all we know, Danielle may have contacted one of them."

Alicia turned as the other women entered the lobby. "Well, I'm pretty sure she goes to Acton-Boxborough Regional High School. Danielle mentioned it to me."

Jillian straightened. "I know someone who teaches there. Maybe he'd have some idea who Bailey hangs out with."

"That's a great idea," Emma said. She looked around. "Everybody ready?"

They all answered in the affirmative.

"Kate, do you want to go with us?" Emma asked.

Kate shook her head. "Thanks, but I'll take my Jeep."

"Heather's staying here," Patrice noted.

"No surprise," Gwen muttered.

"Good luck," Jillian said heartily. "If anyone needs to come back before their driver, give me a call."

# 5

Danielle opened her eyes and squinted at the unfamiliar room. She sat up slowly. Her head still ached, but not as badly as it had last night. She was starving. Where was she again?

The car. The man in the white pickup. The rundown motel.

She groaned. How did she get into this mess? She looked toward the nightstand. Right, she'd lost her phone. A small digital clock blinked 12:00 at her, as though it hadn't been reset since the last time the motel's power went out.

A shower. She needed a shower. But she had no clothes.

*My luggage!*

Danielle let out a puff of air. She needed to make herself presentable and get to the office and figure out a way to reconnect with Alicia and Emma and the others. And get something to eat.

She pushed back the window curtain. The sun was well up. How late had she slept? She hurried into the bathroom. The mirror wasn't kind. Her hair was stringy, and the skin under her eyes was dark. Was that because she'd just woken up, or had she bruised her face in the wreck? She grabbed a washcloth and gingerly washed her face. Still purple under the eyes.

There couldn't be many hotels in such a small town. She'd call them all!

———

As soon as the cheerleaders were out the door and into Alicia's car, Jillian went to the office and pulled out an old school directory. Minutes later, she was connected with a former colleague, Chuck Shaw.

"Hi, Chuck. It's Jillian Tunney."

"Jillian?" His voice rose in surprise. "To what do I owe the honor?"

She chuckled. "I have a question about a Boxborough student. I wondered if you could tell me anything about her."

"What's her name?"

"Bailey Redding."

"She's in my world history class."

"Great. Do you know who her best buds are? Her mother's been involved in an accident, and we're trying to reach Bailey. We know she's staying with someone this weekend, but we don't know who."

"Wow. Is it serious?"

"We're not sure yet," Jillian said. "Apparently Bailey's dad is off on a fishing trip, and the police are trying to get in touch with him too. I thought maybe you could give us some leads on Bailey's friends. If she's not with one of them, she may have mentioned to them where she was going."

"Sure. Let's see ..." Chuck gave her a couple names of girls he thought Bailey was closest to, and he was even able to supply their parents' names and look up one of the phone numbers in the local directory. He pulled another from his personal contacts, saying he and the teen's father were acquainted.

"That's terrific," Jillian said after writing down the information. "I really appreciate your help."

"So, are you still teaching in Bucksport?" Chuck asked.

"No, I retired myself in June. My sister and I are running our parents' hotel in Skirmish Cove."

"The Novel Inn? I always thought that was the coolest place!"

"Thanks. We like it." Jillian chatted for a couple more minutes then excused herself so she could call the numbers he'd given her. No one answered her first attempt, but Bailey's friend Caitlyn answered the second one.

Jillian had thought about how to represent herself to the teenager without scaring her or causing an alarm in the Massachusetts town.

"I'm sorry to call so early on Saturday. I'm Mrs. Tunney, and I used to teach with Mr. Shaw when he lived in Maine."

"I know him," Caitlyn said in a guarded tone.

"I was just talking to him," Jillian went on. "We're trying to locate Bailey Redding about a family event, but she's not home this weekend. Mr. Shaw thought you might know where she is."

"Well, her mom's away for the weekend," Caitlyn said slowly. "Bailey said she was going to have to stay with her aunt."

"Her aunt. That's very helpful. Thank you. Do you happen to know the aunt's name, or where she lives?"

"I think she's named Natalie, but I don't know where she lives," Caitlyn said. "Bailey was all upset about having to go there."

"Why was she upset?" Jillian asked.

"There's a big dance at the school tonight, and she'll miss it because she has to be at her aunt's place. It's not in town, I'm sure of that. If it was, Bailey would find a way to get to the dance."

"Oh, I see. I'm sorry she has to miss it. And thank you, Caitlyn. Are you going to the dance?"

"Yeah, I'm planning on it."

Jillian felt a slight streak of guilt for pumping the girl for so much information. A person with less noble intentions than hers might use it in the wrong way. "I hope you have a good time," she said. "And if you want to check up on me, just ask Mr. Shaw. My name is Jillian Tunney, and he's known me a long time."

"Okay."

"'Bye now." Jillian hung up and called her brother.

———

Kate swung past the police station on her way to the farm. As she had hoped, a white rental car with the front end smashed in on the passenger side was parked just outside the police garage. She got out and walked around it, appalled at the damage.

How could Danielle have walked away from this?

One of the local officers pulled into the parking lot and got out of his patrol car. Kate waved at him. Through Rick, she had met him before. Geordie Kraus, so Rick said, had barely made the height requirement for the P.D., but he made up for his small stature by working harder than most of his colleagues.

He smiled and walked toward her. "Hi, Kate. What are you doing here?"

"I'm on my way to help search for Danielle Redding, and I stopped by. This is her car, right?"

"From the one-vehicle on Heston Mills Road, yeah. Do you know the driver?"

Kate shook her head. "She was booked to stay at our inn last night and tonight."

"Oh, too bad."

Kate nodded toward the car. "That's a lot of damage. Do you really think she walked away from that?"

Geordie frowned and gave a half shrug, eyeing the crumpled front fender. "Well, she didn't call to report the accident or check in at the hospital's emergency room. She could have walked to a house, I suppose, but we've canvassed all along Heston Mills, and so far we haven't found any trace of her."

Kate swallowed hard. "It sounds like she's out in the woods, then."

"That, or she got in somebody else's vehicle."

"Yeah." She pulled her attention off the car and swung around to look at him. "Hey, Geordie, I heard there was an alarm at the Sorenson house last night."

"There was, but I don't think anyone actually broke in."

"False alarm?"

Geordie shrugged. "A raccoon, maybe, or a squirrel."

That didn't sound likely to Kate, but if the security system was ultra-sensitive, she supposed a prowling critter might set off one of the alarms.

"Well, I've got to pick up some equipment for the search. Maybe I'll see you there."

"Sure." Kate stared at the shattered windshield a moment longer and walked back to her car, more troubled than before. She wouldn't want to be in a car that took a hit like that, and Rick had mentioned blood inside.

She drove out to the farm. More than a dozen volunteers milled around the front yard. She recognized several people from the community and walked over to join Sandra Tipton, who was a firefighter. Today she was in civilian clothes— Saturday grubbies, if Kate could judge—and she had a thin teenaged boy with her.

"Hi, Sandra," Kate said. "I should have known off-duty firefighters would be here."

"I couldn't stay home when I heard it." Sandra's glossy, dark hair was caught in a ponytail, and she wore no makeup. "I don't know if you've met my son, Jeremy," she said.

"I don't think so." Kate couldn't remember seeing the boy at the medical practice, where Sandra was a patient. But then, he looked healthy. She extended her hand. "Kate Gage, from the Novel Inn."

"Cool." Jeremy shook her hand and eyed her from beneath the bill of a Seahawks cap. "I heard you have a room that's all full of *Lord of the Rings* stuff."

"We do," Kate said. "We call it the Galadriel Room. There's a guest staying in there right now, but if you come by when no one's using it, we'd be happy to show it to you."

"Awesome."

"Kate is Mrs. Tunney's sister," Sandra told him.

"Oh." He looked a little taken aback, and Kate guessed he'd taken classes under Jillian at the local high school.

She grinned. "I wouldn't want her for a teacher, but as a sister she's great. Jillian and I run the hotel together now."

Over Jeremy's shoulder, she spotted Alicia Boyken's Suburban driving up.

"Excuse me. Several of our hotel guests have come to help, too, and I should speak to them."

Six of the seven cheerleaders piled out of the Suburban. The entire squad minus Heather Saxon had squeezed into the vehicle. Kate hadn't been surprised when Heather opted out.

Beating the bushes for an injured person, or even a dead body, would not be Heather's idea of fun.

"Hello, ladies," she said with a smile.

"Hi," Alicia said. "We stopped for gas."

"You're fine. I just got here myself."

"What do we do?" Patrice asked.

"I think they're going to tell us soon," Kate replied. Rick was talking earnestly to the police chief and the fire department's captain. "There's one thing you might be able to help with." Kate turned to face the group of cheerleaders. "Do any of you know someone named Mickey? Danielle texted this person a few days ago and set up a meeting for this weekend."

Alicia frowned. "Mickey? The only one I can think of that Danielle would know is Mickey Holt."

Patrice caught her breath. "No! Do you think so?" Her brow furrowed.

"Who's this Mickey Holt?" Kate asked.

"He was in school with us," Alicia said.

The others had gathered close, and Emma said timidly, "Danielle used to go out with him. In high school, I mean."

"Long before she met Paul," Gwen put in firmly.

"Let me get my brother." Kate walked over to Rick, who'd finished his conversation, and told him what she'd learned.

Rick frowned at her. "That information was not for the public. I told Jillian in confidence."

"Sorry." Kate scrunched down a little inside her hoodie. Had she overstepped big time? She didn't want him to get in trouble for sharing information about the case. On the other hand, they'd turned up some helpful info, hadn't they?

Rick shook his head and walked over to the group from the inn.

"I understand you had a classmate named Mickey?" he asked in a more affable tone than he'd used with Kate.

Several of the women nodded, and Emma said, "Danielle dated a boy named Mickey Holt when we were in school."

"But that was in Augusta." Alicia looked around at the others. "Does he live in this area now?"

"I don't know," Rick said. "It could be someone else, but we'll check on it. Thanks."

More people had arrived to join the search, and the police chief stepped forward. "Folks, thank you all for coming out," he said. "The critical thing right now is to find the driver from the single-car accident that happened a few yards down the road, near the concrete bridge. Her name is Danielle Redding, and we think she may have some injuries. We want to hear from anyone who may have seen her last night. Until we find out where she went from the scene, we'll keep searching the surrounding terrain too. Let's divide you into groups, so we can cover the woods and fields systematically."

———

Rick stood in silence as the chief gave instructions for the searchers. He was surprised the state police hadn't shown up yet. The county sheriff's deputies were helping, but this case might be too big for them and the tiny Skirmish Cove Police Department to handle.

Of course, if they found Danielle quickly, there wouldn't be a problem, but if she remained missing much longer, they would have to call in the big guns.

While the chief was still speaking, Rick's cell phone hummed. He'd put it on vibrate, and he pulled it from his pocket and stepped away from the civilians.

"Officer Gage."

"Sergeant Michaels here, from the Boxborough P.D."

"Hi. Have you got something for us?" Rick asked.

"A neighbor of the Reddings told one of our officers that Paul Redding is on a fishing trip in New Hampshire. We're hoping we can reach him by cell phone, but it sounds like he's in a remote area. There may not be phone service where he's gone."

Rick sighed. Was it possible Paul Redding was up here in Maine, not fishing at all? "Well, it's something, anyway. Thanks. Keep me posted if you make contact, okay?"

"You still haven't found Mrs. Redding?"

"No, nothing yet."

"There's something else," Michaels said. "You mentioned their teenaged daughter."

"Right. Bailey," Rick replied. "We're pretty sure she wasn't with her mother."

"We've instructed our officers in the field to ask about her," Michaels said. "So far, none of the neighbors and acquaintances seem to know where she is. They don't think she went on the fishing trip."

"Okay. Thanks." Rick closed the connection puzzling over that. The girl had to be somewhere this weekend, but she wasn't at home or with either parent.

A member of the fire department's trained search and rescue team stepped up to instruct the searchers on how to look for Danielle efficiently and how to report anything they found, as well as how to preserve the integrity of the scene if they did find something. Everyone listened soberly.

"Officer Gage," his chief called.

Rick hurried to his side.

"Can you lead this group, please? Take the south side of the road. Make sure all the searchers stay within sight and earshot of each other. We don't want anyone else lost in the woods today."

"Right." His group included Kate and three of the

cheerleaders. They reminded him of their names—Emma, Alicia, and Rachel. They crossed the road together and were about to enter the woods on the other side when Rick's phone whirred again. He glanced at it. "Hold on. It's Jillian."

"Maybe Danielle showed up at the inn," Rachel said.

Rick put the phone to his ear. "Yeah, Jill?"

"Hi. I may have something for you. I talked to a teacher I know at the school Bailey Redding attends. He gave me the names of a couple of her close friends, and I called them. One of the girls says Bailey was going to spend this weekend at her aunt's. She didn't know her name or where she lived, but she was pretty sure she's not in Boxborough. She may even live up here in Maine, where the Reddings used to live. Possible first name Natalie."

"Thanks," Rick said. "I'll pass that information on." He made a quick call to the Boxborough police and shared the tip with them. "Maybe someone on your end can work on that."

"We'll get to work on it," the sergeant said.

Rick signed off and turned back to his somber group. "Okay, that's encouraging. One of Bailey Redding's friends gave us a hint as to where she may be this weekend. Now let's get out there and find her mom."

———

Jillian was making a shopping list when the house phone rang. She grabbed the extension in the kitchen. "Novel Inn."

"Hello," a woman said. "My name is Danielle Redding, and—"

"Danielle?" Jillian all but shrieked. "We were so worried about you. Where are you?"

"I—I'm at a hotel. Motel. They tell me it's on the edge of Skirmish Cove. I had an accident yesterday, and I spent the night here to rest. I'm sorry I made everyone worry. I'm supposed to meet some friends at the Novel Inn."

"Yes," Jillian said. "They're here—Emma Glidden, Alicia Boyken—all of them. They're very concerned about you. In fact, most of them are out helping the police look for you."

"Oh. Well, the name of this place is ... Oceanside Motel."

"I know where that is. Danielle, let me come get you."

"I was going to get a taxi."

"No, just stay put. I'd be happy to come get you, and I'll let the rest of the cheering squad know."

"All right, I guess." She sounded unsure, and Jillian wondered if she was really all right.

"Danielle, have you eaten breakfast?"

"N-not yet."

"Well, see if you can get something to eat. I'll be there in fifteen minutes. My name is Jillian Tunney, and I'm co-owner of the Novel Inn. I'll be right there, okay?"

"Y-yes. I'll be here."

Jillian hung up and whipped out her cell phone. She pushed the buttons to call Rick and grabbed her purse. She was halfway out to her car when he answered.

"Rick! She called. Danielle called."

"Danielle Redding?"

Yes, she's at a motel out near the highway, and I'm on my way to get her. If Kate's with you, ask her to come back and mind the front desk. I'll bring Danielle right back here."

———

After half an hour of hiking through the trackless woods, Kate plodded mindlessly through the trees. She tried to stay alert, but her mind kept wandering to Danielle and possible scenarios of her fate.

She thought she saw the glimmer of water up ahead when a faint shout from Rick snagged her attention. Kate was on the far end of the line, but she ran toward his voice, close behind Rachel. They joined the rest of their group and huddled around Rick.

"Danielle just called the inn. Jillian says she's on her way to pick her up."

Emma gasped.

"Thank God," Alicia said.

"Where is she?" Kate frowned at her brother.

"At a motel on the edge of town. Apparently she spent the night there."

"Was she lost?" Emma asked. "Did she get the wrong hotel?"

Rick shook his head. "I don't know the details. Jillian says she'll bring her back to the Novel Inn. Let's go there."

Kate fell in beside him as they tramped back toward their starting point.

"I have a ton of questions."

"Yeah," Rick said. "Me too. I wish Jillian had told her to stay there and wait for the police to pick her up. I tried to tell her, but she hung up on me. She didn't even give me the name of the motel." He shook his head, and Kate caught a disgusted "Women."

"You know Jillian." Kate gave him a rueful smile. "Besides, she'll get there quicker than we could. If we get back to the inn before she does, I'll make coffee and sandwiches."

Rick said nothing but strode on. The other women had fallen a little behind.

Kate's phone rang, and she pulled it out, expecting to see Jillian's name on the screen. Instead, she saw her former boss's name. Startled, she pushed the talk button.

"Dr. Englebrite?"

"Kate? Is that you?"

"Yes. What's up?" She kept walking, trying not to slacken her pace.

"Kate, we really need you here at the office. Won't you reconsider your decision? We miss you terribly."

"I thought you found someone."

"We thought so, too, but she didn't work out. We had to let her go on Wednesday, and it's chaos here with no one on the front desk."

"I'm sorry to hear that, but I'm sure there's someone out there who's perfect for the job," Kate said. She was pretty sure this was the third candidate they'd let go, but she found it hard to believe that she was irreplaceable.

"We were hoping—I talked to the other partners. We've all agreed we could give you a raise if you'll just come back."

Kate frowned. "No, sorry. That's not going to happen."

"Are you sure?"

"I'm flattered, but I'm certain. I wish you all the best." She clicked off and stuck the phone in her pocket.

Emma had caught up to her and gave her an inquisitive look.

"My old boss," Kate said.

"Sounds like they want you back."

"Yeah. Are you looking for a job?"

"Not me," Emma said. "I sure hope Danielle's okay."

"Yeah."

"Why do you suppose Danielle didn't report her accident last night and have her rental towed? And if someone gave her a ride to another hotel, don't you think she'd want her suitcase?"

Kate hurried so she wouldn't lose sight of Rick. Light showed beyond his swiftly moving figure, and she thought they were close to the paved road. A glance over her shoulder told her that Alicia and Rachel were not far behind.

"I don't know, Emma. We don't have all the information yet. Pray for the best."

———

Jillian pulled in at the Oceanside Motel and swiftly scanned the parking lot. Nobody was waiting outside, so she parked in front of the office. Danielle hadn't given her a unit number.

She didn't like the look of the place. One-star, she thought grimly, if it got any stars at all. The Novel Inn was so much classier than this. She grimaced as she remembered she hadn't left anyone to watch the front desk. Well, she'd be home soon, and chances were, Kate would arrive before she did.

When she shoved the door open and stepped inside, Danielle was sitting on a turquoise plastic chair along the side wall. She rose, eyeing Jillian hesitantly.

"Danielle? I'm Jillian Tunney, from the Novel Inn."

"Thank you." Danielle reached out a hand to her.

Jillian clasped it for a moment, perusing her face. Bruising darkened her eye sockets and one cheek. A scab had formed over a cut on Danielle's temple.

"Are you all right?" Jillian asked. "Do you want medical attention?"

"No, just get me out of here." Danielle's stage whisper held a note of desperation.

"Of course." Jillian flicked a glance toward the pudgy young man behind the front desk. "Are you all set with the motel?"

"Yes, I've checked out." Danielle fingered her leather shoulder bag.

Knowing about the abandoned suitcase, Jillian guessed

that was all she had brought here. "Okay, let's go then." She threw a vague smile at the desk clerk and walked with Danielle to the door, feeling that any minute her companion might fold up on her.

Once they were in the car, she fastened her seatbelt and turned to Danielle. "Did you get any breakfast?"

"I got a packet of nuts out of a machine."

"Well, we can give you a full breakfast at the inn. Your friends will be *so* glad to see you. And I'm sure the police will bring your luggage to you there."

"Thank heaven for that! I can't believe I let that guy bring me here."

"What guy?" Jillian paused with her hand on the ignition.

"Some guy that picked me up after the wreck. He said his name was Bob."

Jillian started the engine. "You'll need to tell the police about him and give them all the details about your accident."

"Of course." Danielle put a hand up to her cheek and winced. "I still can't believe this is happening to me."

Jillian pulled out onto the main road. Beside her, Danielle caught her breath.

"What is it?" Jillian tapped the brake, wondering if Danielle had forgotten something and they should go back.

"Nothing. I thought I saw the truck that picked me up. Bob's white truck."

Jillian's jaw tightened. "You think he's at the motel?"

"No, that's silly. I'm just nervous, I think. This whole thing has me on edge."

"If you're sure ..."

"No, it's okay. That's not the one. Keep going."

Jillian watched her rearview mirror, but no vehicles pulled out of the motel's parking lot. When she made the first turn of their journey, the only vehicle behind her was a blue van.

"Try to relax," she said as cheerfully as she could. "We'll get some good food into you. When you're fed and have your friends around you, you'll feel better."

Danielle's face was still pinched, and she kept watching her sideview mirror.

# 6

W hen Jillian turned into the driveway at the Novel Inn, Danielle let out a little sigh.

"This is perfect. It's just like Emma described it."

Jillian smiled. "I don't see Alicia's SUV. They mustn't be back from the search yet, but they'll all be here any second."

She parked, hopped out, and hurried around the back, but Danielle already had her door open and was climbing out of the passenger seat. "Come right in," Jillian said. "We've got a nice room for you on the first floor. It's all decorated in an Anna Karenina theme."

"My luggage—?"

"Now that you're found, I'm sure the police will bring your suitcase to you."

A vehicle pulled into the yard—not Kate's or Alicia's, but a blue van. Jillian stared at it, her brain rapidly processing the fact that a blue van had been behind her at one point on the way home. Now a similar blue van was rolling too fast into the Novel Inn's small parking lot. A man tumbled out on the passenger side. The driver threw the gearshift into park and jumped out a moment later, his face covered by a light blue mask, the kind doctors wore during surgery.

"No," Danielle said weakly.

Jillian saw the gun then, in the first man's very competent-looking right hand. She grabbed Danielle's wrist.

"Do you know these guys?"

"It's Bob," Danielle gasped and sagged to her knees.

Jillian knelt beside her. "Danielle!" She looked up. The two men came closer.

"Give me your keys," the one with the gun said.

"What?" Jillian felt suddenly stupid. Her heart seemed to have stopped functioning, and Danielle tumbled limply to the ground.

"Your car keys. Let's have 'em."

Jillian's jaw dropped, but her hand moved automatically to the pocket of her pants, where she'd slid her key ring only a moment before. She couldn't give it up, could she? In addition to her car keys, it had hers for the carriage house and the back door of the inn.

"Throw them here." The gunman waved his weapon a little. Jillian assumed he was Bob.

The masked man had approached Danielle and lifted her chin to gaze at her face.

Bob's attention slid to her for a second. "She okay?"

"Out cold," said his partner.

"Well, that makes it easier." Bob sharpened his aim on Jillian. "Come on, toss those keys over here now."

Jillian didn't wait any longer. *Give them what they want. It's not worth risking your life.*

The driver was now lifting Danielle. He carried her like a baby toward the van. Jillian tossed the key ring. It landed a foot from the gunman's left foot. He stooped and retrieved it, keeping his pistol trained on her.

*Blue eyes.*

"Now don't move," he said.

Jillian was shaking all over. Bob went to help the other man hoist Danielle's ragdoll form in through the side door of the van.

*Dark hair, mustache. Maroon shirt.* Everything was happening too fast. She tried to focus on the handgun, but Bob's body hid it from her now. The driver ran around to the other side, and Bob opened the front passenger door. Just before diving inside, he lifted his arm and tossed something— Jillian's key ring—across the parking area, into some long grass growing along the edge.

The van doors slammed, and the tires squealed as the driver made a fast reverse turn and peeled out.

"Dear God, help me!" Jillian sucked in a breath and reached for her other pocket. It took her several seconds to get her phone out, and then she muffed her first try at calling her brother.

"Yeah," Rick said curtly in her ear, so she knew he was driving.

"They've got Danielle. They grabbed her, right here in our yard."

"What? Who?"

"Two men in a blue van. They've kidnapped her. Rick, I was so scared. One of them had a gun."

"Hold on, Jilly. I'm almost there."

"Wait. License plate number! The first three digits are 797. I couldn't get any more than that."

"Okay, good. Hang on."

A siren split the air and grew louder as it came down the road. She stuck her phone in her pocket and ran over to where the keys had landed. The grass and weeds were tall along the edge of the lot. Why hadn't she mowed this strip? With her foot, she brushed the long stems sideways, watching for the glint of metal.

The siren reached a nearly unbearable peak as she spotted the keys and snatched them up. She ran to Rick's SUV. He had cut the siren and was talking into his radio. Kate's Jeep pulled in behind him.

Her sister jumped out of her Jeep and ran toward her. "What's happened? Jillian, what is it? Where's Danielle?"

"Two men took her," Jillian said. "We just drove in, and these two guys pulled up in a van."

Rick was walking toward them now, so she took a breath and waited for him to get there.

"Tell me," he said.

"Two men in a blue van. One had a gun. He was about forty, brown hair, blue eyes, mustache. About your height. The other wore a mask."

"Steel blue van?"

"No, older looking. Kind of navy blue. Not real shiny."

"And you said 797?"

She nodded. "I'm sorry I couldn't get it all."

"Would your video camera catch them?"

She frowned. "I'm not sure. They didn't drive all the way in. They stopped out there." She pointed to where the van had rested.

"Check on it, okay?" Rick said.

She nodded. "And the guy with the gun made me throw him my car keys, and he tossed them off over there, but I found them." She pointed then held up her key ring. "I guess they knew I'd have followed them if I had wheels."

"Which way did they go?" Rick asked.

"They turned left out of the driveway."

"All right, let me call that in. Don't move." He strode back to his SUV.

Kate grasped her upper arms and looked into Jillian's eyes. "Are you all right?"

"Yes. But Danielle fainted. The driver scooped her up and carried her to their van, and they drove off with her." Tears streamed down Jillian's face.

"Oh, that poor woman." Kate put her arms around her and drew her into a fierce hug.

"I should have told her to wait at the motel for the police."

"But ... I don't get it," Kate said. "Why do they want her so badly?"

"I have no idea."

The inn's front door opened, and Heather Saxon stood in the doorway, surveying them. Her gaze settled on Rick's vehicle.

"What's going on?"

"Heather," Jillian snapped. "Did you see the blue van that was here?"

"Huh? No. I fell asleep, and then a siren woke me up. What happened?"

Alicia's vehicle pulled in at that moment, and Jillian was glad she didn't have to answer.

"Can you tell them all?" she asked her sister.

Kate nodded. "You go inside. Get a cup of coffee and sit down in the kitchen. I'll tell Rick where you are. And don't worry about the cheering squad. We'll bring them up to speed. The most important thing is for Rick to get more officers out there looking for that van."

Jillian turned and mounted the steps on legs of concrete.

———

Rick left almost immediately to join the search for the kidnappers. The returning cheerleaders were appalled at the news.

"It happened right here in front of the inn?" Gwen Vale's eyebrows rose almost to her hairline. "I mean—"

Jillian felt sick to her stomach. They would blame her. She'd stood there and hadn't done a thing to stop those men from taking Danielle.

"They had a gun," Kate said.

Emma came over and slipped an arm around Jillian. "You must have been terrified."

"I'm sure you did all you could," Alicia said. She turned to the others. "Look, the good news is that we know Danielle is still alive."

"For now," Heather said, and they others glared at her.

Patrice said sternly, "None of that. We need to keep a positive attitude. There are tons of cops out there looking for her. They'll find that vehicle."

Jillian looked around at the bleak faces. Most of them were trying to put a good face on things, but Emma and Bobbi looked ready to cry.

"Well, listen," Kate said. "The inn doesn't usually serve lunch unless the guests asked for it in advance or request a picnic basket, but I happen to know we've got plenty of food in the kitchen. If you all want to freshen up, I'll make some sandwiches and salad. What do you say?"

"I think I'll go out," Heather said. "There's a café just down the street, right?"

In the end, a couple of others joined Heather, and the remaining four went up to their rooms then drifted into the dining room.

Jillian started to follow Kate.

"You stay out here, okay?" Kate said. "We need someone on the desk, and I'll bring you a plate."

"Are you sure?"

"Yeah. If I need help, I know Emma will jump in."

Jillian sat down wearily. It made sense, but she felt guilty remembering that she'd abandoned her post earlier. Still, it was for a good cause. She'd gone to help Danielle.

A lot of good that did.

The video camera. That was something she could do now.

She fumbled through the commands to show her the saved video for the last half hour. The images of herself and Danielle getting out of her car were clear, but then, she'd parked near the inn's front entrance. Beyond she saw the front bumper and headlight on the passenger side of the van as it rolled into the drive.

Jillian caught her breath. The license plate didn't show. It might be time to invest in a second camera, or to adjust this one's view. But they wanted it to focus on the front steps and people approaching to enter the inn.

She advanced the video. With a sigh, she sat back. The plates didn't show when the van backed out and turned to flee, either. The camera had captured a half decent look at the gunman, though, and the masked guy who picked up and carried Danielle.

She'd only sat brooding for ten minutes when a new couple arrived without a reservation. Jillian gathered her wits and assured them that the Novel Inn could accommodate them. The spacious Hercule Poirot room, overlooking the shore, was available.

The Raynors were delighted with the room and, once they were settled, went out again to explore the quaint town. Jillian gave them smiling recommendations of a couple of restaurants and sat down on her stool when they were gone. The whole process both pleased her and added to her stress.

Kate came through from the dining room and asked, "Are you hungry?"

"Not yet. I may never eat again."

Kate gave her a sympathetic pat on the shoulder.

"Hey, Rachel said she saw someone checking in."

"Yeah," Jillian said. "The Raynors. I put them in Hercule Poirot."

The desk phone rang, and she leaped on it.

"Novel Inn."

"Hi, Jill. It's Diana."

Jillian relaxed and sank back onto the stool. "Hi, Diana."

Kate gave her a knowing nod and headed back to the dining room to check on the guests.

"I wondered if you'd talked to Rick since breakfast," Diana said.

"I guess you haven't heard the news about our missing guest."

"Have they found her yet?" Diana asked.

Jillian sighed. "We did, but we've lost her again." She spent the next five minutes giving Diana an account of her morning and answering her sister-in-law's questions.

"Wow," Diana said at last. "That's a lot. I'm sorry it happened, but I'm really glad you're okay."

"How are you doing?" Jillian asked.

"I'm fine, but I'm afraid Rick is overtired. He was out all night on this. Police officers can make mistakes when they're exhausted, like anyone else."

"That's true. I'm sure the chief will take that into consideration." But she knew Rick wouldn't take a break when they were so close to finding Danielle Redding.

"I'd hate for him to have an accident, you know?"

Diana was a worrier. She'd pushed that aside when she married Rick, but her anxiety surfaced whenever he had a demanding case. Jillian tried to soften her voice.

"Listen, I'm sure he'll call you when he has a chance."

"Sure. And he's never had to fire his gun on duty. He's proud of that."

Jillian shuddered, remembering the horror of having a weapon aimed at her point blank. "Let's pray he keeps that record."

"You'll call me if you hear anything?"

"Of course."

She hung up and sat thinking for a minute. There must be something she and Kate could do while the police were hot on the kidnappers' trail. She still felt like she was the one who'd messed things up.

After Kate and the cheering squad left that morning for the search, she had searched online for a Mickey Holt living in the area. She didn't want to interfere with the police investigation, but finding Danielle was their first priority. She was in worse danger now than she had been yesterday, and if those evil men slipped through the officers' fingers, Danielle could be lost.

It was possible that an officer had already checked on the Mickey Holt lead, but the Skirmish Cove police force was small, and right now they had their hands full. What if Mickey Holt was one of the two who'd kidnapped Danielle?

Her search led to a business called Holt's Auto Body, and a little more browsing had revealed that the owners were named Blaine and Michael Holt.

She hadn't had time to call. The shop wasn't far from the inn, but leaving the front desk unattended again wasn't an option. Jillian drummed her fingers on the desk then jumped up and strode to the kitchen through a now deserted dining room. Kate was loading the dishwasher.

"Hey." Jillian automatically reached for a stack of dirty plates. "I think I've located the guy Danielle was texting with a few days ago—Mickey Holt. He apparently has a garage in town, and I thought I'd run over there."

Kate froze with a bunch of forks in her hand. "And what? See if you recognize him as one of the kidnappers? Bad idea."

Jillian avoided her gaze and bent to slide the plates between prongs on the lower rack. That was exactly what she'd been thinking, but she wouldn't admit it now.

"I thought I'd ask him about Danielle and see if he knew why she wanted to talk to him."

"And what if he's the guy who held a gun on you an hour ago?"

She huffed out a breath and straightened. "Don't you think those guys are busy right now? They've got the cops chasing them. They won't be in a garage working on someone's car."

"They could be changing their license plates or repainting that blue van."

"I doubt it. I'm going to drive by and see if it looks like the place is open. If someone's working in there, I can just—"

"Do *not* go alone," Kate said.

"Well, you can't come with me. We need someone here in case more guests come in, or in case—I don't know. Danielle called here this morning. What if she called again?"

"You think she might be able to get away from them?"

"How should I know?"

Kate's frown puckered her forehead. "If you insist on going, at least take one of the women who knew Mickey back in the day with you."

Jillian nodded slowly. "Not a bad idea."

"And make sure she's ready to call 911 if something goes haywire."

"Right."

78

Jillian thought about it carefully. Alicia was the one who'd come up with Mickey's last name.

"Okay, I'll go see if I can get someone to play backup for me."

She went to the curved stairway and hurried to the second level and down the hall to the Elizabeth Bennet room. After a quiet tap, she waited. Alicia Boyken opened the door. Apparently she was alone in her room.

"Is there news?" she asked.

"No," Jillian said. "I wondered if you wanted to do a little sleuthing with me."

"Like what?"

"It may be nothing, but I think I've located that Mickey Holt guy you went to school with. I thought I'd drive by his place of business and see if I could get a look at him."

Alicia's eyes widened. "You think he could be in on the kidnapping?"

"I don't know. Danielle said one of them was named Bob, but there were two men." Jillian made a wry face. "My baby sister says I can't go by myself."

"Yeah, I'll go," Alicia said. "Let me grab my purse."

"And your phone."

"Right."

They hustled down the stairs and into the kitchen. Kate was still cleaning up.

"Alicia's going with me," Jillian said.

"All right, but call me as soon as you know anything. If Rick calls, I want to be able to bring him up to speed."

———

"What now?" The man called Bob paced back and forth in the open space of the room, wringing his hands.

"We wait," his companion said.

"That's dangerous."

"Well, we can't just do it in broad daylight."

Danielle swallowed hard. Her mouth and throat were so dry they felt as if the skin inside was cracking, but she didn't dare ask for water. In fact, she lay still, hoping to delay the moment when they realized she was awake.

In quick peeks she'd found they were in a large storage room, or maybe a warehouse. Overhead, bare light bulbs glared on old furniture and stacked boxes. Why on earth had they brought her here? What did they want with her?

She considered putting that question to them, but fear kept her paralyzed, lying on a wooden floor between a pile of cartons and some kind of solid old cabinet. Sometime between the moment she and Jillian had driven up at the Novel Inn and when she'd awoken, they'd secured her hands and feet. She couldn't tell what her feet were bound with, and her hands were behind her, forcing her into a very uncomfortable position, but instinct told her not to wriggle.

"Look, it seems like we got away with it," the man who'd driven the van said. She couldn't see him, but she knew Bob's voice by now, and that was the other guy.

"The first part," Bob replied. "So we got her. Getting rid of her is the tricky part."

Danielle felt cold all over, and dizzy, as though she might faint again, even though she lay on the floor. *Get rid of her?* She began to shiver, and she willed her body to stop, but it wouldn't. What had she done to make them hate her?

"You never should have picked her up in your truck," Bob's companion said.

"What was I supposed to do? Just leave her there in her wrecked car?"

"That would have been a better option, yeah."

Danielle could hardly breathe.

"I've got to get over to the store," Bob said. "You stay here."

"Wait! Mark!" The second man's voice rose.

Danielle frowned trying to make sense of that. He'd called Bob another name. Mark. Why? Or maybe it wasn't Bob after all—maybe this was someone else. But she was sure it was Bob who'd pulled the gun on her and Jillian at the inn. And the voice was the same. Her mind whirled.

"What? That shipment from Houlton's coming in. One of us has to be there to receive it."

"Yeah, but have you thought ..."

Their voices faded in the distance. She opened her eyes. If she rolled over, would they notice when they came back? But they might not come back for hours. Cautiously she wiggled and shifted to her back. As far as she could tell, the place was stuffed with merchandise. Not new stuff, old furniture, picture frames, and boxes of bric-a-brac. The overhead lights went out and she froze then relaxed. They weren't coming back for a while.

She rolled again and pushed against the floor with her shoulder. Finally she was able to sit up. Her elbow was skinned, for sure. About five yards away, daylight streamed in through an open door. They wouldn't just leave her here, would they? One of them could be coming back, regardless of the lights. Bob had told the other guy to stay here, but he'd objected.

She looked down at her ankles. Zip ties. Weren't those easily broken? She'd seen something on YouTube. Bailey had called it to her attention. But that was if your hands were bound in front of you. Hers were behind. Still, she might try with her feet.

Footsteps crunched on gravel, and she quickly lay down again, arranging herself on the side she'd lain on when she woke up. One of the men clomped into the room swearing under his breath. Danielle closed her eyes and tried not to think about water.

———

With Alicia tagging along, Jillian hurried out the back door and to her car, which was parked in the drive at the carriage house. It took only about five minutes to get to Holt's Auto Body, during which she gave Alicia all the details she could think of. Several vehicles sat in the parking area, and a wide garage door was up. The noise of power tools reached them from inside.

Alicia craned her neck to look around the parking area. "I don't see a blue van."

"Or any white pickup trucks," Jillian said. "Danielle said the man who picked her up at the scene of the accident had a white truck. Let me do the talking, okay?"

"Sure."

They both got out and walked over to the big door. Two men were busy inside, each working on a vehicle while music pumped from a radio on the workbench. The nearer man looked to be in his mid-thirties. Clad in gray coveralls, he was spraying red paint on the side panel of a pickup truck. The paint underneath was blue. The other man was older, with graying hair. He removed a piece from the front of a minivan, and it clattered to the floor.

Jillian approached the younger man when he paused to adjust his sprayer.

He glanced up. "Hi. Can I help you?"

"I'm looking for Mickey Holt," Jillian said.

"That's me. What can I do for you?" He pushed his safety goggles up onto the top of his head.

He had a charming smile, and Jillian smiled back.

"I'm Jillian Tunney, from the Novel Inn. Did you hear about the missing woman?"

"I heard something on the radio this morning."

"I thought you might know her. The woman's name is Danielle Redding."

His smile faded, and he walked over to the bench and turned off the radio.

"Are you saying Danielle Redding is missing?"

The other man came over. "What's this?"

Mickey glanced at him. "This is my uncle, Blaine Holt. This woman says a friend of mine is missing."

Blaine frowned at Jillian. "Who?"

"Danielle Redding," Mickey said. "I went to high school with her."

"Have you been in touch with Ms. Redding recently?" Jillian asked.

Mickey shrugged. "We've kept in touch over the years, but it's just a casual friendship."

"Did she ask to meet you while she was in town this weekend?"

Mickey hesitated. "She texted me a couple days ago, yeah. We haven't seen each other for a couple of years, and she wanted to get together while she was in the area. We were supposed to meet up tomorrow over coffee, before she goes home."

"That's it?" Jillian asked.

He shook his head, at a loss for more. "You said she's missing."

"Yes. Her rental car was in an accident, and the police haven't found the driver yet."

Mickey swore softly. "Let me see exactly what she said." He unzipped his coveralls and took a cell phone from his shirt pocket. After clicking a few buttons, he adjusted the distance from his eyes and squinted at the screen.

Hey, Mick, I'll be in Sk Cove this weekend. Want to have coffee?

He looked up and met Jillian's gaze. "I texted back, said sure, when and where. She said Sunday 10 a.m., and I named a coffee shop on Main Street. That was about it." As he spoke, he scrolled through the saved messages. "Oh, here we go. 'C u then. Unfinished biz. D.' That's all she said. This came in on Thursday. I haven't heard from her since."

"Unfinished biz?" Jillian said. "What did she mean by that?"

"I'm not sure."

Jillian thought for a moment. "Danielle was coming to Skirmish Cove for a reunion with her high school cheering squad. Do you remember any of the other women?"

His eyebrows shot up. "Who? Alicia and Heather, those gals?"

"Yes. They're all staying at the Novel Inn." She waved Alicia forward. "This is Alicia Boyken. Do you—"

"Alicia! Sure." A smile broke over Mickey's face.

"Hi, Mick."

"Sorry, I didn't recognize you at first."

"It's okay." Alicia glanced around the garage. "You live in Skirmish Cove now?"

"Yeah. With my aunt and uncle."

"They all checked in yesterday except Danielle," Jillian said. "She never made it to the inn."

"Wow."

Mickey's uncle clicked his tongue. "That's too bad. And they don't know what happened to her?"

"Not yet," Jillian said. "My brother is on the police force. He'll let me know when they find out."

"I'm really sorry to hear this, but I don't see that I can do anything." Fine lines crinkled the corners of Mickey's eyes.

"Will it be on the news later, if they find her?" Blaine asked.

"I'm sure there will be something on the local news this evening." Jillian took one of her business cards with the Novel Inn's phone number on it from her pocket. "Look, if you remember what that unfinished business was about, will you give me a ring?"

"Yeah." Mickey took the card. "But I'm sure it was just a friendship thing."

"You two dated in high school." Jillian watched his face, but Mickey didn't seem troubled by that.

"Yeah, but that's ancient history. I figured she just meant catching up, you know?"

Jillian considered how much to tell him and decided she shouldn't let much slip. "Were you here all morning?"

"Yeah, both of us."

"We came in together this morning around eight," Blaine said.

That was earlier than the kidnappers had shown up at the inn, and besides, a perusal of both the Holt men told her that neither of them was as heavy as the van driver who had hefted Danielle into their vehicle.

She nodded. "Okay. The police may come ask you about Danielle because some of the women had mentioned you in connection with her."

"That's kind of scary."

He didn't need to know that Rick had found Danielle's phone and had access to their texts. Rick would surely prefer that she didn't spill everything she knew—and Mickey would hear about the kidnapping soon enough.

"Thanks a lot." She nodded to them.

"'Bye, Mickey," Alicia said, and she followed Jillian out to her car.

"What did you think?" Jillian asked on the way back to the inn. "Same old Mickey Holt?"

Alicia's face scrunched up. "Yes and no. He looks about the same, but more mature of course, and he seemed more serious —but then who wouldn't, with the news we dropped on him?"

"I hope Kate's heard something by the time we get back." Jillian let out a heavy sigh. "I still can't believe Danielle was kidnapped right in front of me."

"Hey," Alicia said sternly. "It's not your fault. Get that through your head."

Jillian nodded, but she knew the scene would haunt her for a long, long time.

———

Kate looked up with relief from the front desk's computer as Jillian and Alicia breezed in through the door.

"Any word?" Jillian asked.

"Not yet. Did you see Mickey?"

"Yeah, we did. He seemed to think it was just a catch-up-with-an-old-friend thing with Danielle, and his uncle alibis him for the time of the kidnapping. They say they worked together in the garage all morning."

Kate huffed out a breath. "Great. Alicia, the other gals went to Auntie's Kitchen for some ice cream. It's a little family-run restaurant that specializes in homestyle food. If you want to join them, here's the address. They've only been gone fifteen minutes." She slid a memo sheet across the desk.

"Thanks," Alicia said. "I think I'll do that."

Kate hadn't eaten yet either, and Jillian admitted she was

hungry at last. She headed for the kitchen to scrounge up some lunch for the two of them. She called Kate into the dining room a few minutes later, and they settled at a table from which they could see out into the lobby in case someone came in.

"I told Mickey the police would probably come talk to him at some point," Jillian said, "but don't tell Rick I went to see him, okay? He'd probably get all bent out of shape."

"Okay." Kate leaned forward as the front door opened. "There he is now."

"Hey, Rick, in here." Jillian waved to him, and their brother strode into the room.

"I'm only here for ten seconds," he said. "We haven't found Danielle, and there's no sign yet of that blue van. We've got someone working on the white truck Danielle told you about, but it would sure help if we knew the make."

"What about the partial license number I gave you on the van?" Jillian asked.

"Working on it. We don't think it's registered to anyone in Skirmish Cove."

"That's weird," Kate said.

"Not really. They could live in another town, or they could have put old license plates on the vehicle so it couldn't be traced."

"That's risky, isn't it?" Jillian said. "If you ran the plate, you'd know right away it didn't go with that van."

Rick sighed. "Yeah, and I didn't say they did that. But in interest of thoroughness, we're checking all blue vans in the area."

Jillian didn't look happy. "Well, I checked the video, and it doesn't show the license plate. It does show the gunman's face from an angle. I don't know if it's good enough to identify him."

"Can you send it to me?"

"What, copy the video?" Jillian asked.

"I know how to do it." Kate got up and walked out to the lobby, and Jillian followed. "Where do I send it?"

"To the desk sergeant." Rick leaned over the desk and scribbled something on the memo cube. "Send it there, and put 'attention Sgt. Watkins' in the subject line."

"Got it," Kate said. "So, what about Danielle's husband?"

"Still looking for him. They contacted one of the fishing buddies' wives, and she gave them a list of places the men had been in the past, but really, they could be anywhere."

Kate nodded, thinking about the lakes and streams in northern New Hampshire. "What now?"

Rick ran a hand through his short-cropped brown hair. "I'm heading out to the motel where Danielle stayed last night. The chief thinks we can get a warrant to search the room she stayed in, and I'm hoping I can get there before they clean it."

"Can I go?" Kate jumped up.

Rick stared at her as if she were a five-year-old. "No, you cannot go. I can't take civilians along when I'm investigating a crime."

She scowled at him. "I guess you couldn't stop me if I just drove out there in my own car, now could you?"

Frustration flared in Rick's eyes. He opened his mouth and closed it. Without another word, he turned and stomped out through the lobby.

"'Bye." Kate breezed past her sister and headed for the door.

"Wait," Jillian said. "I should go."

"You went to Mickey's. Someone's got to mind the desk."

Kate ran out onto the porch and down the steps. No way was she going to let Jillian go while she was stuck here again. Rick was already at the end of the driveway. She managed to reverse her Jeep and get out onto the street before his police car disappeared. Hanging back a little, she let a couple of cars get between them. She knew where he was going, and she didn't want to give him a reason to come down hard on her.

He'd parked the police car in front of the motel's office and was nowhere in sight. Kate pulled up next to it, got out, and went into the office.

The office was smaller and much more cramped than the lobby at the Novel Inn and sadly lacking in atmosphere. The only amenity for guests was a nook with a couple of vending machines in it. A heavyset man of about thirty stood behind the counter working at the computer.

Rick turned and frowned at her. Kate kept her place near the door.

"Hi." Rick stepped up to the desk and introduced himself, but let his uniform do most of the talking. "I understand you had a guest named Danielle Redding last night."

The clerk's eyes widened. "Uh, let me check. We did have a woman check in around five o'clock yesterday." He clicked a few keys on his computer. "Redding, you said?"

"That's right," Rick replied.

He nodded. "Yeah. Her I.D. checked out, so I accepted her credit card and gave her a room. Is there a problem?"

He seemed a bit wary, and Kate wondered if he'd noticed something a bit "off" about Danielle. Surely she'd been shaken up after her accident, and maybe even a little disoriented.

"I'd like to see the room she stayed in."

"Uh, well, we don't usually do that, but—"

"This is a police matter." Rick took out his notebook. "What's the room number?"

"Uh ... fourteen."

"And your name?"

"Ryan McLowry."

Rick wrote something in his notebook. "Did you check her out this morning?"

"No, I don't think she came into the office."

"It's past noon." Rick looked pointedly at a sign reading, "Checkout time is noon."

"Yeah, that's right," Ryan said. "But guests don't have to come in here to check out. We slide their bill under their door during the night. If they want to, they can just leave the key in the room and—"

"The woman who picked her up this morning said she came to the office and met Ms. Redding here. Were you on duty?"

Kate had the impression that Rick was pinning the guy to the wall with his relentless stare.

"Uh ..." The clerk's eyes shifted. "Let me check again." He focused on his computer screen for about fifteen seconds then lifted his gaze to meet Rick's. "Oh, yeah. Sorry about that. I missed it before, but she did bring her bill in here. I remember now. We were crazy busy this morning." His smile wasn't too convincing.

"Uh-huh," Rick said. "So you *were* in here when she was picked up by another woman."

"Well, uh, yeah, but the other woman didn't speak to me. I don't remember much about her ..."

"That's okay. I need to see Unit 14. You got a master key I can borrow?" Rick asked.

"I'll just rekey one of these plastic jobs for you, but it's company policy for me to go with you."

"Fine." Rick waved toward the door. "Let's go."

"Actually, the maid is cleaning that wing now, but she may not be at that exact room." Ryan picked up a key card and ran it through some sort of scanner on the counter then came out into the lobby. He eyed Kate with speculation.

"This is Miss Gage," Rick said. "She's from the Novel Inn, in town."

"Oh, sure," Ryan said. "I know where it is. But you're not —" He looked back to Rick, his face reddening.

"No, she's not the one who picked up Ms. Redding this morning. Your customer had a reservation at the Novel Inn for the weekend," Rick said. He didn't volunteer the information that she hadn't shown up, or that she'd been kidnapped that morning.

"She didn't say that. And it's not our fault if she came here instead."

"I understand that. How did she seem when she came in last night?"

As he talked, they left the office, and Ryan led them down a row of motel units. Kate trailed a couple of steps behind them.

"To be honest, she seemed a little out of it. I figured she'd had a couple of drinks." Ryan paused and turned to glance at Kate. "Maybe that was why she stopped here, instead of going to your place."

*Oh, right. Like she would choose this weaselly place over our inn.* Kate said nothing but gave him a faint smile.

The maid's cart was outside the unit next to Danielle's. Ryan stopped and called inside, and a young woman wearing jeans and a T-shirt came to the door of #15 with a spray bottle of glass cleaner in her hand.

"Did you do 14 yet?" Ryan asked.

"Yeah."

"It was empty, right?" Rick asked.

The maid eyed him up and down. "Yeah. I knocked and no one answered, so I went in. There was no luggage, so I figured the guest had checked out." She looked at Ryan. "What's going on?"

Ryan shrugged. "Don't ask me, but when the cops come sniffing around, we do what they want."

"Oh. Oh!" The maid's eyes flared. "Is she the one I heard about on the news this morning?"

"Could be," Rick said.

"What?" Ryan asked sharply.

"There's a woman missing." The young woman's gaze darted from Ryan to Rick and back.

"Could you please open Room 14 for me?" Rick said to Ryan.

# 7

K ate stayed back, out of the way. She enjoyed watching
Rick at work. He wasn't getting a whole lot of
information so far, but he wasn't giving out much, either. She
wasn't sure it would hurt to say more about Danielle's
situation, since her disappearance after the accident was now
public knowledge, but Rick was trained for this. She was sure
he knew what he was doing.

The desk clerk pushed the door open and stepped aside. He
and the maid waited outside the door, but Kate followed Rick a
few steps into the room. The queen bed was neatly made. He
took a quick look in the bathroom and closet, then opened and
closed the drawers on the dresser and night table. A TV was
prominent, but Kate didn't see any mini-fridge or microwave,
or even a coffee maker or a hairdryer. The only wastebasket
was in the tiny bathroom, and it was empty.

"Too bad we didn't get here earlier," she said softly.

"Yeah." Rick's face was sober as he went outside, and she
followed. Rick stopped beside the maid's cart. "The bed had
been slept in, right?"

"I'd say so. I changed it about twenty minutes ago," the maid replied.

"Can I please see the trash you took out of that room?"

"Oh, sure." Her face wrinkled. "It's all mixed up in the trash bag. I mean, I did four other rooms before that one, and one since. I don't think I could tell you what came from each room."

"Okay, I'll just take the whole bag, then. Do you remember anything unusual while you were cleaning Number 14? Not just the trash—any unusual spills, or anything the guest left behind?"

"Not really. I think there were some candy wrappers in her trash, and maybe a soda can on the night table. Some facial tissue, stuff like that." The maid shook her head. "No bloodstains, if that's what you mean."

"I meant anything at all," Rick said. "Thanks very much. Is this the bag?"

"Yes." The maid unhooked a trash bag from her cart and gave it to him. It was a large plastic garbage bag, about half full of refuse.

"You've been very helpful," Rick said. He looked at Ryan. "Are there any security cameras on the premises?"

"No, sorry. I think the budget's pretty tight."

Kate could identify with that, but her father had always insisted on a working camera at the Novel Inn, focused on the parking area and front steps. She and Jillian had kept it going, since the system was already in place. In fact, they'd discussed putting one in the hallway near the elevator but had decided to wait until they were making a clear profit.

"Well, thanks a lot. And if she contacts you for any reason, please call me right away." Rick gave Ryan and the maid each a business card.

As they walked toward their vehicles, Kate said, "So, that jerk did see Jillian pick her up this morning."

Rick nodded soberly. "Yeah."

"Why do you think he lied about it? I mean, lying to the police—"

"He was probably afraid he'd get in trouble if something happened to her, or that I'd make him go to the station and give a statement. I don't know. Some people are leery of the police. Sometimes with good reason."

"So you'll check him out?" Kate asked, unable to curb the anxiety in her voice.

"Of course. And I need to talk to Jillian again. She said Danielle told her some passerby brought her here and dropped her off last night. She could easily have called a cab to come and get her, but instead she stayed overnight. And this morning, instead of getting a taxi, she called the inn."

"Right, that's what Jillian told me too."

"It seems kind of odd." Rick looked back at the building. "This place is a dump. I'd say the owner runs things pretty much on a shoestring."

Kate nodded. It wasn't just the bleak room décor. Maintenance was sadly lacking. She certainly wouldn't want to stay here.

Rick stopped beside Kate's car and put a hand on her shoulder. "I'm going back to the inn after a bit to see Jillian again, but I need to check in with the station on the way to see if there's anything new. I want you and Jillian—and all those cheerleaders—to stay out of this, you hear me? These guys we're dealing with are not nice."

She swallowed hard, fighting the automatic resentment that washed over her when Rick pulled his big-brother act. They were beyond childhood squabbles. Rick was sincere. And he was right.

"Okay, we'll be careful and stick close to the inn."

"Good."

Before he could turn away, she asked, "Are you going to talk to other guests who stayed here last night?"

"If we think it will help, but we know she walked out of here on her own this morning."

"Someone else could have seen the truck she arrived in."

Rick seemed to consider that. "Unlikely, but possible. If nothing new has turned up, we'll check the other businesses nearby to see if they have cameras that would show part of this parking lot. You go home. I know you and Jill will let me know immediately if you hear anything."

"Of course. It's just ..."

Rick shifted his stance, and his face flooded with exasperation. "What?"

Kate exhaled heavily. "I'm trying to figure this out. Danielle's accident couldn't have been planned."

"I don't think so."

"And the man in the pickup stopped to help her. But when the blue van came to the Novel Inn, Danielle told Jillian that one of those men was Bob, the man who'd helped her get to this motel."

"Where are you going with this?" Rick glanced at his watch.

"I'm just saying, why would he want to harm her? And if he did, why didn't he do it when he had Danielle in his truck yesterday? Hmm?"

Rick huffed out a breath. "All reasonable questions, and all ones the police will take into consideration. Now, please go home. And please, please, stay out of this. Take care of your guests. Do what you gotta do to run the inn. But leave our job to us."

Jillian sat in the office going over the month's financial statements while Kate was gone. They seemed to be doing all right, especially with the numerous guests they'd had this weekend, but it was still too soon to tell if she and Kate could actually turn a profit with the inn. They'd agreed to evaluate their success—or failure—after Maine's tourist season ended at Labor Day. But Jillian wasn't sure she'd be ready to give up if they weren't in the black. She loved the inn.

Her nerves were stretched taut, and she flinched at every sound. The cheerleaders had not yet returned from their lunch foray. She was glad. Only the new guests and Mr. Philson were inside, but the peace and quiet wouldn't last long.

She heard a car in the parking area and rose to look out the window. Her sister parked and walked into the lobby.

"Any news?" Kate asked.

"Afraid not. Did you learn anything at the Oceanside?"

"Not really. They'd already cleaned the room, and they don't have security cameras, so there's no video of the truck that brought Danielle."

"Figures." Jillian made a sour face.

"Rick took the trash away with him, and he says for us to keep out of it and let the police handle it."

"Yeah, that figures too." Jillian leaned back in her chair. "I feel so helpless. I want to do something."

"I know what you mean." Kate sighed. "I had the car radio on during my drive just now. They announced that Danielle is believed abducted, and they asked for anyone with information to call the police."

"Did they mention the inn?"

"No, but it's probably just a matter of time. Do you think it will affect our business if people find out she was kidnapped here?"

"I don't even want to think about that." In the month since they'd opened, they'd managed to attract enough guests to offset their daily expenses, but they needed to increase their income. Bad publicity wouldn't help.

More engine sounds came from outside, and Jillian rose on her toes for a good view. "Looks like the cheerleaders are back. What do we tell them?"

"That Rick and the others are following up on every lead," Kate said. "But he doesn't want them interfering either."

The seven women streamed in through the front door. Jillian and Kate went out into the lobby to greet them.

"Hi. Any news on Danielle?" Alicia asked.

"I'm afraid not," Kate said.

Emma looked to Jillian. "Did they go to that motel?"

"Yes. In fact, Kate just came from there. She can tell you a little bit about that, I guess."

Kate gave them a wan smile. "The police searched the room she used, but nothing turned up. They're following up, talking to people and trying to find some video of the parking lot, but the motel has no cameras."

Patrice Flynn sighed. "We were really hoping you'd have some news for us, Kate."

"So did I," Kate said. "I'm sorry."

Jillian decided she needed to give the women something— an assurance that they were truly trying to find their friend. "I saw Mickey Holt this morning."

"You saw Mickey?" Gwen Vale said.

"What did he say?" Emma asked.

"How's he look?" Patrice seemed more eager for a report on the former high school hero than on Danielle.

"He seemed fine, but he didn't help us find Danielle. He

said they'd scheduled a coffee date for tomorrow, but he hadn't seen her yet. They'd just exchanged a couple of texts a few days ago, nothing today or yesterday." Jillian stepped out from behind the counter. "Can we get you all some coffee?"

"No, thanks," Alicia said, and Kate remembered that she'd gone with Jillian to see Mickey. But apparently she'd kept that bit of information to herself. Rick would be proud.

"I'd like some." Heather stepped forward.

Jillian forced a smile. "This way, anyone who wants refreshment."

Three of the women followed her toward the living room. The others headed for the elevator.

Jillian looked back. "Kate, did you send that video Rick wanted?"

She gulped. "I'll do it right now."

———

Jillian had invited Emma to sit down with her and Kate in the office, and they quietly discussed the best options for the group.

"Heather wants to go home." Emma eyed Jillian anxiously.

"Let her," Jillian said. "We won't charge her for the second night if she doesn't want to stay."

Kate sighed. "I guess it's pretty dismal for you all, with your friend missing."

"In a way. None of us feels like doing the activities we had planned. But most of us don't want to leave until we know Danielle's okay."

Kate caught her sister's eye. "I've been praying for Danielle since yesterday, but I, uh, wondered if you two would like to pray together for her."

Emma's eyes softened. "I'd really like that. Some of the

others don't—well, they don't pray. I've hesitated to suggest it, but I've been begging God nonstop to keep her safe."

Jillian extended a hand to each of them. "Sounds like a good idea."

They each offered a short, heartfelt petition. At the sound of a car approaching, Jillian quickly ended her prayer and rose. "That's Rick in his squad car."

"Maybe they've heard something," Emma said.

Jillian's pulse quickened, and she stepped into the lobby as Rick came through the door.

"Hi," she said. "Have you eaten? Let me get you a plate."

Rick held up a hand, palm outward. "No, I'm not staying. I just wanted to update you, and then I'm going home for a late lunch. Diana is starting to forget what I look like."

Jillian gave him a wan smile. "Did you find out anything?" She glanced at Emma. "Oh, you've met Emma Glidden."

"Hi, Ms. Glidden." Rick pulled out a chair and did not refuse the mug of coffee Kate carried in from the dining room's beverage station. "We haven't got a lead on Danielle yet, but I did have a call from the Boxborough police. They've found Danielle Redding's car."

Kate frowned. "Her car was here in Skirmish Cove. Oh!"

"Not the rental, her personal car, the one she reported stolen yesterday morning before she rented the one that crashed."

"Okay," Jillian said. "Where was it?"

"In Boxborough. But the fingerprints on it all seem to belong to family members."

"So, what does that mean?" Kate asked. "The car thief wore gloves?"

"Maybe. But the most prominent ones on the steering wheel and the driver's door belong to Ms. Redding's daughter,

Bailey." Rick picked up his mug and took a sip. "I gotta say, you girls make good coffee."

"Thanks," Jillian said. "Are you saying the thief didn't wipe the car clean?"

"He would have destroyed Bailey's fingerprints and Danielle's if he had."

"Right." Jillian thought about that. Gloves, maybe.

"So, what now?" Emma asked.

"We still haven't located Bailey, but thanks to you, Jillian, the cops down there got a line on the aunt. They think Bailey is probably with her mother's sister, Natalie Wilson, in Portsmouth. They're going to check it out." He took another swig of coffee and pushed back his chair. "We've got officers from several agencies out looking for Danielle. I'll let you know when we get something more."

"I sent our surveillance camera video," Kate said. She looked a bit guilty, and Jillian was glad she'd reminded her sister.

"Craig looked at it. We may be able to tell the make of the van from that. The facial ID is tricky. He's going to see if the State Police can help with facial recognition, but he said the angle's not good." Rick edged toward the door.

"I'll walk out with you," Jillian said. Her conscience was weighing on her, and she told him quickly about her visit to Mickey Holt as they crossed the front porch.

Rick frowned but didn't comment.

"Are you mad that I went?" Jillian asked.

"It would probably be better if you hadn't talked to him before us. But we'll send an officer over there later to touch base with him."

"I'm sorry," Jillian said. "I thought maybe I could save you some work. And honestly, I was thinking if he knew something, we'd find Danielle sooner."

"Okay, I get it. But no more, right?"

"Right."

"Tell me again what she told you about the guy with the white truck."

Jillian closed her eyes for a moment. "Not much. It was a white pickup. She thought she saw it, or one like it, as we left the motel. She was really jumpy. But she kind of laughed and said it wasn't the one."

"And the guy told her his name was Bob, right?"

"Yeah. She said he picked her up after the wreck—"

"Immediately after?"

"I'm not sure. She was probably in shock. I think she hit her head in the crash. I would have taken her to the ER this morning if she wanted to go, but she just wanted to get to the inn and connect with her friends. Rick, has there been anything like a ransom demand?"

"No. Nothing like that. Complete silence as far as the kidnappers go."

"She may be in really bad shape."

"Yeah."

Jillian couldn't stop berating herself for not insisting on taking Danielle to a medical professional.

Rick opened the patrol car door. "Keep thinking about it, and if you get any more brainstorms, let me know first, okay?"

"I will. I promise." Jillian waved as he turned his car around and drove out, heading toward home. She went back inside.

Kate and Emma had left the office. She found them in the living room, where most of the other cheerleaders had gathered again.

"I just don't understand it." Rachel Barker's voice broke, and tears filled her eyes. "Why would anyone kidnap Danielle?"

"It's not like she's rich," Gwen Vale said.

Emma nodded. "I agree. It doesn't make sense. I have no idea why those people took her, or how we can help."

Heather's upper lip curled. "Some great weekend this turned out to be, thanks to Danielle."

"Shut up," Alicia snapped.

Emma blinked at her in surprise. "Let's all stay calm. Heather, you have no business saying things like that about Danielle. It's not her fault she's had something traumatic happen to her."

"That's right," Patrice said. "Just because she beat you out of the head cheerleader spot twenty years ago doesn't mean you can dump on her."

Alicia directed a scowl at Heather. "I say, keep quiet or leave."

———

The guests remained subdued and, for the most part, quiet through the rest of the afternoon. The former cheerleaders huddled in the game room upstairs. Jillian did a little online browsing and came up with a few suggestions for dinner and evening entertainment. The women agreed to try a new restaurant together for dinner but declined the suggestion of a musical revue.

"I think we're all too tired and discouraged for that," Alicia said.

Jillian couldn't really blame them. She was relieved when Rick came by that evening to bring them all up to speed. She and Kate gathered the cheering squad in the game room on the second floor.

"The Boxborough police have located Bailey Redding at her aunt's house in Portsmouth, New Hampshire," Rick told them. "Danielle left her there on her way up here yesterday. Bailey knew where her father went on his fishing trip, so we hope he's located soon."

"Where is he?" Bobbi Talbot asked.

"Unfortunately, his plans were for camping with two other guys at a very remote lake up in northern New Hampshire. Their Fish and Game Department is sending someone out to find him and tell him what's happened, but they doubt they can have him here before tomorrow afternoon. That's if they find him tonight."

This news was received with quiet moans and sighs.

"Poor Paul," Alicia said softly.

"I suggest everyone try to get some sleep," Rick said.

Again, Jillian walked with him to the door.

"Thank you, Officer Gage," a couple of the women called after them.

"You're welcome," Rick replied.

He had dark half-moons under his weary eyes, and Jillian squeezed his arm.

"Thank you. I know you're doing everything you can."

"We really are, Jill."

She nodded. "I hope you're going to get some rest."

"Yeah, I'm headed home for a few hours."

"I can't help feeling she's close by, you know? And maybe hurt. If those men had good intentions, they wouldn't have come after her with a gun."

"Anything's possible at this point," Rick said.

"Kate and Emma and I had a little prayer meeting for her."

"Don't stop praying. Meanwhile, we keep checking with the hospital and all the clinics and medical services in the area, and we've alerted the State Police. She could be in Boston or beyond by now." His jaw clenched. "I'm still hoping we'll get a break—or that she'll find a way to get in touch again."

———

"All right, it's dark," Bob said. No, Mark said. Danielle squeezed her eyes shut and listened. "There's a moon, but it's cloudy tonight. I doubt anyone will notice."

"Are you coming?"

"I can't. Remember, that auctioneer is coming to the shop to discuss the Burton auction. He wants me to appraise some things."

"I should be there too. We can wait on her until after."

"No, I don't think so. We need to get her out of here as quick as we can—and I don't want to leave her alone that long. She almost got loose this morning when you took her to the restroom."

"I can't do it by myself, Mark."

There it was again. Mark, not Bob. But Danielle was sure that was Bob's voice. Maybe that wasn't his real name.

"Sure you can ... that place we talked about, on the bluff."

A streak of cold lightning zapped through Danielle.

"Can't we just—"

"No. You have to do this while I'm with Channing. I can't miss the appointment. Take her up there where we talked about. If they find her, they'll figure she was out walking and got lost."

"Why do I have to clean up your mess?" The second man's voice rose. He was definitely angry. Danielle didn't like the idea of being alone with him in an isolated area.

"You want me to put her in my van? There's no room in there now, remember?"

"Yeah. I still think that's the best place to keep the X12 until either we're sure we can fix it or else we get rid of it. If it's not repairable, we'll get by with the small one for a while. Anyway, for the job tonight, you'll have to take my truck, I guess."

That was Bob all right. Danielle had no idea what an X12 was, but she didn't want to get back in that truck. She writhed against her restraints, but they were too tight, pinning her hands behind her.

"What if she tries to get out? Maybe we should put her to sleep first. You got anything that would zonk her for a few hours?"

"No, I don't."

The second man swore. "Well, if I put her in the back of the truck, she could climb out at a stop sign."

"And if she was unconscious back there and a cop stopped you because they're looking for a white pickup, what do you think would happen? You're an idiot, Terry."

"I'm not the idiot who caused all this."

Bob swore. "Just do it. Tie her up good and take her in the cab with you. But you'll have to untie her before you toss her."

Toss her? Terror raced through Danielle. She hadn't trusted Bob from the first minute she'd seen him. If only she'd been more careful! Shaking set in, and her legs twitched. Other than that, she couldn't have moved if she'd wanted to.

"What if she fights? I really need you. If she's awake, she could put up a fight, but if she's out of it, I'm not sure I can carry her alone. I don't want to leave marks or anything like that."

Bob-Mark spoke in such a low, sinister voice Danielle could barely hear him, but his words squeezed the breath from her lungs and left her fighting for air.

"So crack her over the head and then do it. They'll think it happened when she fell. Use a rock, and throw it over the edge after her, into the water."

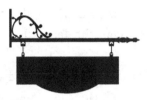

On Sunday morning at breakfast, Kate tried to encourage the cheerleaders. Heather had stayed over with the rest, but the inn's other guests had checked out, except for Mr. Philson. He had gone out after he ate to wander through the picturesque little town.

"I'm going to church this morning," Kate told the other guests. "If any of you would like to go, the morning service begins at eleven. A lot of people will be praying for Danielle."

"Are you going, Jillian?" Emma asked as Jillian refilled her coffee mug.

"No, I'll stay here. We've invited our neighbor over for dinner, so I'll be in and out of the kitchen." She paused and looked around at the women. "I know most of you planned to check out today. If you'd like to stay until Danielle's husband arrives, I'd be happy to make dinner for everyone. I'm cooking a ham, and we'll have plenty."

"Is Bailey coming with her father?" Alicia asked.

"I believe Mr. Redding told the police he'll pick her up on his way here."

Alicia nodded. "It might be nice for her to see someone she knows, even slightly, when she gets here."

"I think that's very kind of you." Jillian gave her a grateful smile.

"Is Paul going to stay here?" Patrice asked.

Kate said, "Yes. We haven't talked to him personally yet, but we had my brother relay a message to him that he and Bailey can stay here for as long as it helps them." Offering the Reddings free lodging was the least she and Jillian felt they could do.

When Kate left for the little clapboard white church, most of the cheerleaders did too. Heather and Rachel stayed to pack. Jillian completed the formal checkout for them, so they could leave whenever they were ready.

"I'd like to stay until we know more," Rachel said, "but I've got a four-hour drive ahead of me, and I have to work tomorrow."

"I'm sure everyone will understand," Jillian said.

Heather offered no excuses. "Can't wait to get home," she announced as she wheeled her suitcase from the elevator to the front desk.

Jillian gave a perfunctory smile. She almost hated to ask Heather, who'd been the main complainer of the weekend, how her stay went. She spoke up anyway, asking her standard question of a departing guest.

"It's been a pleasure to have you as our guest, Ms. Saxon. I hope you enjoyed your stay."

"It would've been better if there hadn't been a drone nosing around outside my window this morning."

Jillian caught her breath. "A drone?"

"Yeah. Was that you people? I mean, whatever happened to privacy?"

"No, it most certainly wasn't us," Jillian said. "We'll look into it."

"Fine." Heather slapped her key card down on the desk. "I assume someone's going to tell us if Danielle turns up?"

"I believe Alicia's taking on that job."

"Huh." Heather shifted her tote bag, grasped the handle on her wheelie, and headed out the door.

"Have a safe drive," Jillian called after her.

The inn seemed very quiet. Jillian spent extra time in the kitchen, making sure dinner would be just right. For Zeb, this would probably be the highlight of his week. She set a small table for three, so that he could eat with her and Kate, and a larger one for the five cheerleaders still in town. Finally everything was done that she could do, and she took a cup of tea out onto the side porch.

A pair of phoebes had started building a nest under the porch eaves, and Jillian settled into a deck chair to watch them. The sun warmed her, and it felt like spring. She hoped next winter would be easier and shorter than the one they'd just come through. Her mother's flower beds were thriving, with daffodils and narcissus in bloom and tulip clusters full of ready-to-burst buds.

Peace. That's what she found here. People often asked if she missed teaching school, but she really didn't. Not when she was able to catch her breath and look around at the gorgeous setting her parents had left her and her siblings.

She sipped her tea and sent up a silent prayer of thanks. An arctic tern wheeled overhead, gliding toward the shore path. She loved the fact that they came to Maine to nest, though they spent their winters in Antarctica.

She checked the time. Better turn on the burner under the fresh broccoli florets. Carrying her mug, she went inside.

Kate breezed into the kitchen just after noon and grabbed an apron.

"Any news?"

"No," Jillian said.

"Rick wasn't at church, so I was hoping."

Jillian took a couple of large serving dishes from the cupboard. "Was Ken Roderick there?"

Kate rolled her eyes. "Ken is always there."

"Oh, really?" Jillian laughed. The church's pianist always made it a point to speak to Kate before or after church—both, if he could manage it.

"The pastor held a special time of prayer for Danielle," Kate said.

"That's good."

"Yeah. Everyone wanted to hear all the details afterward."

"Then I'm glad I wasn't there." Jillian wasn't ready to answer myriad questions about the kidnapping. She heard the front door open and the women's voices as they came in from the parking lot. "Can you mash the potatoes?"

"Sure." Kate reached for the kettle.

Jillian went toward the lobby and paused in the dining room doorway. "Hi, everyone."

"Nothing new, I guess," Patrice said.

"We haven't heard anything new. I'm sorry."

"Oh, man." Patrice and the others looked at each other.

Gwen shook her head. "We were hoping."

"I know. So were we." Jillian gave them a faint smile. "I'm walking over to get our neighbor. If anyone wants to go along, it's just a short walk, and there's a beautiful view of the shore."

"I'll go," Emma said.

No one else volunteered, so Jillian nodded. "All right, then. I expect we'll eat in about twenty minutes, so you'll have time to freshen up."

She led Emma out the front door and along the wraparound porch to the back steps.

"Oh, this is so pretty," Emma cried. "Is that where you live?" She pointed toward the carriage house.

"Yes, it was my parents' home, and Kate and I live there now."

"It's lovely," Emma said, "and so handy."

"It is that. Here's the path."

They strolled along, and Jillian was pleased to see Emma's face light with pleasure.

"You didn't grow up here, did you?" Emma asked.

"No, my folks bought the inn about fifteen years ago. Kate had just graduated from high school, and I was married. After college, Kate took a job as office manager for the medical practice in town. She rented an apartment in an older house overlooking the bay. But she and I moved into the carriage house two months ago, after our parents died."

When they reached the footbridge over the stream, Emma stopped and fingered the smooth railing.

"This is wonderful."

"My dad built it. He and Zeb were great friends, and they liked to visit back and forth." They went over the span, and soon Zeb's compact cabin appeared. The American flag flew on the staff today, flapping in the light breeze off the bay, with Zeb's personal ensign below it. All was well.

"Ahoy, Jillian," the old man called as she approached. He pushed himself up from his deck chair.

"Permission to come aboard, sir."

"Granted, as always."

Jillian grinned and walked up to the front step. "Hi! Been waiting long?"

"No, just sitting out here enjoying the sun for a few

minutes. I figured you'd come when you were ready." He eyed Emma, smiling with approval. "Who's your mate?"

"This is Emma Glidden. She's a former student of mine, and she's been staying at the inn this weekend."

"Oho. Pleased to meet you, young lady. Welcome aboard."

Emma chuckled. "Thank you very much, sir."

"Do you sail?" he asked.

"No, never have," Emma said. "Do you?"

"Zeb was a career naval officer," Jillian said, and Zeb pulled in a deep breath, straightening his shoulders.

"Navy Signal Corps," he said.

"I'm impressed. Do you crack codes and things like that?"

He laughed, his eyes snapping. "You're a bright one. Now, Jillian, how's your daughter doing?"

Jillian smiled, aware that he'd changed the subject on purpose. "Megan? She's fine. She was planning to come home this weekend, but something came up at school, so she decided to stay there. Finals start tomorrow. I think she'll be home by the end of the week."

"Will she be here over the summer?"

"She plans to come home for a week or so, but she's got a job at a place with guest cottages in Belgrade Lakes."

"Well, maybe I'll get to see her when she visits. Say, you've been busy this weekend."

"Yes, we have." That was putting it mildly.

"Now, tell me, do you have anything to do with this woman who's missing?"

"Oh, Zeb," Jillian said. "I should have come and told you about that." She ought to have known he'd have had his television on for the local news.

Zeb shrugged. "You haven't had time, I expect. But is she found?"

"Not yet," Emma said. "And she was an old school friend of mine."

"I'm sorry. I hope she's found soon."

Emma nodded. "Thank you. We all do."

"Are we ready to embark?" he asked in a more cheerful tone.

"I believe we are." Jillian tucked her hand into the crook of his elbow, and Emma fell in behind them on the path. Though Zeb had passed his eightieth birthday, his steps were quite steady. Still, she would hate it if he fell on the way to her house. He probably knew that was why she held on to him whenever they walked together, but they never spoke of it. He just sailed along with his chin up, as though proud to be her escort.

He took obvious pleasure in the attention the cheerleaders showed him before and during dinner.

"My, my, I don't know when I've had the company of so many lovely ladies," he said as Patrice refilled his water glass.

Patrice's face wrinkled, and Jillian supposed she wouldn't put up with such a sexist remark from a younger man, but she said nothing.

"Say, Kate," Zeb said, looking up at her as she held out the platter of ham, "have you folks seen any of those newfangled drone things?"

Jillian's ears perked up.

"Are you thinking of getting one?" Kate asked.

"Me? No. But I'm pretty sure I saw one this morning. It was hovering just outside my bay window. I suppose it could have been a remote control helicopter or something like that."

Jillian hauled in a deep breath. "Interesting that you should bring that up, Zeb. One of our guests saw one outside the inn. She asked me if it was ours while she was checking out."

"What on earth?" Kate threw Jillian a troubled look.

"What do they use them for, anyhow?" Zeb asked.

"Well, some people just like to play with them, but photographers love them, and real estate agents use them to take overhead photos of property they're going to list," Jillian told him.

"Spying," Zeb muttered with a frown.

"You think they were spying on you, Mr. Wilding?" Emma asked.

"I don't know why else they'd hang around my windows if they've got cameras in those things. Just like military spy drones."

"People aren't supposed to use them near houses or airports," Bobbi said. "It's not just the privacy issue. They can be dangerous."

Jillian patted Zeb's hand. "I will definitely talk to Rick about them."

———

An SUV pulled into the Novel Inn's parking lot about two o'clock, and a man and a teenage girl got out. Kate had been sitting behind the desk in the lobby, watching for them. She picked up her cell phone and called her brother.

"Rick? I think the Reddings are here. They're not inside yet, but they're heading for the door, and they fit the description."

"Be right there."

"Okay." She closed the connection and stood as the door opened.

"Hi," the man said uncertainly. "I'm Paul Redding."

Kate walked around the desk. "I'm Kate Gage. I'm so sorry to meet you under these circumstances."

He nodded, a quick jerk of his head. He was tanned, and his dark hair was a little shaggy, his beard about three days' worth of stubble. His anxiety poured from his brown eyes, and deep lines etched the corners, though he probably wasn't over forty.

"The police are on their way here to speak to you." Kate smiled at the girl. "You must be Bailey."

"Yeah." She wore torn jeans, a red crop top, and sandals. Her eyes met Kate's, then flicked away.

"If you'd like to bring your luggage in, I'll take you to your rooms," Kate said. "I'm sure an officer will be here by the time you're settled."

Paul Redding grunted and went out without another word. Bailey hesitated and then followed him.

Jillian came in from the dining room. "Is it them?"

"Yes. Both very quiet."

"Well, let's check them in. I'm sure they'll be ready to talk when they see Rick's uniform."

"I called him," Kate said.

Bailey came in with a backpack slung over her shoulder, pulling a small, wheeled suitcase. Her father strode behind her, bringing a camouflage duffel bag.

"Your rooms are free of charge," Kate said. "We'd appreciate it if you'd register, though."

"Of course." They already had Danielle's home address. Paul gave her his phone number and vehicle plate number.

"Hi, I'm Jillian, Kate's sister." Jillian smiled at them both. "We've decided to put you in the Anna Karenina Room and the Jeeves Room. They're both here on the first floor, adjacent. You'll have some privacy." She reached for Bailey's suitcase, and the girl let her take it.

As she turned to lead them out of the lobby, Emma and Alicia came down the stairs.

"Paul," Alicia said. "I'm so glad you're here. And Bailey. Do you remember me? I'm Alicia Boyken, you're mom's friend from high school."

Bailey shook her head and seemed to shrink into herself.

Emma descended the final step and held out her hand to Paul. "And I'm Emma Glidden. I was at your wedding, but I don't believe I've seen you since. We're all so sorry about Danielle."

"Thank you." Paul cleared his throat and glanced at Jillian.

"This way, Mr. Redding. Bailey."

Tears glistened in Bailey's eyes as Jillian led them out. Emma and Alicia hovered, then moved closer to the check-in desk. Kate resumed her seat behind it.

"I feel so bad for them," Emma said.

Kate nodded. "My brother's on his way here to talk to them. He'll probably want to do that in private, but there should be time for you to talk to them later."

"I'll try to talk to Bailey again," Alicia said. "She looked absolutely wiped out."

"Wouldn't you be?" Emma shook her head. "We'd better give them some space for now."

"I guess you're right." Alicia sighed and followed Emma up the winding stairs.

A few minutes later, Jillian came back to the lobby. "You want to wait for Rick? I'll get some coffee ready."

"Sure," Kate said. "Where do you think they should talk? We want them to have privacy."

"I'm thinking the office. The guests can't just barge in there. We can shut the hall door and that one." Jillian nodded toward the door behind the check-in desk that led into the office. She spent a lot of time in there, especially at the end of the month, but the guests almost never entered that room. They stopped at the lobby desk then breezed on through to the elevator or the dining room.

"Okay, I'll make sure there's plenty of chairs in there." Kate opened the door and looked around the crowded room. Only three chairs. She went to the dining room for another, in case Rick brought a second officer with him. When she got back to the front desk, he had arrived alone.

"Hi." He kissed Kate on the cheek. "You've got Mr. Redding and his daughter?"

"Yeah. Jillian says you can use her office. I'll go tell them you're here."

Bailey was in Mr. Redding's room when Kate knocked.

"Do I have to go?" she asked her father.

"No, it's okay. I'll talk to the police. Why don't you go to your room and lie down?"

Bailey went across the small niche of hallway between their doors and entered the Anna Karenina Room, the one they'd been holding for her mother. Kate hoped she enjoyed the décor, though Bailey was probably too distraught to notice it at the moment.

She took Mr. Redding to the office. Jillian was setting out a coffeepot, mugs, napkins, and a plate of homemade cookies.

"Why don't you two stay," Rick said to his sisters. "You can fill Mr. Redding in on what went on here."

Paul sat down wearily in one of the chairs facing the desk. "Is there any word at all, Officer?"

"There's not a lot," Rick said. "I can assure you, our department is out there right now, trying to find your wife."

"I was told Danielle was abducted right in front of this hotel?"

"That's correct."

"And there was something about a car accident." Paul eyed him narrowly.

"Yes, your wife was involved in a single-car accident late Friday afternoon or early evening. A passerby drove her to a motel—it's about five miles from here, nearer to the highway.

We don't think your wife was badly injured, but her medical condition may have come into play."

"You mean her blood sugar?"

"Yes, and she may have been slightly injured in the accident as well, but she refused medical care. I've talked to the staff at the Oceanside Motel, and the desk clerk said she seemed disoriented. But Jillian here"—he nodded toward his older sister—"got a call from her yesterday morning. She went to the motel and picked Danielle up and brought her here, where her friends were staying."

While he spoke, the sisters had seated themselves, and Jillian took up the tale after a nod from Rick. Kate listened, trying to pick up any nuances. She'd seen a lot of people under stress during her time at the medical practice. Mr. Redding definitely seemed keyed up. With his left hand, he rubbed his clenched right fist.

"Danielle seemed all right when I got there. She did have a small cut here." Jillian touched her temple. "I asked if she wanted medical help, and she said no. She just wanted to get over here where her friends were. She'd lost her phone and couldn't call them, and she was very anxious to be with them."

"But why did she stay at this other motel?" Paul asked.

"The police haven't had a chance to question her yet," Rick said. "We're assuming she was shaken up after her accident and maybe couldn't remember the name of the inn here, where she was booked. Her phone was in the car when we found it, and her glucose monitoring kit was in her suitcase."

"She was at the mercy of the guy who came along and picked her up after the wreck," Jillian said. "I'm sure my brother's right—she wasn't thinking clearly, whether because of her blood sugar or her injuries. But the next morning, she was very eager to leave the motel where she'd slept. I drove over there and met her, and as we left their parking lot, she seemed fearful."

"How do you mean?" Paul asked quickly.

"She thought she saw the truck of the man who'd taken her there, but then she relaxed and said it wasn't him. I told her the police had recovered her rental car and her luggage. We drove here without any problems, but as we were getting ready to go inside, a blue van drove in." Jillian swallowed hard. "Two men jumped out, and Danielle collapsed."

"Collapsed?" Paul gaped at her.

"Yes. She fainted. But first she said, 'It's Bob.' That was the name she'd told me her so-called rescuer gave her the day before, when he happened on her accident."

"So ..." Paul eyed her suspiciously. "You let them take her?"

"Bob had a gun." Jillian's face flushed, and she threw Rick a glance.

"Apparently one of the men held my sister at gunpoint," Rick said. "He made her surrender her car keys while his accomplice picked up Danielle and carried her to their van. They drove away, and Jillian called me immediately."

"I thought there were a lot of people here."

"Actually," Jillian said, "Most of the guests and my sister Kate were out near the scene of Danielle's accident, looking for her, when she called me here. They hadn't returned when we got here. Rick drove in within two minutes after the men in the van left, and the women arrived right behind him."

"We've been following up on the evidence ever since," Rick said.

"But it's—it's been over twenty-four hours since they took her, right?"

Rick sighed. "That's correct. We're focusing on the van and the partial license plate Jillian got."

Paul ran a hand through his dark brown hair. "You've got to find her."

"We'll do our best, sir."

"The police wanted me to wait in Boxborough. I couldn't. I needed to get up here, where she is. That was all right, wasn't it?"

"You need to be where you think you can help your wife the most," Rick said.

Paul's breath came in short, quick bursts. "That's what I thought. I could leave, since I wasn't under arrest or anything."

"Yes, it's all right," Rick said. "I can let them know you arrived here safely."

"Thanks. I had to be near where it happened." Paul darted a sudden look at him. "There hasn't been any contact with the kidnappers, has there? No ransom calls or anything?"

"I'm afraid not."

Kate already assumed the abductors weren't after a ransom —which was not a good thing. According to the little research she'd done while tending the desk, if kidnappers didn't ask for a ransom, it could mean they didn't intend to return the victim.

Rick poured himself coffee. "When did you pick up your daughter, Mr. Redding?"

"I got her about three hours ago, at her aunt's house in Portsmouth. We stopped once for gas."

"How is Bailey taking all this?"

"She was upset, of course."

Rick nodded. "Danielle arrived in Skirmish Cove in a rental car, which she leased down in Boxborough. Did you know about that?"

"Not until last night. The police mentioned it. They said she reported her car stolen Friday morning. Bailey was apparently with her mom when she realized the car was missing, but she didn't know anything about it. She said Danielle tried to call me, but I guess we were out of cell phone service by then, up in northern New Hampshire. Bailey said her mother called the rental place and got a taxi to take them to pick up the car."

"Okay," Rick said. "Do you know anyone who may have wanted to do your wife harm?"

"No," Paul said quickly. "Everyone likes Dani. You think these men knew her? I mean, she'd had an accident, right?"

"We're trying to piece together what happened. At this point, we can't rule out anything. The evidence seems to indicate that someone picked her up after she had an accident in the rental car. Possibly a passerby who'd never met her before. We haven't located that person yet, but we know he drove her to the Oceanside Motel. As I told you, she spent Friday night there. Saturday she called Jillian, who brought her here. That's pretty much all we know."

"Why didn't that guy take her to a hospital if she was hurt?"

"That's yet to be determined. Do you know a man named Mickey Holt?"

Paul shook his head frowning. "Is that the guy who picked her up?"

"We don't think so. Apparently he's a former acquaintance of your wife's from her high school days."

"Holt, was it?"

Rick nodded.

"Dani may have mentioned that name once or twice. I don't really remember it."

"We learned she texted him a few days ago to set up a meeting with him while she was here."

Alarm sharpened Paul's features.

"Jillian, why don't you tell Mr. Redding about the conversation you had with Mr. Holt yesterday," Rick said.

"All right." Jillian cleared her throat.

"Is it okay if I go and talk to Bailey?" Kate asked. "Rick, you can tell Mr. Redding about the motel. I don't really have anything to add, and I wondered if I might reach out to Bailey."

Paul eyed her in surprise.

"We three also lost our mother recently," Kate said. "Both our parents, actually."

"You think Danielle is dead?" Paul asked sharply.

Kate's cheeks heated. "No, not necessarily. I'm sorry. I just meant that I know what it feels like to lose someone you love suddenly like that. I'll try not to alarm Bailey."

Paul nodded slowly. "I guess it's okay."

"What does she like to drink?" Jillian asked.

"Diet Coke."

"I'll get her one," Kate said.

She went to the kitchen and got a can from the refrigerator, then fixed a small tray with a glass and a couple of cookies on a plate. She carried it out through the dining room and around to Bailey's door and knocked.

"Who is it?" came the teen's voice.

"It's Kate Gage. I'm the one who checked you in." After a pause, Kate said, "I brought you a snack. May I come in?"

"I guess."

Kate opened the door. Bailey sat on the wide window seat, facing the side porch and the woods between the inn and the stream.

"Do you like chocolate chip cookies?"

Bailey stirred and turned toward her. "Yeah. Thanks."

"You're welcome." Kate set the tray on a doily on the antique side table, within Bailey's reach. "I'm really sorry about your mom."

"Why can't they find her?"

"I don't know." Kate sat down in the carved wooden chair at the desk. "My brother—the police officer—told your dad they found her phone in the car. She probably dropped it during the crash and couldn't find it. Someone took her to a motel on the edge of town, and the people there said she was disoriented. Without her phone, she may have just gone to sleep and figured she'd contact someone in the morning."

"She could have used the phone at the motel."

"Yes." Kate had gone over it in her own mind many times, and it didn't make sense to her, either. "All we can figure is that she wasn't feeling well or thinking straight, so she went to sleep. When she woke up in the morning, she did call here, and my sister went to get her. We were afraid she'd been hurt when she crashed her car."

"But she was okay when your sister got her?"

"She seemed to be, or at least thinking straight. She'd remembered the name of our inn and phoned from the motel. But right after the accident, she may not have been too alert."

"It wasn't our car," Bailey said.

"No, it was the one she rented. Did she take you in that to your aunt's house Friday?"

Bailey nodded.

"I suppose driving a strange car might have thrown her off kilter," Kate said.

Bailey's face crumpled. "It's my fault."

———

Jillian recounted her meeting with Mickey Holt, stressing that he'd claimed Danielle hadn't contacted him again after reaching the area.

"That's correct," Rick said. "Her phone was in the rental

car, and there were no messages or calls to Mr. Holt on Friday. There were texts a couple of days earlier, when she set up the potential meeting with Mr. Holt."

"I just ..." Paul shook his head, his mouth slightly open. "I can't believe this is happening."

"How have you and Danielle been getting along lately?" Rick asked.

That seemed awfully nosey, but Jillian understood that it was part of Rick's job. She kept quiet as they talked quietly, impressed by her brother's professionalism. She wasn't sure she should be hearing this personal information about the Reddings, but Rick had told her to stay, so she tried to sit as inconspicuously as she could.

"Pretty good." Paul's mouth flexed, and he gave a little shrug. "We had a few squabbles."

"What about?"

Paul sighed. "I've been thinking lately about getting a motorcycle. Danielle doesn't think we can afford it. I was pretty upset one day a couple of weeks ago. I was ready to buy the bike on credit, and Danielle called and canceled it."

"That got you steamed?" Rick asked.

Paul looked a little uncomfortable. "Oh, not enough to harm her, if that's what you mean. I know part of her objection was because she doesn't think motorcycles are safe. She crabbed about the money, but I knew she was worried about me."

Rick nodded. "I notice you had enough for both of you to take trips this weekend."

Paul smiled and pointed one finger at him. "You speak truth. She wanted to come over here and stay two or three nights by the ocean with her friends. I said, sure, if I can have my bike. That didn't go down too well. But then a couple of my buddies asked if I wanted to go fishing with them this weekend."

"Danielle didn't think that was so bad?"

"Well, it's cheaper than a Harley. I mean, really, what could she say? She wanted her little jaunt too. So we compromised. I figured a couple of days apart would give us both time to cool down."

"Okay," Rick said. "I'm going to need your fishing buddies' names and addresses. Phone numbers if you've got them on you. We'll need to confirm that you were with them all weekend."

Paul's eyebrows shot up. "What are you saying?"

"Usual operating procedure," Rick said. "A crime's been committed. Until we get it all sorted out, we can't make any assumptions. We need proof of everything."

"But you know I was at the lake." Paul's face flushed. "New Hampshire state cops came and got me."

"Yes, but did they confirm that you were with your friends the entire time since you left home?"

"I ... I assume so."

"Just give me their contact info. I'll pass it on, and officers down there can double check. We don't want to be caught unprepared later on."

Paul stared at him and shook his head. "I would never hurt Danielle. Ever."

Rick opened his pocket notebook and laid it on the desk in front of Paul. "You can write down your friends' names there. Everyone who was on the trip with you."

"There was only two other guys."

"Okay. The officers who went to get you may already have this data, but I need you to write it down."

Paul picked up the pen and slowly began to write. While he was at it, the door opened. Jillian jumped up. Kate and Bailey entered the office. Tears streamed down the girl's face, and she dabbed at them with a wadded tissue.

"What's going on?" Paul demanded, glaring at Kate.

"Here, Bailey, sit right down." Jillian touched the back of the chair next to her father.

"Sweetie, you okay?" Paul asked.

Bailey's mouth skewed. "I'm sorry, Dad."

"Oh, come on, it's not your fault." Paul stood and reached for her, but Bailey pulled away.

"Yes, it is. I stole Mom's car."

# 9

"What are you saying, Bailey?" Paul Redding stood and stared at his daughter, his face taut.

Bailey grimaced. "I took the car. I didn't want Mom to go away this weekend, and I thought that would stop her."

Shooting Rick a confused glance, Paul stepped toward her. "Sit down. Come on."

Bailey hobbled to the nearest chair and sank onto it. She clasped her trembling hands together between her knees. "I hoped Mom would stay home if the car was missing, and I wouldn't have to go spend the weekend at Aunt Natalie's house and miss the school dance. And now Mom's disappeared!" Bailey crumpled in the chair, sobbing.

Paul pulled his chair closer and sat next to her, engulfing her in his embrace. "Easy now, honey. Calm down. Just tell us what happened."

"Just what I said," Bailey choked out.

Stepping to a file cabinet, Jillian retrieved a box of tissues and carried it over. She held it out to Bailey, and the girl plucked two tissues and mopped her face with them.

"I took the car and drove it a mile or so away and left it in the lot at the park and walked home. But it didn't help. It slowed Mom down all of about ten minutes. She threw a mini fit when she realized it was gone, and immediately called the police, of all things!"

Paul sat back and frowned at her. "Well, what did you expect?"

"I don't knoooow," Bailey wailed.

"But that doesn't make it your fault that she's in danger now," Jillian said, and immediately wished she'd kept quiet. Paul Redding threw her a look that said *someone* was in trouble now, big time.

"If I hadn't stolen the car, Mom wouldn't have had to rent a strange one, and she might not have had the accident." Bailey blew her nose noisily into one of her damp tissues. "Will I have to go to jail?" She darted a weepy glance at Rick.

Jillian's heart went out to her. Yes, Bailey had acted immaturely, but she'd been thinking like a kid. It wasn't that long ago that she and Jack had been through plenty of teen crises with their daughter Megan. They'd all lived through it. Still, without his wife on hand, Paul must be torn up inside. She remembered how hard it had been for her to deal with Megan's emotional outbursts after Jack died.

Paul cleared his throat. "We'll have to sort it out, Bailey. You must know that—" He broke off as Rick's cell phone rang.

He pulled it from his pocket and frowned at it. "Excuse me, folks. I need to take this." Rick rose and stepped out into the lobby, closing the door behind him.

As they waited for him to return, Bailey continued sobbing and sniffing, and her father sat there staring at her with a dumbfounded expression on his face. Jillian was beginning to feel a bit of a fifth wheel.

"Uh, let me go make a fresh pot of coffee," she said. "Bailey, would you like some more Diet Coke?"

"I didn't finish the first one." Bailey sniffed, her face scrunched up like a raisin.

Jillian rose. "Mr. Redding?"

"I'm good."

Jillian nodded and looked at her sister. Kate just shrugged, as though she didn't know what to do either. Jillian stepped out the door that took her into the hall. Rick was pacing the lobby and saying things like, "10-4. Got it. Roger that." She strode through the dining room toward the kitchen. About halfway there, she realized Kate had followed her.

"Man alive," Kate whispered. "What do you think?"

"I think Bailey's in for it."

Kate nodded. "I came out because I don't want to be in there when her father explodes on her."

"Yeah, they needed a private moment."

"What if he goes ballistic?"

"Then Rick will hear him yelling and make him stop." Jillian entered the kitchen. "Maybe we should start thinking about what we're going to eat for supper tonight."

"Are we feeding them?"

"I hope not. You know our policy is that guests are on their own for dinner." With a sigh, she opened the refrigerator and balefully eyed the leftovers from their Sunday dinner. This was all so new, she wasn't sure whether to ignore the meal policy or insist they keep it. Because so many people had eaten at the inn that noon, there wasn't a lot of food left. She and Kate could make do with the leftovers, but they wouldn't stretch to include the Reddings.

She shut the door and turned to Kate. "How did you get Bailey to confess to you?"

"I didn't. She was tied up in knots. She probably would

have spilled it to anyone except her dad. I just tried to calm her down and convince her she needed to tell him sooner rather than later."

"Well, kudos on that. Should we go back in?"

"I don't know. Rick seemed to want someone there. Maybe he's not comfortable with the family dynamic. You've studied psychology and taught teenagers. Maybe you should go back."

"He's a professional," Jillian said. "And he's got a teenage daughter too."

"I know, but—"

"You don't want to go back?"

"I'd rather not," Kate said.

"Okay, wish me luck. I'm going back into the lions' den." Jillian hauled in a deep breath.

"I'll stay out here. I can set up the dishes for the breakfast buffet. If we don't have to feed anyone tonight, let's order a pizza for the two of us."

"Sounds good to me. Andy can snack on the leftovers. Oh, and start some fresh coffee. I said I would."

As Jillian turned away, Rick stepped into the doorway. "You two might want to come and hear what I'm about to tell Mr. Redding."

Jillian looked at her sister.

Kate shrugged. "Okay, I'm coming."

They followed Rick to the office. Paul and Bailey were sitting where they had left them. Bailey was still crying, and Paul's face was red, his jaw set in a hard line.

"All right, folks." Rick walked behind the desk and sat down.

Jillian resumed her seat, and Kate leaned against the closed door.

"I've just heard from one of my colleagues," Rick said. "As we've already told you, we found Danielle's cell phone in the car. The tech officer working on her phone found a bank app on it."

Paul nodded. "She uses that for deposits and things like that. I have the same app. It's handy."

"Yes, well, we've requested her bank records, since you gave us permission. How many accounts do you and Danielle have?"

"Just one. Our joint checking account."

Rick eyed him thoughtfully for a moment. "I wouldn't tell you this, but I'm thinking it might be important. We found your joint account, as well as a second account in Danielle's name only."

Paul's eyebrows lowered, and a crease formed between them. "A second bank account? At the same bank?"

"Yes. You weren't aware of it?"

He hesitated. "No, I wasn't."

His daughter looked over at him, her eyes wide, but she didn't speak.

"Well, it's not a huge account. It only has about eight hundred and fifty dollars in it." Rick shrugged. "My wife has an account in her own name where she puts whatever she earns from her crafts."

"Danielle doesn't have a side job."

"Okay. Well, anyway, she seems to have made small deposits into this account occasionally for the last couple years."

Jillian's mind raced. Had Danielle planned to leave Paul and wanted to have some money stashed to finance her exit? Paul had a thunderstruck air about him, and Bailey's gaze flitted from one person to another and landed on Kate.

"It's probably just her mad money, right?" the girl asked.

"Sure," Kate said. "A lot of women like to have a little cash put away in their own names."

A bad feeling hit Jillian, and she remained silent. She could understand where Rick was coming from. The police would surely see this as a suspicious development. Could the clandestine account be related to the trip to Maine, or to Danielle's appointment with Mickey Holt?

Paul's eyes narrowed and he focused on Rick. "If you're suggesting that Danielle had something secret in mind, like bailing on her family, you're wrong. She wouldn't do that to Bailey and me."

Holding up both hands palm out, Rick said, "I'm not suggesting anything, Mr. Redding. I'm just telling you what the department has learned."

Bailey shook her head. "I just don't believe it."

"What? That she had a secret bank account?" Her father's voice took on a combative tone, as though he had suddenly switched from questioning Danielle's actions to defending her.

"No," Bailey said. "I don't believe she'd leave us."

Paul's lips tightened. "Do you think she'd believe you stole her car so you could be with your friends this weekend?"

Bailey's tears spilled over again, and Jillian held out the tissue box.

"Let's just calm down," Rick said in a soothing, even voice. "I'm sure we all want the same thing—to find Danielle."

Paul had the grace to lower his gaze. "You're right. This isn't about the car, Bailey."

"Of course it is," Bailey gasped.

"No. It's about ... about your mom. Her health is a big concern, and it's got me on edge. I'm sorry I snapped at you. Let's put aside what you did for now. We can talk about that after we find your mom, okay?"

Bailey nodded slowly and wiped away a tear.

Muffled voices came from the lobby, and Jillian was sure she heard the front door shut, followed by a soft knock on the door between the office and the lobby. Kate turned and opened it.

"Hi," Emma Glidden said, her gaze sliding past Kate and into the room. "I'm sorry to interrupt, but Patrice and Bobbi want to check out, and someone else is here to see Jillian."

Jillian stepped forward and looked over Emma's shoulder. She'd expected the two departing cheerleaders to be waiting forlornly in the lobby with their luggage, but they'd abandoned their suitcases to sidle up to Mickey Holt. Poor Mickey, near the door, smiled uncertainly at Patrice and Bobbi. In Jillian's estimation, he looked as if he might turn and bolt at any second.

"It's so good to see you again," Bobbi said, placing a hand on Mickey's arm. She was a bit too excited about the reunion for Jillian's taste.

"Can you handle the checkout?" she whispered to Kate.

"Of course." Kate stepped out to the front desk and spoke with authority. "Ladies, if you're ready to check out, I can take care of you."

Bobbi and Patrice didn't look too happy to leave Mickey's side, but he puffed out a breath in unmistakable relief. Jillian shut the office door behind her and walked over to him. She gave him a smile she hoped signaled welcome but not lightheartedness.

While Kate began the check-out process with Patrice and Bobbi, she placed herself so that Mickey had to turn slightly to face her, taking his attention away from the cluster of women at the desk.

"Mickey. What brings you here?"

"I wondered if there's any word about Danielle. I guess not, huh? Patrice and Bobbi said ..." He stopped with a grimace.

Of course. Jillian had told him of Danielle's plans to come

to the Novel Inn, and he'd come to the inn to find her, rather than approach the police.

"Actually, we have an officer here right now, talking to her family."

"Her family?"

"Yes, Danielle's husband and daughter arrived this afternoon from Massachusetts. My brother Rick is a Skirmish Cove police officer, and he's in the office talking to them."

"Oh. Well, I don't want to interrupt anything. I just wondered—you know."

Jillian nodded. "Of course. Would you like to step into the dining room? It's quieter there, and we have coffee."

"Great. Thanks."

Emma was still hovering between the lobby and the dining room.

Jillian smiled at her. "Would you like to join us, Emma?"

"Sure."

Jillian ushered Mickey and Emma into the dining room, hoping Patrice and Bobbi, who were caught up in the check-out routine, would leave and not try to see Mickey again.

She realized no one had started the fresh coffee and quickly measured out grounds and water for a half pot and started the machine.

"This will just take a sec. And we have cookies." She put half a dozen on a plate and took it to the table.

"Emma, excuse me just a minute. Help yourselves to coffee when it's brewed.

"Sure."

Jillian slipped back over to the office. She opened the door a few inches and caught Rick's eye, giving him a tip of the head to signal that she wanted him to come out of the room.

Rick excused himself and joined her. "What is it?"

"Mickey Holt's here, asking about Danielle. I told him we

had an officer on the premises, and I put him in the dining room with Emma Glidden and the coffeemaker."

"Okay, I'll have a few words with him. Let me just tell Mr. Redding we're done for now, but I'll check in with him later."

"He and Bailey will want you to keep them in the loop."

Rick frowned. "Yeah. I can't tell them everything—for example, let's not tell them Mickey Holt's here. I don't want to risk a confrontation between him and Paul."

"Probably a good idea."

When Jillian went back to the dining room, Mickey and Emma were sitting at the tables where she'd left them with full coffee mugs. Jillian was glad their position put them out of view of anyone in the lobby unless they walked right into the doorway. She fixed herself a cup of coffee and started another full pot while they continued to talk.

"So, the whole squad from our senior year was here?" Mickey asked.

"All but Danielle," Emma replied. "Even Gwen and Rachel. They were juniors that year, but I thought it would be nice to have the whole group that was on the squad together when most of us were seniors. I talked to Alicia and Danielle, and they thought it was a great idea, so I set up this weekend for a reunion."

"Bummer how it turned out." Mickey sipped his coffee.

"Some of the others have left," Emma said. "The police told us we can go home, but we need to be available if the investigators need to ask us more questions. We had to give Officer Gage multiple ways to contact us."

"Wow."

Emma shrugged. "Some of the gals seemed a little uncomfortable with that, but I don't mind. Danielle was a good friend when we were at Cony together. I haven't seen her for a few years—not since our ten-year class reunion, actually."

"Oh, yeah, I went to that in Augusta."

"I remember."

Mickey sighed. "I sure hope they find her. I mean, we weren't close—not since senior year—but, man, this is really weird, don't you think?"

Emma murmured her agreement.

Jillian carried her coffee to their table and sat down. "So, Mickey, how did you end up here in Skirmish Cove?"

"Well, my uncle lives here, and he had the garage. I used to visit him when I was a kid, and he taught me a lot about cars. I love the ocean. He invited me to come work for him after high school, and I've been here ever since. He offered me a partnership a couple of years ago."

"I'm surprised we haven't met before," Jillian said. "If my car needs work, I know where to take it now."

"You taught school here?" Mickey asked. "Emma said you were her English teacher."

"That was before my family moved to Augusta," Emma said. "We were in Bucksport then."

"Yes, I taught in Bucksport, but my parents lived here and owned the inn." Jillian sipped her coffee as Rick walked in.

"Hey, Jillian, I'm sorry, but I've got to go. I just got a call from the station. We may have a new lead." His gaze veered to Mickey. "Mr. Holt?"

"Yeah." Mickey stood, his face filled with anxiety. "I just came by to see if Danielle was still missing."

"Could you come into the police station later and just clarify for us what your contact was with Ms. Redding this past week?"

"Sure."

Rick nodded. "I'll call you later, Jillian."

Before she could get out a question, he was gone.

"Any idea what that new lead is?" Mickey asked.

"No, I don't. But—" Jillian stopped. Mickey was probably still on the suspect list. She shouldn't tell him anything.

"I was hoping to find out what exactly happened to her," Mickey said.

Emma didn't have the same wariness Jillian had. She leaned eagerly toward Mickey. "You didn't hear? Two men in a blue van grabbed Danielle yesterday morning, right outside the front door here."

"Whoa." He looked at Jillian.

No doubt he was wondering why she hadn't told him this the day before. She hoped Emma wouldn't spill all the details. She picked up her mug and took a sip, regretting her thoroughness in sharing with the cheerleaders and avoiding Mickey's gaze.

————

By half past three, the inn was very quiet. All of the cheerleaders except Emma had checked out, and Mickey had left for the police station to give his statement. Even Mr. Philson came to the desk to check out, ending his coastal vacation with reluctance.

"It was wonderful having you here," Kate told him when he turned in his key. "I hope you enjoyed your stay."

"Mostly," he said. "Those women were kind of noisy."

"I'm sorry. They were exuberant at first, and then ..."

"Hm. Well, I'm sorry about their friend."

"Yes, we all are," Kate said.

The big surprise of the afternoon was a visit from the deliveryman for the local florist. He walked in carrying a large bouquet of red roses.

Kate stood up behind the desk. "Wow. Are those for us or one of the guests?"

"Ms. Kate Gage."

"That's me." She smiled, her mind flitting at once to the identities of possible senders. "Put them right here, I guess." She gave him a tip from their petty cash box, and he left. She was about to open the card envelope when Jillian came out of the office.

"Wow! Are those yours?"

"Apparently. My name's on the envelope."

"Who are they from?"

Kate frowned. "Look at this." She held out two tickets.

Jillian leaned in to read the fine print on them. "Hey, lucky you! Those are for the big concert in Bar Harbor next week. Who's the lucky guy?"

"I don't know." Kate opened the envelope again. "There's no card, just the tickets."

"Really?" Jillian took them and studied both the tickets and the small envelope they came in. "I guess he wants it to be a surprise."

"Well, the way things have been happening around here lately, I'm not up for any more surprises."

"Aw, come on. We were just talking about that concert. You know you want to go." Jillian gave her a sudden grin. "Maybe they're from Ken."

"Ken Roderick?" Kate scowled. It was no secret that the church pianist liked her, and while he was a nice guy, Kate wasn't overly enamored of him. "I hope not."

"Why?"

She shrugged. "I'm not thrilled about the idea of spending a whole evening with him. Besides, if he wants to go out with me, why didn't he just ask? This is pretty presumptuous, don't you think?"

"Maybe he was afraid you'd say no."

"With good reason." Kate parted the leaves and stems of the roses carefully in case another envelope was hiding in there. "You don't really think Ken would do this, do you? He's so shy—and he's not made of money."

Jillian cocked her head to one side. "Who else likes you that much? Brent at the gas station always flirts with you."

"Oh, please. He wouldn't do this. And besides, I think he's got a girlfriend now." Kate eyed the bouquet critically.

"Well, whoever sent it is going to ask you to go to that concert with him. And if he doesn't, I'll go with you."

"It's really kind of weird. Guys don't usually do something this flamboyant unless—" Kate stopped searching as things clicked into place.

"What?"

"The doctors. I told you Dr. Englebrite called me yesterday, didn't I? They want me back."

"You really think so?"

"Yes, I do. They probably chipped in on it."

"So call Englebrite and ask him."

"I think I'll do that." Kate shook her head and pulled out her cell phone. "I'm going to give him a piece of my mind."

"Take it easy. You can still enjoy the flowers and the concert." Jillian headed for the door.

"Where you going?" Kate asked.

"I think I'll call Megan. I really miss her, and I should update her on what's going on here. And I don't want to be around when you blow a gasket at your ex-boss." She paused in the doorway and looked back. "But if those aren't from the doctors, you should tell Rick."

"You think it's that creepy?"

"If it's not Englebrite and his partners, yes. I mean, it's Sunday. I'm surprised the florist would deliver today."

Kate paused her movement toward the phone as something clicked. "That's a giveaway. This florist is owned by Dr. Coolidge's cousin."

"Aha. Well, that makes it a little less scary."

"Maybe so, but I'm still mad."

Jillian shrugged and left the room.

Kate sat down at the desk and forced herself to sit still and breathe slowly in and out ten times. The medical practice would be closed today. Finally she took out her cell and scrolled her contacts for the oldest of her three former bosses' personal number.

"Well, hi, Kate. This is a pleasant surprise."

"Hello, Todd. I don't suppose you know anything about a delivery I got this afternoon."

His chuckle told her the answer—and made her furious.

"I told you, I don't want my job back." It took all her willpower to keep her tone civil. "My sister and I are doing fine with the inn, so please leave me alone."

"I'm sorry to hear that. Your efficient presence is badly missed at the office. Anyway, we thought you might need some cheering up."

"What do you mean?"

"Because of all the hoopla out your way. It's all over the news. I was surprised they hadn't interviewed you. Maybe on tonight's broadcast?"

Kate's stomach dropped into the cellar. "They named us on the news?"

"No, but they said a hotel guest was abducted from the parking lot of the Novel Inn."

"Oh, no." She stood and peered out the window. No news crews. Whew. She tried to inject innocence into her voice. "No, nobody's come around here with a camera."

"Well, we all thought maybe some flowers would do you

good—and that concert that's coming up. Jason's cousin was happy to give us a hand."

"You could have put in a card saying it was from you guys. My sister and I freaked out at first."

"Oh, Sorry about that. Jason was probably more focused on getting the tickets in there. You did get them?"

"Yeah, I got them. And thanks, but you don't need to do me any more favors. I'm still not coming back."

He gave a deep sigh. "Okay. Call us if you change your mind."

She hung up without bothering to reply and ambled to the window. They had enough distractions at the inn right now. She didn't need Dr. Englebrite and his two partners coaxing her to return to their office.

Only three cars were in the front parking lot—Emma's, the Raynors', and Jillian's. Her sister hadn't bothered to move her Taurus out to the carriage house.

And a white minivan with the local television station's logo emblazoned on the side was pulling in.

"Jillian!"

No reply. Jillian had gone off to call her daughter. Had she gone out to the carriage house? More likely she'd gone as far as the kitchen, where guests wouldn't follow. Kate dashed across the hall and dining room and through the doorway.

Jillian leaned against the counter, her phone to her ear. "No! Where is it?"

"Jill," Kate cried, "There's a TV camera crew here. What do we do?" The ringing doorbell punctuated her sentence.

Jillian's eyes popped wide. Into the phone, she said, "I've gotta go, Diana. I'll call you later."

"I thought you were talking to Meg."

"I was. Then Diana called. She said Rick called her and said he might be late again. They think they've found the kidnappers' van."

"Wow! That's—" The doorbell rang again and Kate's stomach flipped. "What do we do?"

"We answer the door."

Before they could cross the lobby, the door opened, and a cheerful woman Kate recognized from the regular evening broadcast at the Bangor station poked her head in.

"Hello! Anyone home?"

Kate tried to tamp down her anger. This was a place of business, after all. People were allowed to just walk in—they were encouraged to, in fact, by the *welcome* sign on the porch.

"Uh, we can't talk to you right now," Kate said.

The woman pushed inside, followed by a girl who looked like a teenager carrying a camcorder.

"Oh, no, please." Jillian stepped forward. "We don't wish to appear on camera."

"According to the local police, this is the site of the kidnapping yesterday."

"No comment," Jillian said.

"But it's public knowledge."

"I said no comment."

Kate had a sudden vision of Jillian's pale face splashed all over the evening broadcast as she said over and over, "No comment." She stepped forward.

"I'm one of the Novel Inn's owners, and we do not wish to be interviewed."

In spite of what she said, a red light appeared on the camera.

"Please do not record this," Kate said firmly. "Now, step outside or I will call the police. This is private property."

The reporter gave a deprecating laugh. "It's a hotel—a place of business."

"Yes," Kate said, "but it's also private property."

"All we want is a few words," the reporter said.

"It's an ongoing investigation," Jillian said. "We can't discuss it."

"But you're not police officers."

"No, but we will not discuss it at this time." Jillian looked at Kate, and she gave her a nod.

"That's right. And please do not film the inn."

The young woman with the camera lowered it an inch. "You can't stop us from shooting outside."

"We can stop you from being on the property," Kate said, knowing that news crews could set up camp across the street and probably would.

The reporter smiled and held out her microphone. "We heard one of you was a witness to the kidnapping. Just a few words."

Jillian opened her mouth, but Kate jumped in.

"We neither confirm or deny that. Now, please leave, or my next phone call is to your station manager."

With a sigh, the reporter turned and walked out with the camera operator close behind. Kate shut the door firmly and leaned against it.

"I wonder how long we can dodge them."

Jillian sank onto the chair behind the front desk. "You don't think they'll get tired and go away?"

"Who knows? Now, what were you saying about the blue van?"

"Oh, yeah. Diana told me the police think they've found the van."

"Do you think they'll want you to go identify it?"

"I don't know. I'm not sure I'd be much help."

"Well, you did get a partial plate number. I'm sure that's helped in their search."

"Maybe."

The afternoon was waning. They didn't have any new guests scheduled to come in, so unless they had some walk-ins, it was just the Raynors, the Reddings, and Emma staying over.

"Why don't you go out to the carriage house?" Kate suggested. "Take a break."

"What will you do?"

"Watch the desk and maybe bake some muffins for tomorrow's breakfast."

"You can't watch the front from the kitchen. What if that reporter comes in again—or another one?"

Kate sighed.

Emma came in from the hallway. "Hey. I thought I'd ask Paul and Bailey to go out to supper with me tonight, but I wanted to check with you first."

"That's good of you," Jillian said. "I can't speak for them, but I don't know of anything that would keep them here. And we can always call you or Paul if there's any news."

"Okay. We wouldn't go for a couple of hours, but I'll ask them. Although Bailey was so depressed, I'm not sure how much she'll eat tonight." Emma headed toward the hall and the ground-floor guest rooms.

Jillian's phone rang, and she looked at her screen.

"Diana?" Kate asked.

"No, Rick." Jillian put the phone to her ear. "Hi, Rick." She listed for several seconds, and her eyes widened. "Okay, I'll come right over."

# 10

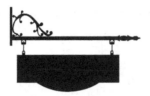

The small frame house could have been anywhere in New England. It sat in a quiet residential neighborhood, and without knowing, Jillian wouldn't have guessed it was less than a mile from the bay. She pulled in behind the police SUV and got out. Rick came from the attached carport to meet her.

"Hey," he said. "The man who rents this house works at the auction barn in Bucksport. We've sent a car to bring him in for questioning. Geordie's on his way with a warrant to search this vehicle."

As they walked toward the carport, Jillian's chest tightened. The squarish front of the van looked all too familiar.

"Either that's it or they're off the same assembly line."

"Okay. As soon as the warrant gets here, I'll open the back door. I want you to take a look."

"You said on the phone that there's some kind of machinery in there. How do you know if you haven't been allowed to open it yet?"

Rick held up his flashlight. "I looked through the back window."

She nodded.

At the sound of an approaching car, he turned toward the street. "There's Geordie now."

A squad car—the town police department's second vehicle—drove in and parked behind Jillian's Taurus. The officer jumped out and strode toward them.

"Here you go." He held out a folded paper.

"Thanks," Rick said. "I think you know my sister."

Geordie nodded. "Jillian, right?"

"Yeah. Good to see you."

Rick skimmed the warrant and nodded. They all walked into the carport, and he said, "You got your tools? You can go ahead and open one of the doors."

Within a couple of minutes, Geordie had the passenger side front door open. He climbed in and disengaged all the locks. Jillian walked with Rick around to the back of the van.

"You ready?"

She nodded, and he swung the rear door open. She half expected to see a corpse inside, but there was no sign of Danielle, just a pile of crumpled metal.

"What is it?" She frowned, trying to figure out what she was looking at.

"Tell me what you think it is."

She remembered Zeb's words about remote control helicopters. "Is it a drone?"

"I'd say so." He leaned in over the wreck. "A smashed drone."

Jillian tried to puzzle it out and gave up. "What does it have to do with Danielle? I don't get it."

"That's because you haven't seen her car."

"Oh, wait." She sought his eyes. "Kate said her windshield was smashed."

"To bits."

"You think ... Really? You think this drone flew into her windshield?"

"It's a possibility. We can't jump to conclusions, but you can bet the lab in Augusta will be testing it tomorrow for traces of paint from Danielle's car and any other evidence that's there." Rick looked around for Geordie. "Get a big bag and let's get this on its way."

Jillian let her shoulders sag, thinking about what Danielle had experienced. "Wow. It hit her, and she crashed. Then the guy with the pickup came along. How long was it between the wreck and when he put her in his truck?"

"We don't know. She could have blacked out for a while."

"She didn't say anything to me about a drone."

"No. She may not have realized what hit her."

"And it was Bob, the pickup truck guy, who took her from the wreck to the motel, not the guy driving the van when I saw them."

Rick nodded. "I have a lot of questions for Terrence Isles. Ever hear of him?"

She shook her head.

"He's a partner in the auction business, and he owns this van."

"Antiques," Jillian said. "That kind of auction?"

"Yeah. We need to find out who owns the drone and about a million other things."

"They have to be registered, right?"

"Any this big have to be, with the FAA. We should be able to get a name on the drone's owner quickly."

"It *is* Sunday."

"Yeah. I don't think that will hold us up too long. Come on." He put his hand on Jillian's elbow and guided her out of the carport toward her car. "You okay? You might as well go home now."

"I feel fine," she said. "But, Rick, a reporter came to the inn, and a girl with a video camera. We don't have to talk to them, right?"

"You don't. Tell them to contact me, or better yet, Sergeant Watkins at the station."

"Okay, we just refer all questions to Craig Watkins?"

"That'd be best, I think."

"Thanks." She'd met Craig before, and he was a levelheaded man. She stood on tiptoe and kissed Rick on the cheek.

He made a wry face. "Drive carefully—and watch out for low-flying drones."

———

Kate tried to amuse herself with a game of solitaire on the computer, but she soon lost interest. She was tired of minding the front desk. Nothing was happening. Andy Cummings, their night clerk on the weekend, wouldn't arrive until nine o'clock. That wasn't for another four and a half hours. At least the gaggle of reporters that had lingered outside had given up and left.

Ironic how her social life had dwindled to practically nothing since she'd moved here with Jillian. When she'd lived in her own apartment and worked at the medical office, she'd had plenty of friends nearby and weekend dates. Now she spent time with few people besides her siblings and the inn's guests. Yet going back to her old job wasn't attractive. She and Jillian would just have to make more of an effort to be involved in the community.

Bailey Redding came in from the hallway with Emma Glidden.

"Hi," Kate said. "Are you going out to eat early?"

"Actually, we thought we'd take a walk on the beach," Emma said. "Anything new?"

"My sister's out looking at a van they think might have been involved. I don't have any details, but she may know more when she comes in."

Bailey looked at Emma. "Should I tell my dad?"

Emma considered that for a moment. "Let's take our walk and not bother him. He was going to try to get a nap. If this van thing turns out to be important, Kate will tell him."

"I sure will," Kate said.

"And call us on our cell phones?" Bailey's huge eyes pleaded with her.

"Sure." Kate smiled and hoped some news actually would come in.

"The moon was full last night," Emma said. "I was thinking of taking a walk later, but I wasn't sure it would be safe."

"You should be fine," Kate said. "Low tide was about an hour ago." Her father had made a practice of checking the tide tables in the morning, in case the guests asked about it, and Zeb had reminded her and Jillian to do it when they took over the inn. "Don't want any unfortunate accidents," he'd said.

"Do they have neat shells here?" Bailey asked.

"Some. And starfish and sea urchins. Oh, and our beach turns up some pretty polished glass sometimes."

"Awesome."

"We'll watch for it," Emma said. "Jillian showed me the path down to the shore earlier, but which way should we walk?"

"Well, you can go toward town and the marina, or, if you

want better scenery, go past Zeb's house. The bank gets really high and turns into a cliff. I think it's more interesting to walk along under the cliff. Just allow yourselves plenty of time to get back before the tide comes in again."

Emma looked at her watch. "If we turned back in an hour, would we be okay?"

"You should be. The weather's fine. Wish I could go with you."

"I wish you could too. Bailey's dad said we should be back here before dark."

Kate nodded. "You might want a jacket. We had snow on the ground a month ago, and it still gets cold here in the evening."

Bailey grinned at Emma. "Be right back." She tore off for the hallway.

"This should be a good distraction for Bailey," Kate said to Emma with a smile.

"Yeah, she seemed pretty depressed at lunch. I think she's still feeling guilty about taking the car. Hey, I'd better grab a sweater myself." Emma hurried out.

Kate wished she could do something to help Bailey and Paul feel better, but nothing would bring them out of this morass until they knew what had happened to Danielle.

Emma and Bailey were just returning to the lobby more warmly dressed when Jillian returned.

"Oh, hi." Bailey bounded forward to meet her. "Kate said they might have found the van?"

Jillian nodded, her face sober. "They think so. It sure looks like the one I saw, and the license plate is right."

"What about the owner?" Emma said.

"He wasn't home. I'm sure they'll catch up to him soon."

"Anything else you can tell us?" Kate asked. "Mr. Redding's keen to hear any details."

"Well, this is kind of odd, but there was a wrecked drone in the back."

They all stared at her.

"That's kind of crazy," Kate said at last.

"It is. And they don't know that it's related to any of this, but—"

"What?" Emma asked.

Jillian shook her head. "It's too weird, but Rick thinks a drone could have hit Danielle's car and caused her to crash."

Bailey let out a little moan, and Emma grabbed her arm.

Jillian's brow furrowed. "I'm sorry, Bailey. I shouldn't have told you that."

"No, it's okay," she said. "I just ..." She looked around at the three women. "I'd better tell my dad."

"I can tell him if you still want to go for your walk," Kate said.

"We were going to walk down on the shore," Emma said to Jillian.

"It's a nice time for it." Jillian looked at her sister. "You've been stuck here all afternoon. Why don't you go along? I'll stay at the desk."

"You wouldn't mind?" Kate asked.

Emma's smile returned. "Do come with us. You know the beach here. You wouldn't mind Kate coming along, would you, Bailey?"

The girl frowned. "No, but what about my dad?"

"I'll tell him about the van," Jillian said. "Go on."

Emma checked the time on her phone. "We'd better if we don't want to have to hurry to beat the tide."

"Thanks, Jill." Kate dashed into the office for a sweatshirt, and the three went out the front door.

"Come this way." She led Emma and Bailey around the side porch. They walked briskly toward the carriage house, then

Kate took the quickest path down to the pebble beach below. The smell of the salt water and exposed ground was stronger, though not as pungent as it was in areas with mud flats.

"This is so cool," Emma said as they reached the rocky shore. A gull rose and winged its way out over the water. "Do you swim here?"

Kate laughed. "Not yet. We've only lived here about two months, and it hasn't been warm enough."

"What about when your parents lived here?" Emma asked.

"Oh, I guess I waded a few times, but I never had anyone wanting to go in the water with me."

"I'll probably get my sneakers wet," Bailey said, eyeing the surf as a wave rolled in.

Emma chuckled. "If you do, they'll dry. And that's better than sandals for a place like this."

"Yeah," Kate said. "You don't want sandals on rocks." She guided them to the right. "The bank gets a lot steeper the farther you go along here. It turns into a real cliff if you go far enough. If you walk the other way, toward town, it's not so bad, but they have steps leading down from the park. By the time you get to the marina, it's all flattened out again."

She kept well in from where waves washed the beach, and her companions stayed close to her. Soon Bailey was squealing and picking up periwinkles and small scallop shells.

Emma gazed up to the top of the steep rocks. "It that Mr. Wilding's house?"

"Yeah. He has a terrific view of the bay from up there. Another reason I like to go this way is because there aren't many houses."

Across the bay, the sun was lowering in the western sky. Its rays gleamed bright off the window in Zeb's living room.

Kate took a few steps. "Oh, watch your step."

They'd come to the place where the stream bridged on the

path above met the shore. At low tide and for a couple of hours either side, Kate had no trouble skipping across the water on large rocks. She scampered across, and Bailey followed with a happy shriek as she landed without slipping off the steppingstones. Emma followed more sedately.

Beyond the stream, more boulders were strewn on the shingle. Kate picked her way between them until the rocks were so close together she had to walk across them.

Bailey stopped by a small tide pool and stooped for a shell about an inch wide and four or five inches long. "What's this?"

"That's a razor clam shell," Kate told her. They walked on, and she said, "Look carefully and you may find a sand dollar."

Emma joined Bailey's search, and both of them collected half a dozen shells. Emma dropped hers into a pocket and smiled ruefully. "We should have brought plastic bags."

"Maybe this is far enough," Kate said. "We don't want to get our feet wet going home."

Skirmish Cove was located on the west side of one of Maine's many fingerlike peninsulas, and across the water, the sun lurked behind a band of low clouds. Bits of pink stained the clouds near the horizon, though sunset wouldn't complete for at least an hour.

Watching several shore birds wing across the sky, Bailey sank onto the nearly flat surface of a rock. "Oops. Bad decision. My seat's getting wet. But what a view." She stood and brushed off the back of her jeans with a grimace.

Kate stood beside her, drinking in the sight and smells she loved. No sounds reached them down here except the surging waves and the distant chug of a boat's engine as it headed for the marina. In that moment, she had no doubt she'd made the right decision when she left her old job.

"I see a little crab." Emma climbed down between the rocks

and began poking about for more shells. "Hey, sea glass." She passed a small item up to Bailey.

"Oh, wow." Bailey held up the bit of amber glass, polished smooth by the constant working of the sea against pebbles and sand.

"That's a good one," Kate said.

"Is it okay to keep it?"

"Sure."

Bailey looked up at her. "Officer Gage asked Dad if he could think of anyone who'd want to hurt my mom."

"That's right," Kate said. "They have to ask questions like that. But your dad said he couldn't."

With a frown, Bailey said, "There's her cousin Becky."

"She doesn't get along with your mom?"

"No. When Grandma died, she left Mom a necklace that Becky really wanted. She was really mad."

"But surely not made enough to harm her?"

Bailey let out a big sigh. "I don't suppose so. And I did see her Friday, after I got to Aunt Natalie's house. So she couldn't have been up here that day."

"I don't think this is about family stuff."

For a long time, Bailey stared out across the water. "Do you think they'll find my mother?"

Kate grasped her hand for a moment. "I do. A lot of people are praying for her, Bailey. Don't give up hope."

"We don't pray much," Bailey said stiffly. "I just don't know ..."

Kate took a deep breath. "I do believe in God."

"What if she's dead?" Bailey's eyes were round as she brushed wind-whipped hair from her forehead.

"Then God is still there. Bad things do happen—horrible things sometimes. But God is there for us. I trust him to get me through those times. Like when my mom and dad died—"

Emma's squeal interrupted the thought. Kate whirled toward her. Emma had gone another ten yards, picking her way among the boulders and closer to the cliff looming over them.

"What is it, Emma?"

"It's a—It's a man."

Kate's stomach dropped. Quickly she assessed the best way to get to where Emma stood, her face a stark white.

The swash from the waves oozed between the rocks, bathing the ground below the big boulder where they stood. Kate waited for it to recede then jumped down. Water squished from beneath her shoes as she landed. She hurried toward Emma, leaving Bailey to scramble down on her own.

"Where?" she asked as she reached Emma's side.

Emma pointed behind her, not looking, hooking her thumb like a hitchhiker.

Kate took a few more steps inland and caught her breath. It was a man, all right, or rather, a man's body. Fully clothed, it lay twisted in a niche between boulders. The feet were nearest her, and one shoe was missing. He lay mostly on one side and she couldn't see his face, but she could tell his head had been battered on the rocks. His wet hair looked black. She fumbled in her pocket for her phone.

Beside her, Bailey gasped.

"Get back, Bailey." Kate pushed 911 on her cell and waited. Nothing.

She turned to the others. Emma had come closer now, crowding in beside Bailey.

"I can't get service here under the cliff. Can you, Emma?"

Both the others took out their phones and checked them.

"No," Emma said, and Bailey shook her head.

"Right. I'll stay here with him. You run back to the inn and call the police."

Bailey opened her mouth, but Kate shook her head. "Hurry! The tide's coming in."

Emma and Bailey turned and scrambled over the rocks. Kate could still see them as they hopped over the makeshift bridge at the stream below Zeb's house and reached the smoother beach beyond. As they ran toward the inn's path, the waves' nearest reach was still twenty yards from the base of the cliff, and ten from where Kate stood, though each breaker seemed to stretch and feel its way toward her.

She looked down at the man. She couldn't tell much about him. A tourist? Vacationers flooded Skirmish Cove and the other coastal towns in summer. But he could be a local. She and Jillian had grown up farther north along the coast. They'd visited after Rick and their parents had moved here, and then Kate had worked in the next town, but there were still a lot of people in the area she didn't know.

She gazed back along the shore. The police might come from the inn, the way she and Emma and Bailey had. Or they might take a boat from the marina, in light of the incoming tide. Either way, they probably wouldn't arrive for at least twenty minutes. She started to pray silently but stopped, at a loss for what to ask.

Jillian had always been the strong one. She was the oldest, and she always knew what to say, what to do. On the terrible night when their parents died in the car crash, the three siblings had sat together in the hospital waiting room. Jillian was the one who held them together. They'd all cried and held each other, but then Jillian had wiped her tears, squared her shoulders, and said, "They're gone. Now we need to pray a different prayer. One for wisdom on what to do."

Her eyes stung, whether from emotion or the salt spray she didn't know. Looking around, she couldn't spot anything that would help her secure the body or mark the spot if the tide rose over it. She hoped Rick and his colleagues would arrive before that happened and before the light faded.

She looked back to where the corpse lay. What would Jillian pray if she were here? That man must have a family. *Lord, comfort those who've lost him. And give the authorities wisdom and speed.*

# 11

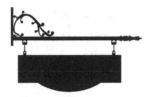

Jillian sat in the office after advising Paul Redding about the drone found in the van. She'd left the door to the lobby open and pulled out a paperback mystery to keep her occupied. She'd read a chapter before the front door flew open and Bailey charged in, skidding to a stop in front of the desk.

"Bailey, what's wrong?" Jillian stood and hurried out of the office. Emma strode in through the front door, panting.

"Call the cops," Bailey gasped. "We found a dead man."

"What? Where?"

"Down on the shore. Kate's stayed with him, but she said to hurry. The tide will come in."

Jillian hesitated only a second between 911 and Rick's private phone. She chose Rick.

"They're sure it's a man, not Danielle?" he asked.

Jillian looked hard at Bailey then shifted her gaze to Emma. "You said it's a man?"

"Yes," Emma said. "It's awful. Like he got all beat up on the rocks."

159

"Which direction did you walk?"

Bailey pointed vaguely.

"We went past Zeb's house, down on the shore," Emma said.

"And how far did you go before you found the body?" Jillian asked.

"Not far beyond there."

"The rocks got real big," Bailey said. "We were walking on them, but the man is down in between."

Jillian said into her phone, "Rick, it sounds like it's below the cliff not far beyond Zeb's house. Kate's down there now, and the tide's coming in."

"Right. Have the others stay at the inn, and we'll get right out there."

He disconnected.

Jillian took a deep breath. "Okay, Bailey, you and Emma did a good job. Let's go tell your dad what's going on. Officer Gage said for you to stay here. He and some other officers are on their way."

"Will Kate be okay?" Bailey asked.

"She should be." Of course, the tide had turned two hours ago. "How far out was the body from the cliff?"

"Not far," Emma said. "It was in between some big rocks, maybe twenty or thirty feet out. I was looking for shells, and then I saw something whitish. I was curious, so I walked over to it. And it was ..."

"It was gross," Bailey finished for her.

"Right. Come on." Jillian led them to the door of the Jeeves Room.

Paul Redding's face blanched when they broke the news. "Are you sure—" He stared into his daughter's eyes.

"It's not Mom," Bailey said quickly.

"It's probably totally unrelated," Jillian told him. "It

sounds to me as if someone hiked too near the edge of the cliff and fell over. It's quite a drop-off along the stretch of road up above."

"But it's not right up against the cliff wall," Bailey said.

"No, but the tide could have carried it a short way, and then it lodged in the rocks."

"Or maybe the man fell off a boat and drowned, and his body washed in," Emma suggested.

Bailey was looking a bit green by now.

"All right," Paul said. "I'll keep Bailey with me until we hear more."

"Da-ad!"

He laid a hand firmly on the girl's shoulder.

"Please," Jillian said, "help yourselves to the snacks I laid out in the dining room and drinks from the refrigerator. I can make fresh coffee if you'd like some, Mr. Redding."

"It's Paul. But no, that's all right. I don't drink caffeine this late."

"Well, make yourselves at home with the TV and the library—whatever you like."

"Thank you."

She turned back toward the front desk, and Emma followed. "I wonder if I can get our night clerk, Andy, to come in early tonight."

"You want to go down there?" Emma asked.

"I hate to leave Kate there alone."

"I could watch the desk for you."

"Are you sure? It would only be in case the phone rings— you could take a message. And if anyone came in wanting a room without a reservation, you could ask them to wait until Kate or I got back."

"Sure. Easy peasy."

Jillian smiled. "There's one couple staying here tonight

besides you and Reddings. They're up on the third floor, but they went out for dinner."

"Okay," Emma said with a slight frown. "Should I tell them anything when they come in?"

"Only if they ask. If they've heard sirens or seen lights down on the beach. Stuff like that. And Andy should come in at nine, but we may be back by then."

"Got it."

Jillian drew in a deep breath then gave Emma an impulsive hug. "Thank you."

"Go. I know you don't want Kate down there alone with him."

"Thanks."

Kate had taken the flashlight she kept in her desk. Jillian ran through the kitchen and storage room, grabbing another flashlight they kept for walking back and forth to the carriage house after dark and an old Red Sox sweatshirt. She pulled on the sweatshirt and went out onto the side porch.

She sprinted down the path onto the beach and turned right. She couldn't see her sister until she crossed the stream, then she spotted Kate among the boulders beneath the towering cliff. No other people were visible, and she was glad she'd come. Rick should arrive soon, but it could be a bit longer.

Jillian jogged along the shore until the rocks made it dangerous and then slowed to a walk.

"It's me," she yelled when she thought Kate could hear her.

Kate waved, and Jillian returned the signal. As she approached Kate's position, she heard an engine, and a boat motored around the curve of the shore from the direction of the marina.

"You didn't have to come," Kate said, but she folded Jillian in a hug.

"Are you all right?"

"Yes. Emma found him. Bailey and I were busy watching the bay, and I was going to suggest we turn back. If Emma hadn't gone shell hunting, we wouldn't have seen him." Kate nodded toward a jumble of jagged boulders a few feet away.

Jillian picked her way cautiously between them. Something was there, at the base of the rocks. Another rock? A mound of seaweed and debris? Without knowing it was a body, she wouldn't have guessed until she was only six feet away.

She swallowed hard. "I need to look at him."

"Why?"

"To see if it's the guy with the gun—from yesterday, you know?"

"Well, you can't see his face the way he's lying, and I don't think you should touch him."

Jillian hesitated and decided she was right. "Okay."

"I think that's Rick in that boat." Kate's gaze was fixed on the oncoming cabin cruiser.

"It looks like the warden's boat." Jillian climbed up on a rock that gave her two feet of extra height and waved at the boat's pilot.

The engine cut out, and the boat eased in with the next wave, until the bow gently scraped bottom. The anchor splashed just offshore. Rick and another man jumped out and waded in.

"This the spot?" Rick asked.

"Right over here." Kate led them toward the corpse, and Jillian hung back. There wouldn't be a lot of room for them to work.

Rick bent over the body for several minutes then stood.

"Okay, we need to remove him quickly. I've called for the medical examiner, but it will take a while for him to get here. If we don't want this body under water again, I think we'd better take him out now with the boat."

"Right," said his companion. "We can mark the spot with a buoy."

"Good." After trying unsuccessfully to contact the police station on his phone, Rick said, "I guess I need to get out on the water, away from the cliff. Jill, Kate, you'd better go back to the inn."

"The water will be in here very soon," Jillian said.

"It will. We'll have to remove him ourselves, but I want a hearse to meet us at the marina."

"We could call the station from the inn," Kate said.

"No, we'll handle it. The boat has a radio." Rick nodded toward the man who'd brought him. "This is Calvin Binns. He's the local game warden." He looked at Calvin. "My sisters, Jillian and Kate."

"Glad to meet you," Calvin said. He was a few years younger than Rick, maybe Kate's age, taller and broader through the chest and shoulders, and he stood with his boots planted firmly on the rocks.

"I hate to move the body," Rick said, frowning down at the corpse.

"We don't have a choice, do we? The tide's rising." Calvin hopped down from his rock and stood shoulder-to-shoulder with Rick. "I don't have a body bag, but there's a tarp in the boat."

"Right." Rick looked toward the bay and scrutinized the reach of the breakers. "By the time the M.E.'s here, he'll be underwater. Let's do it." He threw Kate and Jillian a meaningful look.

"I thought maybe I could look at him more closely and see if he was the kidnapper whose face I saw," Jillian said.

"I don't think this is the time or the place. If we need you to do that, you can go to the morgue tomorrow. But first we'll try to establish the victim's identity. Once we're sure who he is, we can show you pictures of him when he was alive."

That made sense to Jillian. She'd recognize him best if he looked the way he did when she saw him in her driveway, not with his face all bruised up and part of his head bashed in.

"Guess we'd better go," she said softly. She hated to leave, but that was her nature—always wanting to help. Maybe they could look around for the man's other shoe.

Kate hooked her hand through Jillian's elbow. "Come on. Rick won't be happy till we're gone."

"Yeah." Jillian pulled in a deep breath. Maybe she had a touch of shock. She didn't seem to be thinking straight.

Calvin threaded his way through the rocks to the ever-oncoming waves, presumably to get the tarp. Jillian lifted her gaze to the top of the cliff. Had the man really tumbled all the way down from the top? And would they ever really know?

A small spot nearly three quarters of the way up caught her eye.

"What's that?"

"What?" Kate asked.

Jillian pointed. "Way up there. Do you see something?"

Squinting, Kate tried to follow the trajectory from her hand to the cliff. "I don't know—oh, wait. You mean that gray-looking patch?"

"Yeah. Just to the left of that part that juts out. It's a different color."

Kate turned on her flashlight and aimed it at the spot, but it was too far away. "Hey, Rick," she called.

He looked up at her. "What?"

"Up there. Do you see something?"

Rick stood and squinted up at the rock wall. "Where?"

While Kate patiently described the spot for him and

adjusted his angle by placing her hands on each side of his face, Jillian climbed a higher rock.

"Oh, yeah," Rick said. "Do you think that's something?"

"Well, it's different from all the rocks around it," Jillian said. "Do you have binoculars?"

"No, but Calvin might have some in the boat."

Rick slogged his way toward the water. Calvin was already out of the boat, wading through the surf with a gray tarped bundled in his arms.

When Rick yelled at the warden, the wind blew his words back toward Jillian and Kate, and he shook his head and hurried on to meet Calvin.

A few seconds later they met. Rick took the tarp and turned back toward them, while Calvin headed once more for the boat. This time he lifted the anchor and brought the vessel in a little closer then anchored again. When he jumped out, he had a case hanging around his neck by a strap. Rick took the tarp close to where the body lay, and Kate scurried over to help him unfold the unwieldy bulk.

"Wind's picking up," she yelled.

Rick nodded and gave her some directions Jillian couldn't hear.

As Calvin came closer, he opened the case and removed binoculars. "Who gets these?"

Jillian bent down to take them from his hand then straightened, standing tall on the boulder. She panned the cliffside and focused in on the odd-colored patch she'd spotted. The light was fading fast, but she could still make it out.

"There's more men coming down in a small boat from the marina," Calvin called to Rick. "I asked them to send more officers if they could to the inn and down your path too."

"We've only got a half dozen on duty." Rick frowned and looked up at Jillian. "See anything?"

"It might be cloth. I'm not sure."

"See any movement in the wind?"

"No." She held out the binoculars, and he stretched to take them.

Jillian looked for the best way down from her perch and was surprised that the waves were now purling around the bottom of her boulder.

"Here." Calvin held out both hands. "I got you. Jump."

She caught her breath and hopped down, and he caught her around her waist and swung her onto a lower, almost flat rock.

"You two had better get out of here while you can." He nodded toward the shrinking strip of shore.

"Yeah, go, so you can get over the stream." Rick handed the binoculars to Calvin. "We need to move this guy pronto."

"Do you think we could see anything from up above?" Kate asked. "Jill and I could go up the road and look down from there."

"No, don't go near the edge," Rick said. "We'll figure out something later."

"There's a rescue team in Bar Harbor. They climb down and rescue hikers who've taken a tumble." Calvin trained the binoculars toward the cliff. "Oh, yeah, I see it. You're right, that's not rock."

"Maybe the guy had a coat or a backpack when he fell," Kate said.

"I don't know." Rick scowled at them. "Go. Now."

"We're going. Come on, Kate." Jillian jumped to the nearest clear spot and set her course for the more hospitable pebble beach. As they headed back toward the inn, the breaking combers crowded them closer to the bank. The high cliff wall above them gradually grew lower. They reached the stream, and the rocks in it protruded only a few inches from the surface.

"Go quick," Kate said.

Jillian took a running start. Her left foot slipped and she barely caught herself, saving herself from a dunking.

"It's slippery." She reached the far side and turned, but Kate was right behind her. "Good, you made it. My shoes are soaked." She looked back for a moment. Rick and Calvin were tiny figures among the rocks, wading through the water toward the boat, supporting the weighted tarp between them.

"A couple of real, live swashbucklers," Kate said.

"Right." Jillian's gaze lingered on them.

Kate touched her shoulder. "Let's go get some cocoa."

At the top of the path, they paused beside the carriage house.

"Come on," Jillian said. "I left Emma on the front desk. We should invite her to have supper with us."

Kate hung back. "I was just thinking."

"Thinking what?"

"Well, Rick said he didn't want us near the edge of the cliff, but we could just drive up there and see if it looks like anyone's been there recently."

Jillian hesitated.

"I promise I won't go near the edge," Kate said. "There's a railing up there anyway, to prevent accidents."

That much was true, but the railing wasn't very high. More of a warning than a fence.

"If you don't want to go, I could take Emma."

Kate had that determined look, and Jillian made a quick decision.

"Let's call Andy and see if he'll come in early tonight."

When they walked into the lobby, Emma jumped up from behind the desk. "Everything okay?"

"Yeah," Kate said. "Thanks for doing this."

"No problem. The only person to call was Zeb Whiting. He saw the activity on the shore, and he wanted to know what was going on, so I told him. I hope that's okay."

Kate shot Jillian a questioning glance.

"I think so," Jillian said. "It happened closer to his house than ours."

"I'd want to know too," Kate said.

Emma nodded. "I figured. And Paul took Bailey out to get some burgers. I think he was a little claustrophobic."

"Oh, and you were supposed to have dinner with them." A load of guilt poured down on Kate. "I'm sorry."

"No, it's okay. They were fine with it, and I've been snacking."

Kate eyed Emma, speculating on how game she was. "Listen, Jillian and I want to go up the road above the cliff and see if we can find any trace of someone being up there. We won't go near the edge."

Jillian said quickly, "I thought I'd see if Andy, our night clerk, could come in early tonight."

"Oh, okay." Emma looked a bit uncertain. "I can stay on the desk if you want."

"No, let's ask Andy," Jillian said. "You've been here an hour or so already."

Andy answered the summons with alacrity. "Sure, I'd love to put in a few extra hours. I can be there in fifteen minutes."

Kate knew that meant paying him for the extra time, but she felt it was worth it.

"Fifteen minutes," she told Jillian and Emma. "Let's see what we can scrounge up in the refrigerator."

When Andy arrived, they'd all eaten sandwiches and were ready to head out the door.

"I don't get it," he said. "Is something happening in town?"

"A body was found down on the shore," Kate said.

Andy's eyebrows shot up. "For real? That's so wild."

"Yeah. We won't be out long, but we want to check on something."

The three women headed outside and piled into Kate's rather dirty Jeep.

"You should wash this thing," Jillian said.

"I never seem to have the time."

Jillian laughed, and Kate felt the urge to defend herself, but she could see her sister's point. She had time to sniff around potential crime scenes, but she couldn't wash her vehicle.

It didn't take long to reach the stretch of gravel road above the cliff. Kate pulled over to the side, leaving enough room for a vehicle to pass without danger, but this road didn't get much traffic.

"Now, everyone be careful," Jillian said in her schoolteacher voice as they all climbed out of the Jeep.

"Yes, Mother." Kate rolled her eyes at Emma.

Jillian frowned at Kate. "I'm serious."

As Kate threw a leg over the guardrail, Jillian cried, "You promised you wouldn't go near the edge."

"I won't."

Bushes and weeds grew in the three or four yards between the road and the cliff's rim. The soil on top of the rock formation wasn't thick enough to support trees. Kate crossed it gingerly, with Emma and Jillian a couple of steps behind.

"Kate, that's far enough," Jillian said, a note of panic in her voice.

"Okay, okay. We should have brought a rope."

"You are *not* going down there." Jillian stared at her as if she was insane.

"I meant so we could tie it to something and hold on to it while we look over the edge."

"Well, we didn't bring one."

"It's too dangerous," Emma said. "I can't see anyone down on the shore."

Of course, they couldn't see directly below them, all the way to the bottom of the cliff. Kate noted that the relentless tide now covered a lot of the rocks they'd walked on. From this vantage point, she couldn't see any remaining land below—just water, swirling around the boulders jutting up from it.

Jillian looked toward town. "See that boat out there, heading for the marina?"

"Yeah." A pinprick of red light showed on its stern.

"That's the local game warden and Rick. When we left them, they were getting ready to take the body away in Calvin's boat. They'd called for the medical examiner and a hearse to meet them at the marina."

"Oh, okay," Emma said.

Kate gave a big sigh. "It'll be dark before we can get anyone up here with equipment."

"Too bad we don't have a drone," Jillian said.

Kate swiveled her head around. "That's brilliant. This is the perfect job for a drone."

Jillian shrugged, looking a little embarrassed. "Any kid would have thought of it when we were down below."

"Maybe. Who do we know with a drone?"

"I know someone in Augusta," Emma said, "but that won't help."

"I could call that real estate agent on Main Street," Jillian offered.

"The office would be closed tonight." Emma puffed out her cheeks for a moment. "Well, anyway, we should suggest it to Rick."

"Okay." Kate looked out over the water. Across the bay, the sun had sunk behind the trees and houses on the western shore, and just a few slashes of fuchsia and orange across a low band of clouds remained.

"Gorgeous sunset," Emma said.

"Yeah. We'd better make the call." Jillian pulled out her phone.

Kate turned and walked back to the railing. She climbed over it beside the Jeep. Emma followed and walked around to the passenger side.

Her gaze flicking to the opposite side of the road, Kate stopped. "Hey, what's that?"

"What?" Emma looked toward her.

She pointed off into the trees on the other side of the road. "It looks like a car."

Emma hurried around the Jeep's hood and stood next to her.

"I see it now."

Kate squinted at the light-colored vehicle. Why hadn't she noticed it when they arrived? Probably too focused on the railing and the cliff edge. "Come on."

She and Emma strode across the gravel road.

"Hey, where are you guys going?" Jillian yelled from behind them.

Emma turned. "There's a vehicle over here."

Jillian hopped over the rail and trotted to catch up.

"Rick says they're docking at the marina. He thinks a drone is a good idea. He has to stay with the body, but he said to call the desk sergeant."

The three of them stopped on the far side of the road. A

white pickup truck was parked off the shoulder, partly hidden by bushes and two bushy pine trees.

"It can't be," Jillian said.

Kate gulped. "The guy who picked up Danielle had a white pickup truck."

"Yeah."

Emma's stress showed plainly on her tight face. "Can you call your brother again?"

"Better yet, just call the station," Kate said.

Jillian was already dialing.

# 12

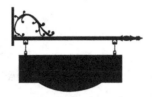

"Jillian, that's quite a find," Sgt. Watkins said over the phone. "Good job!"

Jillian felt warm inside. Praise from Craig Watkins was much better than a quick acknowledgement from Kate. And at the end of a long, exhausting day, it gave her spirits a bigger boost than a mug of hot chocolate would.

"Thanks. Actually, Kate spotted it. And the truck may not be related to the body down below, but—"

"Given the location and the timing, I think there's a pretty good chance," Watkins said. "Rick had already asked for officers to search that area, but it's starting to get dark, and we probably would have put it off until morning."

"Oh." That was a disappointment.

"But not now."

Her heart popped up again. "So you'll send someone up here tonight?"

"You betcha. I've already got someone running the license plate number you gave me to find out who owns it. Just stay back and don't let anyone touch anything. We don't even want you flattening the grass or maybe walking where the driver left footprints when he parked there."

She gulped. "Well, we did walk over to the truck and try the door handle. It's locked. But we didn't mess with it other than that." She squinted into the twilight. Emma had come back out near the road with her, but Kate stood at the pickup's tailgate, leaning over and peering into the bed. "I'll tell everyone what you said."

"Great. Thanks. We should have someone up there within ten minutes. Great call on the drone too. The department doesn't have one, but I'm sure we can find someone who does and would be willing to help us out."

Jillian thanked him and smiled as Watkins signed off in a warm voice, like somebody draping a warm blanket around her. The thought made her realize the air had cooled noticeably since the sun set, and she shivered.

"Hey, Kate?" she called.

"Yeah?"

"Sgt. Watkins says to keep away from it. An officer's on the way."

"Okay." Kate plodded to her. "I saw something in the back of the truck."

"What?"

"I don't know. A small piece of metal. And there's a bolt loose in there too, just lying in the bottom."

"You didn't touch them, did you?"

"No. I didn't even touch the side of the truck." Kate held up both hands. "Made sure I didn't leave any prints."

"Good, because I told the sergeant we only touched the door handle."

A few minutes later, Geordie Kraus and another officer showed up in the squad car.

"Hi, Jillian. Kate." Geordie walked over to them with his companion. "Do you know Officer Hall?"

"I don't think we've met." Jillian held out her hand. "Hi. I'm Jillian Tunney, Rick's sister. This is our sister Kate Gage, and one of our guests at the inn, Emma Glidden."

"Hi." Dave shook hands all around.

"Dave's our department's newest officer." Geordie looked around in the fading light and spotted the truck. "I take it that's the pickup in question?"

"Yes," Kate said. "We spotted it as we were leaving."

"What were you doing up here?" Geordie asked.

Jillian swallowed hard.

Kate said, "We thought we'd just look around, since we'd found that man's body on the shore earlier. "We wanted to see if there was any evidence that he'd been up here and fallen off the cliff." Geordie said nothing, just nodded, and Kate added, "As opposed to falling out of his boat or something."

"I see. Well, thank you for calling it in. You can leave if you want to."

"Is it all right if we stay a while?" Jillian asked. "We thought we saw something on the cliff when we were down below. Rick and the game warden saw it too."

"Hmm, I don't know about that," Geordie said. "The sarge just told us to come up here and process this truck and then, if we can't get hold of the owner, to arrange towing to the station."

"But, what if …" Jillian hesitated.

"We think the owner might be that dead man from the shore," Kate said. "And white isn't the most popular color for trucks in Maine. It could be the same one Danielle Redding rode in after her accident."

Geordie nodded. "It's a possibility. We hope we'll find out

who the owner is soon." The radio on his shoulder crackled and a dispatcher rattled off some numbers. "Excuse me."

"Of course," Jillian said.

Geordie stepped aside to take the incoming call.

"So what will you do now?" Emma asked the other officer.

"We'll check for fingerprints—"

"I touched the driver's side door," Kate blurted.

Officer Hall smiled. "We understand. Once we've dusted, we'll open the door and check for the registration and see what we find inside."

"I saw a couple of little things in the back," Kate said. "A bolt and a piece of metal. Do you think they could be significant?"

"You never know," Hall said with a big smile. "We'll make sure to bag them and have the lab take a look."

"Great."

Jillian had the feeling Officer Hall was enjoying the interview with her sister more than he would most of his on-duty encounters with witnesses. While he seemed like a nice young man, he was way too young for Kate, who'd turned thirty-three on her last birthday.

She cleared her throat. "So, Officer Hall, if this truck turns out to belong to the—the dead man, that would make it pretty conclusive that he came from on shore here, not from a boat or anything like that, wouldn't it?"

"That's what it looks like right now," he said with an air of caution. Police officers never wanted to commit to a scenario until they had proof, Jillian realized.

Geordie came back and glanced at the women. "The sarge says they got a name on the vehicle's owner."

Jillian caught her breath. She didn't say anything, but Kate was quick to ask.

"Can we know?"

"I don't see why not." Geordie gave Kate an approving nod. "You found it. This truck is registered to a Mark Edson."

"Mark," Kate said with a blank look.

"That's right."

"Not Bob?" Jillian asked.

"Not Bob. I read Rick's report about the kidnapping. Bob was the name of the guy who picked up the victim after her accident, right?"

Jillian nodded.

"Well, the owner of this pickup isn't named Bob or Robert. We'll take a look at the papers in the truck, assuming there are some, but this may not be the same man as the one involved in the kidnapping."

"Right." Jillian couldn't help it, she was disappointed. She gave herself a mental kick. Had she expected them to solve the entire puzzle, from Danielle's abduction to the mysterious body in the surf, in one evening?

"I guess we'd better let you get to work," Emma said.

Kate opened her mouth, as if she'd like to keep asking questions, but she nodded. "You're right."

"We might as well go back to the inn," Jillian said. "They're just going to process the truck. There's nothing more we can do, and it's getting cold."

Emma rubbed her hands together. "Yeah, I thought I was done with mittens for the year, but I wish I had a pair now."

Jillian hoped they weren't going to have a late frost. All the flowers that had started to bloom would be ruined.

"What about the drone?" Kate asked the policemen. "It's getting dark. Don't you want to see what's down there on the cliff tonight?"

Hall threw Geordie an uncomfortable glance.

"You'd have to ask Sergeant Watkins about that," Geordie said.

"Can we just call him?" Jillian asked, not sure she really wanted to bother the sergeant again. But that light spot on the cliff had her very worried.

Geordie shrugged. "He probably wouldn't mind. If he can't tell you anything, he'll say so."

"Let's go get in the Jeep and warm up a little," Kate said.

"Thank you!" Emma trotted toward the vehicle, and the sisters followed more slowly.

"You call him, okay?" Kate said. "You know him best."

"I don't know him. I've only met him once that I remember."

"But you called in tonight and talked to him."

Jillian sighed. "All right, I'll call him."

She placed the call, and as the phone rang, she cleared her throat.

"Skirmish Cove Police Department," said a woman's voice.

"Hello, this is Jillian Tunney. Is Sergeant Watkins still there, please?"

"One moment."

Quicker than she'd thought possible, the sergeant said, "Hello, Jillian."

"Oh, uh, hello. I was wondering if you have any news about the use of a drone? My sister and I are still up here on the cliff. Officers Hall and Kraus are here, and they're working on the white pickup truck, but I'm a little worried about whatever's down on the cliff face."

"You think it may be Mrs. Redding, don't you?"

"Well, yeah. Possibly."

"We're concerned too. I've been working on getting a drone since you called in, and I actually have a man on the way with one. Officer Gage just checked in with me, and we're planning to come up to the scene right away. Will you still be there?"

"If we won't be in the way." Jillian met Kate's eyes then Emma's, and they both nodded.

"Fine. Sit tight. We should be there in just a few minutes."

———

At nearly nine o'clock, Rick and Sergeant Watkins arrived at the top of the cliff, where Mark Edson's pickup truck had been abandoned.

"Hey," Rick said as the three women climbed out of Kate's Jeep.

"Thanks for keeping us in the loop," Kate said.

Jillian nodded to the sergeant. "Hi. This is my sister Kate and my friend Emma Glidden, the one who actually spotted the body on the shore."

"Craig Watkins." He shook Kate's hand, then Emma's. "Thank you, ladies, for your diligence."

"Everyone's been working hard today," Rick said. "The sarge let a couple of the officers go home and offered to come out here with me."

"What did you find out about the dead man?" Kate asked.

"Quite a bit, actually. The victim you gals found was Terrence Isles. His wallet was still buttoned into his back pocket."

"Wait a sec." Kate held up a hand to stop Rick's words from flowing. "It wasn't Edson, the guy who owns the truck we found?"

"Apparently not. However, we think this man—the one on the shore—is the one who owns the van used to kidnap Danielle Redding yesterday."

Jillian frowned. "So vehicles are interchangeable with these guys? First Bob in the truck, then two of them with the van, and now the van owner is here with the truck."

Rick gritted his teeth. "We're still sorting it out. But we think Isles was in the water between twelve and thirty-six hours. The medical examiner may be able to pinpoint it closer than that when he's done the complete autopsy."

"Nobody reported him missing?" Emma stood with her arms hugging herself, even though she wore a jacket. "That seems odd."

"Well, he's divorced and lives alone. It hasn't been that long, really, since he died."

"But he was there through a couple of tides?" Kate tried to make sense of that.

Rick arched his back in a stretch. "You saw where the body was. He wasn't too far from the cliff, and he was caught among the rocks. If it had been a smooth beach, the tide probably would have carried him out into the bay. We were planning to comb the area around the truck and examine the cliff face at sunup, but now we think it's urgent. We're guessing Isles went over the cliff sometime yesterday or early this morning."

"And nobody noticed." Jillian's gaze lost its focus, as though she was trying to follow the logic. "Don't you think that's strange?"

"It could have happened in the middle of the night," Watkins said. "The truck's off the roadway, and people don't walk along this road much. Even if someone was up here, the body wouldn't be visible at high tide. The fact that it was out a few yards from the base says it may have shifted some in the first tide or two, but from what Rick tells me, once it lodged where you found it, it probably didn't move much."

"What about his injuries?" Kate asked.

"The doc will have to tell us," Rick replied. "He's sure the cause of death wasn't drowning, and I'm guessing he died from the fall. But don't quote me on that—I'm certainly not an expert. I probably should have said we're not ruling it out."

"Do you think it was suicide?"

"Not really, but I can't say for sure without more information." Rick looked down the road where the gleam of headlights was visible. "Someone's coming. Let's hope it's our man with the drone."

"Should we tell the Reddings about this?" Jillian asked.

"No. There's no reason for that at this point," Rick said.

Watkins nodded. "He's right. We don't know for sure that this is pertinent to Mrs. Redding's kidnapping, and the fewer people here at the scene, the better."

He stepped away and walked toward the approaching vehicle. Rick started to follow.

"Wait a sec," Kate said.

Rick turned expectantly toward her.

"That name, Terrence Isles."

"Yes?"

"I think I recognize it."

Rick's mouth skewed. "You do or you don't?"

"I'm pretty sure he was a patient at the medical practice where I used to work."

"Okay. Anything we should know?"

She shook her head. "It's probably irrelevant. But I seem to remember he had some chronic condition that kept him coming back every six months or so. I couldn't see his face out there on the beach, but if it's the guy I think it is, he may have been a drug user too."

Rick took out his pocket notebook. "This was at Coastal Family Practice?"

"Yes." Kate squinched up her eyes. "He would make some crude remark to me every time he came into the office. I really hated to see him coming."

"Did you tell your bosses?"

"Yes, and Dr. Englebrite told him to quit it or he'd have to find another physician."

Rick inhaled slowly. "Anything else?"

"Not that I can think of."

"Okay, I shouldn't tell you this, and I expect you to keep it quiet, but I've actually run into Terrance Isles before. You're right about the drugs. We busted him once when he made a buy." He hesitated.

"What else aren't you telling us?" Jillian asked.

Rick said slowly, "Danielle Redding—did she have her purse when she was kidnapped?"

Jillian's face crinkled as she thought about it. "I think she had it on a long strap across her body."

Rick nodded.

"What?" Kate jumped up and stood less than a foot away from her brother. "Spill it!"

"I'm not—"

"Oh, come on! You're saying this guy's death is related to Danielle's abduction."

Rick raised both hands, forming a shield between himself and Kate. "Take it easy. Okay, the guy had one of her credit cards in his wallet."

# 13

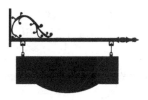

Jillian stared at her brother. "If that's the case, how can Sgt. Watkins say there may be no connection to Danielle's kidnapping?"

"Take it easy." Rick sighed. "We try not to give out too much information until we have our evidence lined up. Can you imagine what would happen if the press got hold of it? This place would be crawling with reporters, and we'd end up having to rescue ones that fell over the edge trying to get a good picture."

"Okay, got it," Kate said. "And we won't notify the Reddings unless something more direct turns up."

"Hey, Rick," Sgt. Watkins called, "Mr. Lane's here."

"Brian," Rick acknowledged, walking toward the newly arrived SUV.

"Where do you want the drone?" the driver asked.

"Right over here." Rick pointed and then turned to look sternly at his sisters. "I'm serious about you all keeping out of the way. This man will need room to operate. We'll be close to the rim, and we don't want any distractions."

"Right," Jillian said, and Kate gave him a thumbs-up.

The darkness was complete now, but the officers set up a couple of battery-operated spotlights near the rim to aid them in their work. Geordie helped Mr. Lane carry his equipment from his vehicle to the cliff's edge. The sea birds seemed to have settled down for the night, but an owl gave its eerie call some distance away on the inland side of the road.

"Brian Lane," Kate said pensively.

"Isn't he the real estate agent?" Jillian asked. "I see him in TV ads now and then."

"Oh, right. Moffet & Lane. Their office is on Ocean Drive, isn't it?"

"Yeah, I think so." Jillian watched the lanky man prepare to operate his machine. It was smaller than the wrecked one she'd seen in the back of the blue van, a compact, neat apparatus.

Lane started its motors, and she could barely hear its propellors turning. Bright lights shone from the fuselage. It rose, and Lane guided it over the edge of the cliff and out a few yards. Jillian couldn't see it any longer, but a glow from its lights showed at the rim.

Rick leaned in over Lane's shoulder to view his small screen on the remote controller board as the machine buzzed up and down the rock face below them, and the sergeant stayed close to them.

"There," Rick said. An eerie silence hung over them as the operator made adjustments.

"Looks like you're right," Lane said. "That's definitely a person down there."

Jillian's pulse sped up. She reached for Kate, and they clasped hands.

"Can we communicate with them?" Craig Watkins asked.

"Not via the drone," Lane replied.

"It wouldn't be safe to lean over the edge here," Rick said.

Lane was frowning, and his words reached the onlookers clearly. "I don't see any movement."

Emma took in a quick breath.

"Do you see that?" Lane asked softly.

Rick and Craig bent closer and murmured their agreement. Rick said something Jillian couldn't decipher and then took out his cell.

The sergeant turned and walked over to the women.

"It appears there's a person lodged on a ledge about twenty feet below the rim. And from what we're seeing on the screen, we believe it's a woman."

"Danielle," Jillian said.

"We're not positive, but no other women have been reported missing in the area this weekend, and we have a tentative connection between Mrs. Redding and the owner of that pickup truck over there. I'd say the chances are pretty good it's her."

"Is she alive?" Emma's eyes were huge in the moonlight.

"We don't know yet. We're not even a hundred percent sure it's a female. But the cliff rescue team is on the way. They should be here in less than an hour."

Rick came over and laid a hand on Jillian's shoulder. "It may be time to inform Mr. Redding and Bailey."

"Right. Are you going to do that, or do you want me to go tell them?"

"We will. Mr. Redding's friends have verified his alibi, so we're ready to bring him in on this." Rick looked toward Watkins.

"Why don't you take Jillian with you?" his sergeant said. "The family will be a little more comfortable that way."

Rick nodded. "The inn is only a few minutes away. We should be back here before the team arrives."

Holding out her key ring, Kate said, "Take my Jeep. It'll be easier to get it out than your rig right now."

Rick squinted toward the vehicles that had lined up on the edge of the road. Lane's SUV was blocking his from pulling out easily.

"Okay, thanks. You staying here?" Rick took the keys.

"Emma, you want to stay?" Kate asked.

"I might ride back with you to get something warmer," Emma said. "I don't suppose you have gloves I could borrow?"

"Yes, and a parka," Jillian said. "Come on. Paul and Bailey will probably be glad you're there."

"I'll stay here," Kate said.

———

Kate huddled in the back seat of the patrol car at Geordie's suggestion. The others were gone more than a half hour, but they still beat the rescue team. And they brought a round of hot coffee for everyone who waited—a popular gesture for which Jillian received fervent thanks.

Rick introduced Paul Redding and Bailey to Sgt. Watkins, Brian Lane, and the other officers. Paul refused coffee and seemed eager to talk to the sergeant, who stood waiting for the rescue team, his steaming mug in his hands.

"Officer Gage says this spot is right above where Bailey and the others found a body."

"That's right, Mr. Redding," Craig said. "There's someone on a ledge partway down the cliff, and we have a rescue team coming to try to bring them up."

"You think it's Danielle?"

"We don't know," Craig said.

"Can we go over there, Officer Gage?" Bailey asked Rick,

pointing beyond the guardrail, to where Lane had his equipment set up.

"You need to stay back here behind the rail," Rick told her. "It's for your own safety, and to give us room to work."

"Honey, we'll be fine right here," Paul said. "How soon before you'll know for certain if it's Danielle?"

"The climbing team should be here in about ten minutes," Rick said.

"And is there any sign—" Paul coughed. "Jillian said you couldn't tell if this person is dead or alive."

"That's right, Mr. Redding. I'm sorry."

"Don't you have a sensor or something that you can lower down there? A microphone, maybe, to see if you hear any breathing?"

Rick looked helplessly at the sergeant.

"All we have right now is the drone camera," Craig said. "We could try to get something like you've described, but the rescue team will be here before we could put that in place. I think the best thing to do is wait for them. When they arrive, it should only be a few minutes until we have some word."

Paul nodded and drew Bailey close to him. "Okay. I understand."

Rick swallowed hard and looked at Paul. "Mr. Redding, as I told you at the inn, we have reason to believe that the man whose body they found had a connection to your wife's kidnapping."

Nodding grimly, Paul stood without speaking again, his face set like a statue.

"Is this rescue team like a ski patrol?" Bailey asked.

"Sort of," Rick said. "They help out in Acadia National Park."

Paul frowned. "Help out how?"

"Finding lost hikers," Jillian said.

"That's right." Rick met Paul's gaze with sober brown eyes. "Terrence Isles had one of your wife's credit cards in his wallet, and ... well, we don't know yet who the other person is lying on the ledge down below. It could be Danielle, or it could be someone else. The man who picked her up after her accident Friday evening, for instance. He's still missing. There's no path down to the ledge, so we just need to wait."

Kate started to speak, but Jillian laid a hand on her arm. She drew Kate aside and whispered, "Rick didn't tell them yet that they think it's a woman. He told me on the way over the hair's pretty long, but there are lots of long-haired men. Bailey was right there, and he was afraid it would be too much for her if he shared that."

"Okay," Kate replied. They would all know soon, and she schooled herself to keep quiet.

But Bailey had no such inclination. "You think it's my mom down there on the side of the cliff, don't you?" Her voice rose in a plaintive howl.

Paul hugged her shoulders. "They don't know, sweetheart. He just said that."

"But Jillian said they saw her from down on the shore when they came to get that guy's body."

"We saw a patch of color is all," Jillian said quickly. "Something lighter than the rocks on the cliff. We couldn't tell if it was a person or not. It could have just been some cloth— maybe a jacket or a blanket—caught in a crevice."

"Until the drone camera showed us, we didn't know for sure it was a person," Rick said.

"Can we see the pictures?" Paul asked.

Bailey crowded close to him. "Yeah, maybe we'd recognize her clothes."

Rick seemed to consider that and nodded slowly. "I'll ask Mr. Lane if he can show you. If he says no, please be patient."

"I'll speak to him," Craig said and walked toward the drone operator.

"What about down on the beach?" Bailey asked. "We could go down there and watch from below."

"No, the tide's too high," Kate said. "The place where we found the man is under water now."

"Oh."

Kate had a quick vision of Bailey watching her mother's body being hauled up the cliff. She stepped closer to the girl. "Let's just wait, like Officer Gage said. It could be somebody else altogether."

"But he said that dead guy had Mom's credit card!"

"That's right," Rick replied, "but that's the only possible link we've found between him and your mother."

"What about the truck?" Kate asked, and her brother scowled at her. "Sorry," she mouthed.

"We're trying now to establish whether it's the one Danielle rode in on Friday."

"Where is it?" Bailey asked.

"It's over on the other side of the road," Jillian said, "but we can't go near it. The police officers are working on it, and they'll probably tow it later."

Paul cleared his throat. "Officer, Danielle was kidnapped yesterday morning. I believe the coroner said the man on the beach had been there at least twelve hours."

"Yes, that's what Dr. Smithson said."

"Then if that is my wife on the cliff, she may have been there twenty-four hours or more—a whole day, maybe a day and a half."

"Just stay calm," Rick said as Craig Watkins returned. "We're doing everything we can, as fast as we can."

"And we've had people tracking Terrence Isles's movements this weekend," Craig said, stepping closer to the

Reddings. "We've found witnesses who saw him alive late yesterday afternoon. We're trying to locate his business partner, to bring him in for questioning."

"Who's that?" Jillian asked.

"Mark Edson."

Kate's heartbeat doubled as she heard the name, but she didn't speak up. She'd keep her mouth shut this time and let the police make the connection for Paul.

Sgt. Watkins went on, "Terrence Isles didn't own that white pickup truck. His business partner did. So of course we want to talk to him as soon as possible. Now, Mr. Redding, if you'll come with me, Brian Lane will show you the footage from the drone camera."

Kate thought Bailey would protest that she should see it too, but she stood watching bleakly as her father walked with Watkins.

A black minivan rolled up a few minutes later and stopped on the shoulder behind the other vehicles. Officer Hall spoke to the driver for a moment, and then four people got out. They approached carrying safety helmets and climbing gear.

"That's the rescue patrol," Rick said.

Paul came back to Bailey's side. "He's right. They can't tell much from what the drone saw, but these people will find out more." He put an arm around Bailey's shoulders, his lips pressed tightly together.

Two men and two women comprised the team. They discussed the situation with Rick, Craig, and Brian Lane in a quick, terse conversation, and Lane showed them what his drone had revealed on the cliff face.

The rescue patrol's leader, Barney, was a man in his mid-thirties who looked fit and was tall and muscular. "Right, so we'll send Amy down first," he said. "She can take a good look and tell us how things stand."

Amy was a small-framed, slender woman in her late twenties. "She's the lightest member of the team," Kate whispered.

Jillian nodded.

Geordie Kraus approached and said to Rick, "Better check in with the station. Someone turned in a purse they found in a Dumpster at Anne's Apparel shop."

"And it's significant to this case?" Rick asked.

"It has Danielle Redding's car rental agreement in it, along with an empty wallet and some makeup."

Paul stepped forward. "They found my wife's purse?"

"Easy, Mr. Redding," Rick said. "You can go over to the police station later if you wish and speak to the officer on duty about this."

"Okay," Paul said, and Bailey nodded.

"I'll give them a quick call," Rick told them. "If I learn anything more, I'll tell you." He put his phone to his ear and walked away, toward the drone operator and the others near the edge of the cliff. He didn't turn back with new details, so Kate figured Geordie's report was complete for the moment.

Jillian grasped her hand. "Prayer time?"

"Always." Kate looked at Emma, and she nodded.

Kate stepped closer to the Reddings. "We're going to pray for Danielle. Would you like to join us?"

"I think I'll just keep watching," Paul said.

Bailey met her gaze. "I would."

Kate put an arm around her shoulders and led her off a few steps, to where Jillian and Emma waited. They joined hands.

"Lord, watch over Danielle wherever she is," Jillian said. "Let her be found soon."

"Yes, Lord, and keep these men and women safe as they work to find her," Emma added.

Bailey sniffed.

"We thank you for bringing Bailey and her dad here," Kate said, giving Bailey's hand a squeeze. "Please comfort and encourage them."

Jillian gave a firm amen.

"Amen," Bailey whispered and swiped at a tear.

Kate gave her a quick hug. "We're here for you, no matter what happens."

"Thanks." Bailey blinked hard and walked to her father's side. Paul glanced at her and put an arm around her, hauling her in close. He whispered something in her ear, and Bailey slid her arm around his waist.

"Don't stop praying," Kate said.

Jillian nodded. "I won't."

Barney and his teammates set up the equipment to belay Amy over the rim. One of them fitted her with a headset and tested it with her to be sure she could communicate. They were ready in only a few minutes, and Amy backed up to the rim and gave them a thumbs-up. With a hop back, she was over the side and out of sight.

"Okay," Barney said into his microphone. "Good." He looked at the second woman on the team. "Another ten feet. Right." He held up a hand, and everyone waited.

Jillian held her breath, waiting for him to speak.

"It's a woman, as you thought," Barney said. A few more agonizing seconds passed, and then he looked around and grinned at them. "She's alive!"

"Thank God," Kate breathed.

Paul hugged Bailey so hard, Jillian feared he would hurt the girl.

Bailey pushed away from him, laughing while tears streamed down her cheeks.

"My mom's alive!"

"Yes!" Jillian accepted a bear hug, and Bailey went down the row, embracing Kate and then Emma.

Rick was already on his radio, calling for the ambulance they'd put on standby earlier and giving directions. "Right, we should have her up off the rock by the time you get here."

Pulling her phone from her pocket, Emma said, "I'm calling Alicia. I'll keep her updated, and she can let the others know."

"Maybe you'd better wait until they make an ironclad I.D.," Kate said. She wanted to believe it too, but how devastating would it be if they put out the word that Danielle was found and then were disappointed?

Emma's brow wrinkled. "It has to be her. Who else could it be?" Still, she held off.

The team lowered more equipment, and they all waited for Amy to secure the woman so she could be lifted to the rim. As soon as they had her up and on solid ground, Paul jumped over the guardrail and rushed forward.

"Danielle!" He knelt beside her and broke out in loud, wracking sobs.

# 14

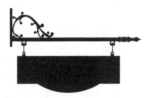

K ate stood by her sister, watching the paramedics load Danielle Redding into the ambulance.

"She's barely alive."

"They said she's hypothermic—it got pretty chilly last night," Jillian said.

"Yeah. I wouldn't have wanted to stay out all night without a coat." Kate shivered.

She overheard Amy, the rescue climber, talking to Rick and Craig.

"She was really jammed into a crevice. I don't see how she could have fallen into it."

"So what do you think happened?" Rick asked.

Amy shrugged. "Maybe she landed hard on the ledge and managed to pull away from the edge. There's not much room there. She may have seen the crevice and worked her way into it to keep her stable. If she was conscious when she landed on that ledge, she wouldn't want to risk falling over while she was asleep or disoriented. And if this happened last night, the wind was pretty sharp. The crevice would give her some minimal cover."

"Wow." Kate whispered.

"And they suspect her blood sugar's extremely low." Jillian looked toward the parked vehicles. "Mr. Redding's riding in the ambulance with her, and Emma's taking Bailey to the hospital in Paul's car. I guess we might as well go back to the inn."

"I suppose so. They probably won't be able to talk to her tonight." Kate started for her Jeep.

Jillian veered off as they came near one of the officers. "Sergeant Watkins, Kate and I are going back to the inn. Thanks for everything you did tonight."

"You're welcome, but it's part of the job. And please, call me Craig."

Jillian smiled. "I was wondering if your people have found the man who owns that pickup."

"Not yet. We've checked his house, and he wasn't there. I had someone check the auction barn and the antique store attached to it, but everything's locked up tight."

Kate's mind whirled, and she stepped closer. "I was thinking ..."

"Yes?" He turned to face her.

"What if that Bob guy, or Edson or whatever his name is, was with Terrence Isles when he came here."

"Then the logical thing would have been for him to drive his truck away," Craig said.

"Right. But he didn't. I mean ... what if Bob went over the edge too, and he got pulled out with the tide?"

Craig let out a sigh. "It has crossed my mind."

"Can they tell who was driving the truck last?" Jillian asked.

"We're working on it. Kraus and Hall have lifted prints

from the steering wheel and other parts of the truck. They also found some long hairs on the passenger side, and some zip ties that had been sliced through, but please don't let that information out, not even to the family. Once the lab is up and running in the morning, we may have more answers, and we'll talk to the Reddings."

"Sure." Jillian looked at Kate. "Ready?"

"Yeah, let's go."

"Goodnight," Craig called after them.

They passed Rick on their way to the Jeep.

"Hey," Kate said. "Are you going to the hospital?"

"Yeah. I need to speak to Danielle as soon as she's able." Rick sounded tired, but that was nothing new.

"What if she's not able to talk to you for a long time?" Jillian asked.

He let out a long sigh. "I want to get the doctor's opinion. If it looks like she'll be unconscious for a while, I'll go home and get some sleep." He rubbed his eyes with the back of his hand.

"Do the EMTs think she'll make it?" Jillian peered at him closely.

"They're noncommittal. She was out here a long time."

Kate stood still, watching him walk toward his department SUV. "We need to pray for Rick and the other officers," she said to Jillian.

Andy seemed wide awake when they walked into the inn's lobby, though it was nearly midnight. They quickly filled him in on the drama out on the cliff, and Jillian asked him if he was still willing to spend the night at the desk.

"Yeah, I'm okay. And I need the extra pay. If that's okay with you."

"Tell you what," Kate said, "call my cell at five and I'll come relieve you. You can leave a couple hours early and catch some Zs."

Andy shrugged. "How about I do that if I can't keep my eyes open?"

"Deal," Kate said. "Just keep them open long enough to call me."

"Right, boss. Oh, and there's a family of four coming in Thursday for a long weekend. They want two rooms—one for Mom and Dad, and one for the two girls."

"Terrific," Jillian said. She and Kate headed out the back for the carriage house.

Kate crawled into bed with aches in nearly every muscle in her body. It had been a long day, but still, she'd thought she was in better shape than that. Poor Danielle, cramped up in a crevice on that cliff for hours and hours—what had she endured? Kate decided she had nothing to complain about. But she still wondered about the man called Bob. Where was he now?

———

Kate woke refreshed and ready for a new day's work. Andy hadn't called her early, and she was glad for the extra hour's rest that gave her. She knocked on her sister's door, and Jillian gave her a sleepy, "Yeah! I'm up."

Kate smiled. "Sure you are." She headed for the bathroom.

Andy was slouched in his chair behind the front desk when they got over to the inn to start breakfast.

"So, you didn't call me early," Kate said.

"Nope, I'm good."

"Well, let me give you your check before you go." Jillian went into the office and wrote out the check for his weekend's work, which Andy was happy to pocket.

"See you Saturday night," he said on his way out the door.

Kate went to the kitchen and took a pack of juice

concentrate out of the freezer. While she readied the juice dispenser in the dining room, Jillian strolled in yawning.

"Andy's heading out. I think I'll pick some flowers for the breakfast buffet. Mom's daffodils and hyacinth are looking good out there." Jillian poured what was left of Andy's nighttime pot of coffee down the drain and started a new one.

"Sounds good," Kate said. "If Danielle's allowed visitors later, we can take them over to the hospital."

"I like it. Double value." From a drawer, Jillian took a pair of kitchen shears and headed back outside. She was back in less than a minute.

"Kate, did you take your Jeep down to the carriage house?"

"No, I left it out front." Kate closed the top of the juice cooler and turned around.

"It's not there now," Jillian said.

"What?" Kate strode past her, through the lobby, and out the front door. She stopped on the porch, staring at the parking area. Her stomach twisted as she gazed stupidly at the empty spot next to Jillian's Taurus. "I don't understand."

Jillian caught up with her. "Me either. *My* car's still here."

Kate swung around, studying Jillian's car, one of only two in the lot at the moment. The Reddings and the Raynors were their only current guests. The Raynors' car, with a New York license place, was sitting where she'd seen it last night.

"Paul and Bailey must have stayed all night at the hospital," Jillian said.

Something wasn't right. Kate whirled on her. "Did I take the Jeep down to the carriage house and forget?"

"I don't think so. We both got out up here last night, talked to Andy, and walked down to the house, remember? And I didn't see it down there this morning."

They both walked around the corner on the porch. At the far end was a widened area with a grill and a couple of small tables where they could barbecue and eat outside. Kate almost ran to the grill and stared out over the railing, toward the carriage house.

Jillian joined her at a more sedate pace. "Well?"

The driveway and the space immediately in front of their snug home was empty.

"It's gone."

"Maybe you put it in the garage." They had a two-car garage their father had added beside the carriage house.

Kate shook her head vigorously. "I'd remember that."

"Okay. Where are your keys?"

"In my purse in the kitchen."

They hurried in through the side door and the storage room. Kate pulled her small purse from the cupboard where they sometimes kept personal items and unzipped it. She rummaged through it and looked up in dismay. She patted the pockets of her pants.

"I must have ... Oh, no. I must have left them in the ignition. Jillian, my Jeep's been stolen!" Kate's face heated, and she feared she was going to cry.

"Hold on." Jillian laid a calming hand on her sleeve. "Why don't you call Andy? He was here all night. Maybe he knows something. Your Jeep was definitely here when we came in last night. I was with you, and you're right. It was out front, right beside my car."

"Right." Kate took out her phone and pulled up Andy on her contacts. "Hey, Andy?"

"Yeah?" He sounded half asleep already, but he hadn't even had time to get home.

"Do you know where my Jeep is?"

"Uh ... well, some guy came to get it."

Kate jerked her head back. "What do you mean, 'some guy came to get it'? I didn't tell any guy he could take my car."

"Uh ... he said your brother okayed it."

"My brother. You mean Rick?"

"You have another brother?"

Kate huffed out an exasperated breath. "No, just the one." She clicked off and swiped to find Rick's name.

"What's going on?" Jillian asked.

"I'll tell you when I find out."

The tone in her ear rang three times.

"Rick was going to the hospital," Jillian said. "He may have had to turn his phone off."

It rang again.

"Well if he doesn't answer, I'm calling the station." Kate's jaws were painfully tight.

"Hello?" Rick said.

"Rick, my car's been stolen."

"Well, hello to you, too, Kate."

"Did you hear me? My Jeep was in the front parking area, and it's gone. Andy said you had something to do with it, but I'm one millimeter from calling your desk sergeant and reporting grand theft."

"Easy, easy," Rick said. "It wasn't stolen. Dr. Cusack called me and asked if I'd help him and his partners give you a little gift."

"What are you talking about?"

"He wanted to send your car to be detailed. I didn't think you'd want to turn it down, but he said they wanted to surprise you."

"So they stole my Jeep? That's their idea of a surprise? You're out of your mind."

"I told you, they didn't steal it."

"What, you gave them my keys?"

"I knew where you kept your extra set, and since I have a key to the carriage house, I didn't think you'd mind."

It was all Kate could do to speak. No way would she admit he could have skipped the housebreaking, since she'd left the keys in the vehicle. "When did you have time to do that? You keep complaining about how little sleep you've had this weekend."

"Well, that's true, but I made a little detour the last time I was at the inn. It probably wasn't smart of me, but all of our officers have been so harried, I just didn't take time to think it through. Kate, those guys are dying without you. Cusack said you organized a really cool filing system when you worked there, but the temps they've tried can't figure it out. They're going nuts."

"Are you saying I should leave the inn and go back to work for them?"

"No, I just … I don't know. He was begging. It's painful to watch a guy beg."

Kate heaved out a deep breath. "So you gave them my keys, and one of them came and got it while Andy was on duty late last night."

"Apparently. It's at the garage now. And it's a reputable place. They'll do a great job."

"I've had it with those guys," Kate said. "I don't care how many letters they have after their names, they're brazen male chauvinists, car thieves, and bribers. And you're guilty of something, too, but I haven't figured out what yet. Accomplice to something or other." She hung up on Rick.

"Wow," Jillian said. "What did they do to the Jeep?"

"Took it to a detailer."

"Another little act of kindness to sweeten the pot, I guess?"

"Yes, and I am furious. Do I look it?"

Jillian eyed her thoughtfully for a long moment. Kate was sure she saw a scarlet face, blazing eyes, and taut muscles in her face and neck.

"Yeah, you do." The desk phone rang, and Jillian picked it up. "Oh, hi, Emma. Any word on Danielle's condition?"

Kate caught her breath, hating that she'd vented at her brother and forgotten to ask about Danielle.

"Okay. Well, you're welcome to come back here for lunch with us if you want. Paul and Bailey probably want to stay there, but they're welcome too. I'll make sure there's plenty of food around here."

A moment later she hung up.

"Well?" Kate asked.

"Danielle's still unconscious. They're monitoring her, of course. She's dehydrated, and Emma said they're giving her fluids but she had some injuries—bruises and scrapes mostly. There's a contusion on her head, and they want to do a scan. She could have a concussion. Mostly it's a wait-and-see situation."

"Man, I feel so selfish." Kate drew in a shaky breath. "Danielle might die, and here I am ranting about my Jeep."

Jillian walked over and put an arm around her. "Try to relax. Get yourself a cup of tea or something. Maybe you'll think of a way you can help the docs without selling your life to them."

"Well, I'm sure not going back to work for them."

"Good." Jillian grinned. "I don't think I could handle this place without you."

"What are you going to do?"

"I think I'll go online and see what I can find out about Terrence Isles."

"What about the guy who owns that pickup truck?" Kate asked.

"I don't know. I didn't get his name."

Kate frowned. "Edson, right? Let's see ... Mike? No, Mark.

Do you think Rick will get upset? He wasn't very happy about us poking around yesterday without asking him first."

"Yes, I know he was upset when I told him I'd talked to Mickey Holt, and I think he wished I'd called him before I went to get Danielle at the Oceanside and let the police handle it."

"And he wasn't happy that we went up the cliff road last night, even though we found the truck." Kate sighed.

"I know what you're thinking," Jillian said.

"What am I thinking?"

"That this wouldn't have happened if I'd called Rick Saturday morning and said, 'She's at the Oceanside Motel,' and then stayed out of it myself."

Kate shook her head. "No, I don't think that. Those guys in the van must have followed you after Danielle got in your car at the motel. It couldn't have happened any other way. So if you'd called Rick and stayed home, what do you think would have happened in the ten or twenty minutes before the cops got to the motel?"

At Jillian's blank look, Kate went on, "I'll tell you. The guys in that van would have snatched Danielle from the motel the minute she stepped outside, instead of here, and you wouldn't have seen them and gotten that partial license plate."

"I suppose," Jillian said.

"That Bob guy has to be the one who owns the truck," Kate said. "Mark Edson. What did he look like again?"

"Brown hair, mustache. I think his eyes were blue. Not brown, anyway. Lighter. I guess they could have been hazel or gray." Jillian squinted for a moment and seemed to be looking past Kate, through the living room and out the window toward the bay. "I'm thinking he just told Danielle that his name was Bob to make sure she couldn't identify him later, and to gain her trust."

"Why would he want to hide his identity from someone who'd just been hurt?"

"Why would he want to kidnap her the next morning? None of it makes sense to me." Jillian walked over to the peg rack and took down her favorite apron. "Craig Watkins said last night they planned to bring Terrence Isles's business partner in for questioning, but they couldn't find him. He's the guy with the pickup."

"Yeah." Kate leaned on the counter. "They were driving around together Saturday in the van."

"And Sunday, either Isles borrowed Edson's truck or they were both riding around in it."

"They must be close friends."

"Well, they *are* business partners." Jillian took a dozen eggs and two pounds of bacon from the refrigerator.

Kate heard a whirring sound from the elevator. "Oh, somebody's up already."

The Raynor family was soon enjoying breakfast. Kate and Jillian were still busy serving their guests when Sgt. Craig Watkins walked in through the lobby and looked around the dining room.

"Good morning, Sergeant," Jillian called across the room. His uniform looked fresh, and his hair was shiny and clean. She guessed he'd been home and slept, or at least showered and changed. "Would you like a cup of coffee?"

"I'd love one."

She went to the coffee station and filled a cup—ironstone, not the takeaway type. Craig had come here for a reason, and she didn't think he'd turn around and walk out with his cup of java.

Kate, who had just refilled the warmer tray with sausage links, sidled up to her and picked up another cup. "He sure cleans up nice."

Jillian blinked at her in surprise. "You interested?"

"I meant for you."

Jillian hadn't consciously given it a thought, but now she felt the blood rush to her face. She hadn't really thought much about romance in the four years since Jack died.

"Hush," she whispered. "He's probably married." She grabbed a small tray and put the mug on it with a couple of creamers and two packs of sugar.

Kate laughed. "Nope. Per Rick, he's free as a bird."

"Shut up." Jillian picked up the tray and carried it toward the doorway where Craig still hovered, hoping she wasn't blushing. "Did you want to talk?"

"If you've got a minute."

"Sure. Do you want Kate too?"

He looked at her sister, who stood by the Raynors' table, laughing at something one of them had said.

"That's okay. You can fill her in after."

"Okay, let's go in my office."

He took the mug, leaving the creamers and sugar on the tray. "I take it black. Thanks."

Jillian set the tray on the nearest flat surface, catching a glimpse of Kate's waggling eyebrows. She turned quickly away and led him across the hall and into the office. "Have a seat."

Out of habit, she took the desk chair. Craig set his mug on the surface and swung over one of the straight chairs then settled into it. After a sip of coffee, he smiled at her.

"That's good stuff."

"White Mountain," she said. "The guests like it."

"I'll bet. Well, listen, I came around to tell you we don't think Mark Edson was driving his truck yesterday—or whenever it was left at the top of the cliff."

"What about Isles?"

He nodded. "The fingerprints support Terrence Isles as the driver."

Jillian blew out a big breath. Craig took another swallow from his mug.

"So where's Edson?" she asked.

"That's what we'd like to know. I sent your brother home to sleep for a few hours, but we've got a lot of people on this now. The State Police have sent four officers, and with ours and the entire county sheriff's department, we've got a pretty good team."

"I hope you find him soon."

"Well, if he knows what happened to his pal, he may be on the run. There are troopers at the entrance to the Piscataqua River Bridge checking every vehicle that goes through, in case he wants to get into New Hampshire and beyond."

"The morning commuters must love that," Jillian said.

"Yeah, well, we thought it was expedient."

"What about the Canadian borders?"

"All the customs stations have been notified. And he'd need a passport to cross. Unless, of course, he crossed on private property, where there's no border patrol. Personally, I think he's still in this area."

Jillian sat back in her chair. "I wonder what he'd be driving. You've got his truck and Isles's van now."

"I have a theory on that. See, the van was used for the auction business. Isles had another car, a Chevy Malibu. We can't find it, but we're looking. And we're watching Edson's house, in case he goes back there."

"Does either of these guys have a family?"

"Both divorced. We've notified Isles's ex-wife, and she's going to make a formal I.D. on the body later this morning. Edson's ex moved out of state a year ago. Vermont. Haven't spoken to her yet."

"Okay. And what about Danielle? Last we heard, she hadn't regained consciousness."

"That's right. Mr. Redding agreed to notify us as soon as she's awake. Listen, Jillian, I've already spoken to Mr. Redding and his daughter about this, but you and Kate need to know. We managed to keep the rescue from getting out on the late news last night, but reporters are in a frenzy this morning. We haven't announced yet that Danielle Redding was rescued alive."

Jillian gulped. "You mean ..."

"We thought it might help us if Edson doesn't know his friend failed to kill her."

"But you just said you think he's on the run."

"I know, and he may have heard somehow. But please don't tell people."

"I'm afraid we notified all of the cheerleaders last night. That is, Emma Glidden did."

Craig sighed. "Well, it may be general knowledge then. I suppose it soon will be. Can't be helped, I guess. But I'm pretty sure it didn't make today's morning papers. Things could be different by this evening."

She thought about it. Those reporters were persistent. Too many people knew Danielle had survived to keep it quiet for long.

"There's actually one other thing Rick and I discussed," Craig said.

"Oh?"

"You need to be alert at all times," he said slowly, as though choosing his words carefully.

"What do you mean?"

"Terrence Isles wore a mask when you saw him here at the inn. Mark Edson didn't."

Jillian frowned, thinking about that. "Why do you suppose that is?"

"Obviously Isles didn't want to be recognized or identified later. In a lot of kidnapping cases, the perpetrators wear masks so the victims can't identify them."

"Right. But Edson figured Danielle had already seen him, so it didn't matter."

"It was a mistake on his part." Craig eyed her gravely. "Jillian, you hadn't seen him before, when he first made contact with Danielle. But you did see him when he came here with a gun and kidnapped her."

She sat very still, gazing into his steady brown eyes.

"Edson and Isles decided they had to get rid of Danielle," Craig said.

"You mean, because she knew who they were?"

"She knew who Edson was, anyway. And the two of them were business partners. They knew if one of them was caught, it wouldn't be long before the other was too."

"So ... Mark dragged his friend into a bad situation and made it worse."

"I really think Isles was already involved in illegal activities with him. The drone is registered to Isles. They used it for business."

"In the antique business?"

He sighed. "There have been a lot of antique thefts in the region lately."

"Yeah." She stared at him. "A guest said a drone was hovering outside her window here."

"The thieves have been very savvy. When they target a house, we think they know exactly what they're going to steal."

"So they're using drones to case people's houses."

"We think so. Rick worked it out. Mrs. Redding's accident

wasn't far from the Sorenson mansion. We sent an officer out there the other night, when an alarm went off, but he didn't find anything."

She nodded slowly, thinking of the movie magnate's home and its position a few miles to the south, overlooking the ocean. "So it wasn't a raccoon. It was a drone. They'd been casing the house for antiques to steal."

"It's a possibility. And when they finished, they wouldn't want anyone to see the drone. Edson could have flown it low and fast, back to where he was waiting in his truck."

"But Danielle's car got in the way of the flight." Jillian closed her eyes, imagining it. "It smashed through her windshield." She opened her eyes. "How did she not see it afterward?"

"Everyone who saw her after the accident says she was very disoriented, and she has a concussion. She may have passed out at the time of the collision. If so, it wouldn't be difficult for Edson to scoop up the wrecked drone and toss it in the back of the truck, maybe throw a tarp over it. Then he played the roadside hero and went to her rescue."

"Wow. Does Paul Redding know about this?"

"We have no proof. So far it's only a theory. But if Danielle is able to speak to us, we may get some answers. In the meanwhile, we're keeping this quiet. If the press got hold of it and it turned out differently, we'd have egg on our faces. Besides, we don't want the antique thieves to know we've thought of it."

"That's understandable."

"It could be someone else entirely who's after the antiques," Craig said.

"Wait a sec. If that drone crashed into Danielle's car on Friday ..." She frowned, thinking about the weekend's events.

"One of our guests complained about a drone outside her window on Sunday morning."

"Maybe they had a second one. It wouldn't surprise me. Or maybe the one the guest saw was totally unrelated to the Redding incident."

"But still, those two men run an auction house." She winced. "I guess I should say ran, past tense."

"Yes. Isles is dead, and Edson will never run the auction again. What he did to you and Danielle is enough to put him away for a long time. If we can also nail him for the stolen antiques—we're talking hundreds of thousands of dollars' worth of goods."

"Grand theft."

"Exactly. And he knows that now. Which is why I'm telling you to be careful. You recall that a woman was killed a couple of months ago during a burglary?"

"Yeah. You think it could have been these auction guys?"

"I'm just saying, stay alert. Don't go out alone. Don't even walk the short distance from here to your house alone, especially at night."

"Don't worry. I've seen what he can do in broad daylight."

Craig drained his coffee mug and stood. "All right then. I'll get going. Thanks for the coffee, Jillian."

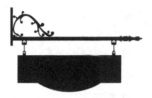

E mma returned to the inn that afternoon, reluctantly
telling Jillian she had to check out.

"I really hate to leave now, but if I don't make it to work tomorrow, I'll have a real mess on my hands. I stretched it by taking today off."

"I'm sure that Paul and Bailey understand," Jillian said.

"Yes, but I'd so hoped to stay until Danielle woke up. Bailey's promised to text me, but it's still hard to walk away now."

"I'll call you. Would you like that?"

"I sure would. Thank you."

When she was gone, Kate listlessly took the checklist for the Anne Shirley room. "I'll go over the room. Not that Emma would take anything."

Jillian stayed near the front desk, restless and discontent. Danielle was found, but the case wasn't solved, and the loose ends bothered her.

At two o'clock she heard a car drive in and looked out the window, surprised to see Kate's Jeep being parked neatly in the front lot. She fingered her cell phone, debating whether or not to alert Kate, but after a moment's thought she decided not to. Instead, she hurried out onto the porch as a dapper man climbed out of the Jeep and another car pulled in from the street. Jillian recognized them at once and strolled out to greet them.

"Dr. Cusack! I see you've brought Kate's Jeep back."

The physician smiled at her. "Yeah. Looks great, doesn't it?"

"It sure does."

The second man left his car and walked over. "Hello, Mrs. Tunney. Is Kate around?"

"It's Jillian, and I'm not sure she'd want to see you two right now."

"Oh?" Cusack's eyebrows shot up.

"She was quite upset when she realized her vehicle was missing. She thought it had been stolen."

"Oh." Cusack had the grace to flush.

Dr. Englebrite, on the other hand, gave a raucous laugh. "That's Kate for you. Jumping to conclusions."

"Well, we've had a lot going on here," Jillian said, and both men sobered. "This might not have been the best time to pull a surprise on her."

"We just wanted to do something nice for her." Englebrite's tone was wheedling, and she realized why Kate had grown so exasperated with him.

"It would have been much better to ask her. She was on the verge of calling the police."

He grinned and pointed a finger at her. "We had that covered. I actually got the keys from a police officer—your brother."

"Yeah, we know that now, but we had a few very tense minutes, and I don't think that's what you intended for Kate."

"Well, no." He looked away.

Cusack stepped toward her and held out a placating hand. "Our intentions were good, Jillian."

"Were they? She thinks you're trying to bribe her into taking her old job back."

"Bribe her? Well, no. We are willing to raise her salary if she'll come back."

"We really need her," Englebrite said. "We've tried out two new receptionists and a couple of temps since she left, and we're convinced no one can replace her."

"What about Dr. Coolidge?" Jillian asked.

Cusack said quickly, "Oh, Jason agrees. He couldn't come with us this afternoon— had a consult at the hospital—but he wants Kate back too. If you can think of anything that would convince her ..."

"Why would I do that? Kate and I are partners running the inn now. She loves it. She doesn't want to go back to the office. She's made that very clear. She also thinks it was really low of you to use our brother to abscond with her Jeep. She was furious when Rick explained it to her."

Dr. Cusack swallowed hard. "I'm sorry we caused her distress." He gave Englebrite a nervous glance. "Come on, Todd. We should leave."

His partner frowned. "Tell Kate we meant it as a good thing —a gift. And if she changes her mind—"

"She won't."

He nodded and turned on his heel.

Cusack scratched the back of his neck. "The keys are in it. Two sets, actually. And again, I apologize."

"I won't speak for Kate, but I accept your apology." Englebrite had started his car, and Jillian smiled tightly. "You'd better go, or he may leave you here."

She watched them pull out then went back inside. Kate was coming out of her office.

"I thought I saw Dr. Cusack out the window."

"Yeah, he and Englebrite just brought your Jeep back."

"Why didn't you tell me? I wanted to tell them off!"

Jillian chuckled and put her arm around Kate's shoulders. "That's why."

Kate gave her a rueful smile. "Right. Actually, I've been thinking about it, like you suggested."

Jillian's jaw dropped. "About going back?"

"No, no. But I thought maybe if I offered to go in for a couple of afternoons to train someone new, that would help them out and get them off my back."

"It's generous of you. I suppose it might be a solution."

Kate nodded. "I'll let them stew overnight and call them in the morning. What now?"

"I'm thinking we should consider some ads. With Emma gone, the Raynors are our only paying guests left, and they could leave any day. I guess they're staying tonight—I mean, they'd have checked out by noon if they were leaving today, right?"

"Presumably. That's the official checkout time."

Jillian nodded and sat down at her computer. She opened the reservations file. "There's that family of four that Andy booked coming Thursday, but up until then, we've got nothing. That's not enough to cover our expenses."

"And half our current guests aren't paying." Kate grimaced. "Do you think this is going to work, Jill?"

"You mean long-term? I certainly hope so. I liked teaching, but I don't want to go back to it now."

"Well, I'm sure not going back to the office."

Their eyes met and Jillian nodded. "Right. Ads it is, then."

"That's expensive."

"I know. I wonder if we could barter for it somehow. A free night at the inn in exchange for a box ad in the paper, something like that."

"Well, first you should find out how much those ads cost. And the local paper's been giving us plenty of publicity the last few days anyway. The Bangor paper, too, and Sandra Tipton told me she saw it on Saturday night's news about Danielle being kidnapped here, and on this morning's news about Terrence Isles going over the cliff. They didn't name him, I guess, but still ..."

"Not exactly the kind of publicity we want. And Edson seems to be on the run. Craig told me this morning they haven't been able to find him yet."

"They've got his truck, and his friend's van. What's he driving?"

"Possibly his friend's second vehicle. I don't know, but Craig said to be careful. There'll be more on the evening news. They'll probably highlight the fact that Danielle was found alive. Edson isn't going to like that."

"Man, all this cloak-and-dagger stuff," Kate said. "Maybe we're in the wrong business."

"What, we should be cops like Rick?"

"I was thinking private detectives."

"No way. But maybe we should change our room names to all detectives, to go along with Hercule Poirot. Zeb suggested a Sherlock Holmes room."

Kate's smile was back. "We could do Miss Marple and Lord Peter Wimsey."

"Campion and Stephanie Plum."

"No, I don't think so. It would narrow the market, not expand it. With the names we have now, we're hitting a huge cross section of readers. But I do think we should get rid of Anna Karenina."

"Why?" Jillian asked.

"Who reads Russian novels anymore? They're so depressing."

"Hmm. I hadn't thought of it that way. I kind of like Tolstoy. Speaking as a former English teacher, it gives us a literary air for serious folks, don't you think?"

"Maybe." Kate shrugged. "Anyway, I'm going to finish cleaning Emma's room."

"You don't think we should call Mindy in?"

"For one room? I thought you were trying to save money. Besides, I'm all done except for the bed and refilling the shampoo."

"Okay. Want help with the bed?"

"I can handle it." Kate strode off toward the linen closet.

She hadn't been gone a minute when the phone rang.

"Jillian? This is Bailey Redding," said a very youthful voice.

"Hello, Bailey! How is your mother doing?"

"That's why I called. She's awake."

"Oh, Bailey, that's wonderful."

"Yeah. My dad's in with her now. He asked me to call you and Emma."

"Did you get to see her?" Jillian asked.

"Uh-huh. She's still kind of out of it, but she knows who my dad and I are. The nurse said that's a really good sign."

"I'm sure it is. Listen, if Kate and I came over would we get to see her?"

"I don't think so—not yet. The doctor said one person at a time, and Officer Gage wants to talk to her."

"Oh, my brother is there?"

"Yeah, he just got back."

"Hmm." If Rick interviewed Danielle, maybe she could get some information out of him afterward. "Hey, maybe I could bring over some flowers, and you or your dad could take them into the room."

"Mom would probably like that."

"All right. I'll see you in a bit." Jillian replaced the receiver and thought about it for a moment. Then she called Kate's cell phone.

"Hey," Kate said. "What's up?"

"Danielle's awake. I thought maybe we'd take some flowers over."

"Well, I don't think they'll let us take flowers into the ICU."

"I'll bet you're right." Jillian frowned.

"But we should still go," Kate said. "Well, we can't both go. I mean, the Raynors are out for the afternoon. We can't just lock up and leave."

"One of us then. Do you want to go?" Jillian asked. "I can stay here on the desk and do some research on those ads we talked about."

"You sure?"

"Yes. Just don't forget when you get there to discreetly pump Rick for anything he's learned from Danielle, okay? Bailey said he's waiting to talk to her."

"Okay," Kate said. "Give me ten minutes to finish the room."

———

Kate found Bailey sitting in the waiting room outside the intensive care unit. She hurried to the girl, and Bailey jumped up when she saw her.

"Hey, Kate!"

Kate glanced around at the empty waiting room. "Is your dad in there now?"

"No, Officer Gage is. Dad went to get something to eat. He's going to bring me a sandwich and a drink."

"Oh, good." Kate sat down beside her.

"Dad is so happy. It's like he hadn't smiled since—well, forever. Since he left on his fishing trip, anyway. But now he's so happy. Wait until you see him."

"I'm glad."

"I don't think they'll let you in the room, though. They said only family for now. And the police, of course. Officer Gage has been really nice, and he thinks they'll find out who did this."

"That wouldn't surprise me. I know they're working awfully hard on it."

"He told my dad they're almost positive that dead guy on the beach was one of the men that kidnapped her."

Kate nodded. "That's what Jillian and I thought too. And that truck we found up on the cliff is probably the one the other man came along in when Danielle had her accident."

"Does it seem weird to you that it was a different guy driving the truck?" Bailey asked.

"Yeah, kind of. But Rick said they work together, so they're probably good friends. They could even be related, I suppose." Kate looked up as her brother walked into the waiting room and jumped up. "How is she?"

"Well, she's still a little addled, and they've given her painkillers, so she's kind of groggy." Rick looked at Bailey. "I guess you can go in now, unless your father wants to."

"He went to get lunch. I'll go in for a few minutes. Dad can come boot me out when he gets back."

Kate watched her go then turned to Rick.

"Spill it," she said.

Rick laughed. "Well, we've got a ways to go. She told me a few things, but she's not a hundred percent back to herself yet.

In fact, the doctor wanted me to wait, but I told him, the faster we wind this up the better."

"Okay. So sit down for a minute and tell me what she was able to tell you."

Rick glanced at his watch. "Five minutes. No more."

"I'll take it."

He eased down on one of the padded chairs, and Kate settled in next to him.

"She's mostly lucid, but very sleepy. I didn't have the heart to keep waking her up. She needs to rest."

"Does she remember the accident?"

"Not really. She remembers driving the rental car, and then waking up in some guy's pickup. I asked her if she could describe it, and she went all fuzzy on me. But she remembers the man. She said she was terrified to be in a moving vehicle with a complete stranger. She was afraid she was going to be raped."

"How awful for her."

"Yeah. But then she backtracked and said she remembered getting into his truck. She's still confused, I'm afraid. I guess she saw the motel sign at Oceanside and made him let her out there. She couldn't remember the name of the Novel Inn, but she didn't feel good, and she figured she'd rest a bit and then maybe she'd feel better. But she basically wanted to get away from Edson, to a place where she could lock the door and feel safe."

"Thank God he did let her out," Kate said.

"Yeah. In my opinion, if he'd thought about it longer, or if he'd talked to his buddy about it, he would never have let her go. She said he wanted to take her to the hospital, but when he told her it was in the next town, she said no. She was afraid he was trying to string her along so he could get her off somewhere, where he wouldn't be caught."

"Do you think he just didn't want to be blamed for the wreck?"

"I'm not sure. Right now I'm thinking he and his partner are behind all the antique thefts we've been having, or at least some of them. If she saw the drone and put two and two together, it could go hard on Edson and Isles. Anyway, he did stop at the motel and let her out of the car. She got inside the office, and it was too late then for him to do anything."

"But he and his friend came back in the morning to try to intercept her there with the van."

"I think so. And they followed Jillian home."

"That much was obvious. Did Danielle say anything else?"

"Uh, let's see, she got a candy bar and crackers and a Pepsi from the vending machine in the motel office. And she does remember them grabbing her at the inn, but she kept nodding off. I'll want to talk to her again later today or tomorrow morning. I want to know if she remembers where they took her when they kidnapped her. They didn't throw her over the cliff that morning. I could see restraint marks on her wrists. They held her somewhere."

"They must have," Kate said. "At least for the rest of the day. I hope you can find Edson."

"You, me, and everyone else. We're getting a search warrant for his house, and we've got a ton of cops looking for him." He checked his watch and stood. "I've gotta move."

"Okay. Hey, I got my Jeep back."

"Oh, good. Am I forgiven?"

She made a fierce face then let it morph into a smile. "I guess so." She reached for him.

Rick gave her a quick hug. "Thanks. Catch you later."

Danielle opened her eyes and squinted in the bright light. Slowly she turned her head. That was—yes—her daughter Bailey sat in a plastic chair next to her bed.

"Hey," she said. Her mouth was drier than if she'd eaten a spoonful of flour.

"Mom!" Bailey leaned close, grinning. "How are you doing?"

"Can you get me a drink?"

"Sure." Bailey stood and poured water from a pink plastic pitcher into a glass with a bent straw.

Danielle remembered that a police officer had been in to talk to her. Had she told him everything? She couldn't remember much about the conversation.

Bailey held the straw to her lips. "Need to sit up more?"

"No," Danielle whispered. She sucked in cold, refreshing water with only the faintest ambiance of plastic. She let the straw go and leaned back, exhausted.

"Kate Gage is here. She and Jillian are worried about you."

She couldn't process that, though she tried. "Who?"

"Oh, sorry. The ladies from the inn. Jillian is the one who picked you up at the motel the other day, and Kate is her sister."

"Motel ..." Bits and pieces swirled through her mind, but still her brain seemed out of sync with her body. "How's your father?"

Bailey sat down beside her. "He's okay, Mom. He went to get us some lunch. But he's a little bit on edge."

Danielle frowned and tried to focus on the girl. "Because of the car?"

"Well, that and the money."

"Money?"

"He found out you have an extra bank account he didn't

know about, and that upset him." Bailey's face was drawn, definitely worried.

Danielle tried to reach out to her, but plastic lines were attached to her wrist. "That's my motorcycle fund."

Her daughter's eyebrows shot up. "Whaaat?"

"I want to buy your dad a motorcycle, but not until I've saved up enough so we can pay cash for it."

Bailey huffed out a breath. "Wow."

"Don't you tell him."

"I think you'd better tell him, Mom. Soon. He knows about it."

"How did he find out?"

"The police were poking around, trying to find a reason someone would kidnap you. They looked at the bank accounts and phone records, things like that. And they told Dad about it."

"... A reason ..." The pieces fell into place then, and suddenly she was back in the warehouse, lying on the dusty floor, tied to the leg of a heavy breakfront. "Those men ..."

"What?" Bailey bent over her, staring into her eyes.

"Did they catch them?"

"No. Well, one of them—" Bailey stopped short. "Hold on." She dashed out of the room.

# 16

Bailey ran straight to Kate and grabbed her wrist.

"Where's Officer Gage? My mom is talking about those bad guys." Her eyes bulged.

"He just walked out. But I can catch him." Kate ran out into the hallway. Rick stood forty feet away, waiting for the elevator.

"Rick!"

When he looked toward her, Kate beckoned frantically. He strode quickly toward her.

"What's up?"

"Bailey wants you for her mom."

He walked ahead of Kate into the waiting room. "Bailey, what's going on?"

"I need you to talk to Mom again."

"Sure." He hurried with her into the hallway.

Kate followed cautiously as Rick accompanied Bailey back to the ICU. No one stopped her, and she all but tiptoed behind them to the door of Danielle's cubicle.

Rick told Bailey, "You'd better go back to the waiting room and tell your dad when he gets there."

"Okay." Bailey hurried past Kate, shooting her a sidelong glance but not speaking. Kate waited until Rick was inside the room. Apparently he hadn't noticed her or hadn't thought it was crucial to send her away. She stood in the open doorway, keeping an eye out for watchful nurses.

"Hey, Danielle," Rick said quietly, taking the chair next to the bed. "Are you feeling a little better?"

"I'm not sure." Danielle's voice was hoarse.

Rick reached for the water glass on the nightstand. "Water?"

Danielle nodded, and he held the cup so that she could capture the bent straw with her lips.

"Better?" he asked when she released it.

She nodded, and he put the glass aside.

"Bailey told me you were saying something about the men who kidnapped you on Saturday."

"Did you catch them?" Danielle asked.

Rick hesitated then said, "One of them was found. The other's not."

"Was it Bob?" she asked.

"Funny thing about Bob," Rick began, but she interrupted him.

"That's not his real name."

"Oh? How do you know?"

Danielle gave a little cough and reached toward the bedside table. Rick handed her a tissue. After a moment, she said softly, "I heard them talking. The other one called him Mark."

"That's right. His real name is Mark Edson. And the truck he used to take you to the motel is registered in his name."

"Why did he say his name was Bob? And why did they come after me?"

"We're still working on it," Rick said, "but I think I can answer your first question. He gave you a false name at the accident because he didn't want you to be able to identify him later. Danielle, we think Mark Edson caused your crash."

After a long moment, Danielle said, "On purpose?"

"No. I think it was truly an accident, but it may have been caused by his recklessness. Do you remember something hitting your windshield?"

Her brow wrinkled, and she squeezed her eyes nearly shut. "Sort of. Something smashed into me. My car."

"That's right."

"I thought I hit a tree or something. My sugar ..."

"Well, the car did hit a tree after it left the road, but we believe it did that because it was first impacted by a drone. It smashed your windshield and set off your airbag. That caused you to lose control, and the car swerved into a tree."

She was silent for several seconds. Blinking, she focused on Rick's face. "I didn't see any drone when I got out of the car. There was glass everywhere, though."

Rick nodded. "We're not positive, but here's what we think happened: the impact knocked you out for a few minutes, and the man who'd been operating the drone came along in his pickup, looking for it. He found it entangled with your car. He was able to get it out and put it in the back of his truck. Later we found a couple of small pieces of it in the truck bed. Then he approached you and asked if you were okay and offered to take you somewhere."

Her hand rose to her forehead, and she carefully fingered the bandage on her head. "The hospital. He offered to bring me here, I guess."

"Right. But he didn't, did he?"

"No. I ... I didn't trust him."

Rick took out his pocket notebook and pen. "What did you do instead of going to the hospital?"

"Let's see ... He mentioned a friend of his that lived nearby, but I wouldn't let him take me there. He was scaring me, and I just wanted to get out." She met Rick's gaze. "I saw a motel, and I told him I wanted to go there."

"Do you remember the name of the motel?"

"Not really. It was some awful little dive. The first place I saw. I had to get away from him."

"You were wise to do that," Rick said.

Danielle sighed. "I'd have been smarter to call the police right away, wouldn't I?"

He shrugged with an air of sympathy.

"I couldn't remember where I was supposed to end up, and I thought I'd just get something to eat and rest a bit and then, when I felt better, I'd call someone. I didn't think I was seriously hurt."

"I understand. Danielle, do you remember what happened later?"

"I think I slept the whole night, but I wasn't sure. I called the other hotel in the morning." She put a hand to her forehead with a grimace. I don't remember the name now, but someone came to get me. Your sister, you said?"

"That's right."

She let out a breath and nodded slowly. "She took me to the right hotel, and then ... He had a gun. Bob. Mark. He had a gun, I remember that."

"Do you remember anything else?"

"A van. Blue, I think. He wasn't driving, though." She frowned. "The other guy ..."

"Yes?"

"He had on a mask. A light blue one. A surgical-type mask.'

"Yes, that's what Jillian said too. Anything else? Take your time."

Danielle lay there for a moment in the propped-up bed, looking utterly lost.

"No. I think I must have fainted."

"You did, but it's okay. Now, I want you to think carefully. When you woke up, where were you?"

"I don't know." Her brow wrinkled. "Some sort of warehouse, I think. They talked about a store, though."

"Who talked about it?"

"Bob and the other man. Only he called Bob Mark."

"Good. Now, did you catch the other man's name?"

"I don't think so." The frown was back, as though she groped for something teasing her mind.

"What sort of things were around you in the warehouse?" Rick asked.

"Furniture. Boxes. All sorts of stuff. It looked like a storage room. Not a storage unit, it was bigger than that. But a place where they kept a lot of stuff. They had me tied up, and the rope was tied to the base of a big, old-fashioned cabinet."

Rick made a few notes. "Those two men owned an auction business together, and they also have—or had—an antique shop. Is there anything else you can tell me about where you were held? I'd like to be certain. I'm thinking I know where they kept you, but if you can tell me something specific that you saw, it may help us."

"I'm sorry. I was scared, and from the position I was in, I really couldn't see much. They were talking about getting rid of me and—and it sounded like maybe drugging me. Do you think that's what happened? I don't remember, but the next thing that's clear was when I woke up in the open air. I was cold and hurting. Someone dragged me over the ground."

Rick resumed his notes. "Good—I mean, it's good that you remember. What else? Was it daylight?"

"No. It was dark. I … heard waves breaking. I'm pretty sure that was it. Water noises. I tried to scream, but I couldn't. Then he was pushing me, shoving me sideways."

"Mark?"

"No, the other one. And all of a sudden I thought, 'He's going to push me into the ocean.' I don't know how I did it, but my foot slipped over the edge of a drop-off, and I grabbed his ankle—" She stopped, gazing past him into space.

"What, Danielle?"

"He must have untied me. No, not tied. They used those plastic zip ties. Anyway, I grabbed his ankle and hung on. He lost his balance, I guess, and went over the edge. I fell too. I thought I was going to die." She paused for a moment.

The horror Danielle had experienced washed over Kate, and she swiped at her tear-filled eyes.

"But you landed on a ledge," Rick said quietly.

"I guess so. I think I was out of it for a while. When I started to be aware, my head hurt something fierce. I was freezing. It was dark, and I could barely move. And then I realized I was on a narrow shelf and the water was way down below. I was terrified. The waves just went on and on, and I wondered if he'd fallen all the way down there, into the water." She put a bandaged hand to her side and grimaced.

"You have a couple of cracked ribs," Rick said.

"Yeah, the doctor told me. And cuts and bruises. But she said I'll get better."

He nodded.

"I was petrified I'd fall. I just tried to lie still, and I think I slept some," Danielle said. "Then I woke up again. I tried to yell, but I just couldn't." She looked up at him quickly, her lips parted.

"What?" Rick asked.

"It was daylight then. And I was afraid to try to sit up or move much. But I tried to work my way as much as I could away from the edge. There was a little niche in the rocks, a kind of crease, and I stuck my head and shoulders in there." She sighed. "That's about all I remember. I don't know how long I was there."

"That's okay. You've done well. We think you may have been there twenty-four hours or so. And I'm sorry we didn't find you sooner."

"It's not your fault." She swallowed hard. "Can I see Paul and Bailey now?"

"Of course, if you're up to it."

"I'm tired, but I want to see them again."

"Sure. I'll tell them you're asking for them. Thank you, Mrs. Redding."

Rick walked quietly toward the door. He raised his eyebrows at Kate, and she tiptoed into the hall and waited for him. They fell into step together.

"You heard?" he asked.

"Yeah. That was quite an ordeal."

"We're gonna get Edson."

"I know you will." She slipped her arm around her brother as they walked toward the waiting room.

———

That evening Jillian called the hospital and learned that Danielle had been moved from the ICU into a semi-private room and would most likely be discharged the next day. She picked a bouquet of white lilacs and tulips from her mother's garden and left Kate to mind the inn while she drove to the hospital. She hurried to the new room and joined Bailey and Paul at Danielle's bedside.

"Those are pretty," Bailey said when she saw the flowers.

"They're beautiful," Danielle said. She frowned slightly. "I think you're Jillian."

"Yes. You look much better, but are you sure you're ready to leave?" she asked.

"I can't wait to get out of here," Danielle replied.

Paul looked up at her apologetically. "We thought we'd stay at the inn a couple more nights, if we're not in the way."

Jillian almost laughed, since only one room was occupied besides the Reddings'. "Of course. Stay as long as you like."

"Well, we figured Dani would rest better there than here in the hospital, but we don't want to hit the road right away. Home's about four or five hours' drive."

Jillian nodded.

"We can pay for the room if—"

She held up a hand to stop him. "Nope. I told you, those rooms are yours as long as you need them. And to be honest, since you're providing your own meals, it hardly costs us a thing to have you stay a bit longer." She made a mental note to talk with Kate again about the low occupancy rate. If they wanted to make a go of the inn, they'd have to do something soon about advertising, and she'd come up with a few possible avenues but hadn't finalized anything.

"Thank you," Danielle said. "And thanks for the beautiful flowers. Are they from your own garden?"

"My mother's garden, actually. She was much more of a green thumb than I am, and her flowers have really cheered me up this spring."

Danielle nodded. "I'm sorry I missed the reunion. It would have been nice to see all the girls again."

"Well, that Mickey guy's still in town," Bailey said saucily.

"Mickey? Oh, yeah, Mickey Holt."

"Who is he, anyway?" Paul asked with only a bit of an edge to his voice.

Danielle smiled. "He was a friend in high school. We actually went out for a while senior year."

"He said you mentioned some unfinished business." Paul wasn't smiling, and Jillian wondered if she ought to leave the room.

"Oh, that." Danielle laughed. "I was rummaging in the attic a couple of weeks ago, and I realized I still had his letter sweater and I wanted to return it. I'm sure it means a lot more to him than it does to me now."

"How come I've never heard of this guy before?" Bailey nearly shouted.

Paul shook his head. "I had no idea you had some other guy's letter sweater."

"It means nothing." Danielle laid her hand on his wrist, and Paul grasped it.

"Did you bring it with you?" Bailey asked.

"It was in my suitcase."

"An officer dropped your luggage off at the inn this afternoon," Jillian said with a smile. "You can mail it to Mickey after you get home."

"Well, since you were planning to buy me a motorcycle, I guess we can overlook that." Paul gave his wife a sheepish smile.

Danielle shifted and hit the button on the bed rail to raise her head a little more. "I wasn't going to tell you until I had enough, but I'm kind of glad you know now. I've been putting away a little here and there for the last two years, hoping one day we'd have enough to do it without going into debt." She sighed. "I had over a thousand at one point, but I had to dip into it when the refrigerator went bust."

"That doesn't matter right now," Paul said. "What matters is that you're safe."

"And you're going to be okay," Bailey added.

Danielle smiled. "Yeah. We're going to be okay."

A short time later, Jillian left and drove back to the inn. Only one car sat in the front parking area. A rainstorm was predicted, and the sky was already dark with no stars peeking through. She decided to drive on down to the carriage house and leave her Taurus in the garage.

She hit the remote, and the door ran up. After she rolled inside next to Kate's Jeep and turned off the engine, she opened her door to climb out. Just as she swung it to, she realized she wasn't alone.

# 17

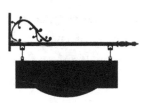

Mark Edson walked in and approached Jillian between the two vehicles. Down beside the leg of his jeans, he held something that glinted of metal. Rick had told her they'd found a .38-caliber pistol in his house. Did he have another gun?

She stared at his hand and realized he held a tool. Not just any tool. He held the hatchet they used to split sticks of kindling off firewood logs for the fireplaces. How did he get hold of that? Had she or Kate left it outside? Or had he brought along his own tools and this only resembled their hatchet?

"I see you found your car keys," he said.

She jerked her gaze from the hatchet to his face. "Yes, Mr. Edson."

"You know who I am."

"Of course I do. Everyone in Maine knows who you are now. The police are looking for you, in case you didn't hear."

"Oh, I heard."

He took a step toward her, and she backed up. Would he kill her here, in the garage? Maybe. He must realize by now that

237

he'd made a huge mistake in letting Danielle out of his sight in the first place, and then in letting Jillian see his face. Maybe she could rattle him.

"Tomorrow your face will be plastered all over the TV news and every newspaper in the state."

"Oh, really?" He spoke casually, as if that didn't bother him a bit.

She shuffled back another step, edging toward her father's workbench. Rick took some of Dad's tools, but most of them were still here in the garage. If she could get hold of a hammer, say, or a heavy wrench ... How much farther? She was even with the Taurus's front bumper. It couldn't be more than a couple of feet to the bench.

Edson took another step toward her and hefted the hatchet. Jillian's chest tightened, and she sucked in a painful breath. Was she kidding herself? She'd never stop him. There must be something she could do!

"She's alive, you know."

He froze. "Who?"

"Danielle Redding," Jillian said.

"Terry threw her over a cliff. He fell too."

"That's the story the police put out."

"What do you mean?"

"Danielle did fall," Jillian said slowly, drawing out the sentence, "but she landed on a ledge. She's alive, and she's told the police everything. What you did to her." She hoped she wasn't putting Danielle in further danger, but at the moment anything that would save her own life was paramount.

She eased back a little farther, and the edge of the workbench brushed her back, just above her belt. Slowly she moved her hand behind her and up. What would be lying there? Had they been too neat and hung up all the tools they'd used recently?

"Jill?" Kate said from the darkness beyond the open garage door. "Hey, I saw you drive in. What's up?"

Edson flinched. His mouth closed in a thin line, but he didn't turn around.

Jillian's fingers found a cylindrical handle only half an inch or so in diameter. She didn't dare take her eyes off Edson to look beyond him, but she said, "Kate, stay back."

Her sister didn't reply. She must see the man and realize who he was.

Jillian forced herself to concentrate on the tool behind her. She leaned back a bit, and her hand closed around it. The cool plastic handle was grooved, and she had a mental image of the screwdriver she'd used a few days earlier to tighten the hair dryer holder in the Rip Van Winkle Room's bath. She'd been in a hurry when she returned it.

Slowly, deliberately, Edson lifted the hatchet chest high, then shoulder high.

"What are you going to do?" Jillian's voice trembled. "You'll have to kill my sister too. That's a bit excessive, don't you think?"

"What difference does it make now?"

Kate's voice, firm and clear, reached them. "This is Kate Gage. Send police to the Novel Inn right away. And an ambulance."

Jillian swung both hands up, her left to deflect Edson's arm with the hatchet as much as possible, and her right to thrust the screwdriver into him.

Her block slowed the hatchet, and it gave a glancing blow to her shoulder. Pain seared through her arm and shoulder as she shoved him away hard and let go of the screwdriver. Its yellow plastic handle stuck incongruously from his torso, just left of center. Blood seeped through his gray Colby College T-shirt.

"Jill! Get away from him."

Jillian was vaguely aware of Kate's shrill cry echoing from the rafters.

Edson let out a slur and pitched forward. Jillian jumped out of the way, and he grabbed the edge of the workbench. As Kate reached her, the hatchet fell to the concrete floor, thumping Jillian's little toe through her shoe. She grimaced and backed away, her heart pounding. She swooped in to grab the hatchet handle as Edson went to his knees, pulling in horrible wheezes.

"Kate!" She was shaking all over.

"I'm here." Kate grabbed her hand and yanked her back between the cars. "They're on the way. What?" she said into her phone. "Oh, Tracie, is that you?" She smiled then sobered as she answered a question from the dispatcher. "My sister was attacked in our garage. The man had an axe. She stuck him with something, and he needs medical attention fast. Can I hang up? All right." She made a face at Jillian and mouthed, "She says hang on."

"You know the dispatcher?" Jillian whispered, keeping an eye on Edson. Her head whirled. This whole thing was crazy. How could Kate be so calm?

"Yeah," Kate said. "She works in the call center."

Edson sprawled on his side, one hand clutching the screwdriver's handle.

Jillian's heart wrenched. What had she done? "Can't we do something?" She turned to Kate, hoping she'd have a solution to the entire harrowing situation.

"They're coming. Can you hear the siren?"

She could, actually. The wail grew louder even as she became aware of it. "But ... he might die."

"And he'd have killed you if you hadn't defended yourself." Kate put an arm around her shoulders. "There's nothing we can do. Let's step outside." She put her phone back to her ear. "Tracie? Tell them to drive around the inn and down to the house in the back."

Jillian let Kate guide her out of the garage. The sirens were loud now, and flashing blue lights seeped around the edges of the inn's silhouette. A moment later the blue lights went out and harsh white ones swept over them as the first police vehicle rolled down the gravel drive to the carriage house. It had barely stopped when Rick leaped out the passenger door. Geordie Kraus followed more slowly after parking.

"Who's on the front desk?" Jillian asked.

Kate eyed her as if she was crazy. "Don just got in before I came down here."

The night desk clerk. "We should have told him and the guests," Jillian said.

"I'll call him now." Kate said to the dispatcher, "Tracie? They're here. I'm hanging up."

"What happened?" Rick demanded.

Jillian found she couldn't speak. She pointed inside the garage, and her brother charged inside.

Geordie approached her more tentatively and looked her up and down. "Are you okay?"

"Yes," Jillian said.

Kate stepped away, talking on the phone, and bits of her conversation reached Jillian. "Yeah, don't worry ... please do tell them ... Rick's here now."

The town's squad car and an ambulance rolled up before the garage.

"I think you're bleeding," Geordie said.

"What?" Jillian asked.

He pointed toward her collar.

"Right. He hit me with the hatchet." She looked down and

realized she still held it. With numb hands, she held it out to Geordie. "Here. My prints are all over it, but he swung it at me."

"You'd better sit down, Jillian. Come on, let's get you over to the ambulance and let the EMTs take a look at you."

She let him take her arm and walk her toward the ambulance, but Rick was already yelling for the EMTs to hurry inside.

"I'll stay with her," Kate said.

Geordie nodded and strode toward the garage.

"What if I've killed him?" Jillian looked helplessly at Kate.

"Then we'll deal with it. Here, sit down." The back of the ambulance was open, and Kate pushed her gently to a seat on the steps. "I don't think your wound is too serious, but let me take a look."

Jillian pulled her sweater and the collar of her blouse aside.

Kate bent close and squinted in the light from inside the vehicle.

"It doesn't look too deep, but your blouse may be ruined. Let me get something to put over it, so you don't get blood everywhere." She squeezed past Jillian and opened and closed cupboards inside without compunction.

Jillian bowed her head and cradled it in her hands. She hurt now. He must have slashed the muscle on her shoulder.

"Here we go." Kate scrambled down to the ground and tore open a package of gauze. She pressed a pad against the wound, and Jillian sucked air through her teeth. "You many need stitches."

"Can you find out how bad off he is?"

Kate scowled at her. "I don't care how bad off he is. He tried to kill you." Tears glinted suddenly in her eyes, and she grabbed Jillian's hand and squeezed it. "I didn't know what to do. I felt like I should whack him over the head, but I didn't have anything handy. All the shovels and hammers were way at the other end of the garage, near you. All I had was my phone, so I called 911."

"It worked. It was enough of a distraction."

"Oh, Jill!" Suddenly Kate was sobbing. Jillian put her arms around her, and they held each other and wept.

———

Rick came out of the garage and strode straight to where his sisters huddled.

"She needs to go to the hospital," Kate said. "Should I take her? I mean, they need the ambulance for—"

"I'll take her." Rick put a hand firmly under Jillian's elbow. "Up you go, Sis."

"Don't you need to stay here?" she asked.

"Craig's on the way, and Geordie can handle it until he gets here. They're going to load Edson quick and take him to the hospital, and I need to go there anyway, so I can talk to him the minute he's able."

"He'll be okay then?" Jillian blinked up at him.

The small yard in front of the carriage house was crammed with emergency vehicles, and the lights cast Rick's face in odd relief, then dropped shadows over him.

"We don't know yet."

"I can wait—"

"Nope. Kate says you need stitches, and I believe her." He shoved her gently along to the police SUV.

"Do I have to ride in the back?"

"You're special. You can sit up front with me. Just try not to bleed on anything."

She climbed in and grimaced as she fumbled for the seat belt.

"Let me do that." Rick found the latch and clicked it with

ease then went around to the driver's side. He handed her a clean handkerchief. "Here, just in case you need it."

Kate was already walking up the driveway to the inn, and Jillian lifted a hand as they passed her. She hoped the guests weren't too upset. Poor Don. He'd probably had a million inquiries.

The twenty-minute ride was drenched in haze.

"Here we are."

She jerked her head up, unable to believe she'd dozed off. Or had she lost consciousness for a few minutes? Rick came around to help her down. The movement in her shoulder sent stabbing pain through her chest and down her arm.

"Easy."

She climbed slowly out of the SUV, into Rick's supporting grip. She'd never known her brother to be so tender.

The dispatcher had called ahead, and a team burst out from the ER entrance with a gurney.

"Mrs. Tunney?" the nurse in the front asked.

"That's right," Rick said.

Jillian could hear the ambulance's siren now. It cut off as the vehicle turned into the hospital's parking lot. She grimaced with pain as the nurses settled her on the gurney, but it was a relief to be able to lie back and do nothing but breathe.

No waiting room tonight. They whisked her right into an exam room.

"Let's take a look." A nurse carefully removed Rick's handkerchief and the gauze Kate had put in place. Jillian was surprised to see how much of her blood had soaked it. She felt a little muddled, but it didn't matter. She was lying flat on her back.

"What are you smiling about?" Rick asked.

She hadn't realized he'd come into the room with them, and she focused on his face. "I can't collapse. I'm in bed."

"Oh, yeah, that's real funny."

She could hear commotion out in the emergency unit as the ambulance's passenger was brought in.

"Okay, the doctor will have to take a look at that," the nurse said. "I'm going to put some more gauze on it because it's still oozing."

Jillian cringed and caught her breath as the new bandage was applied.

"Sorry. We'll give you something for the pain after the doctor sees you."

"Will someone stitch me up?" Jillian asked.

"Probably, but they'll want to evaluate the damage to the muscle first."

Oh, great, Jillian thought.

"I'm going to give Kate a call," Rick said.

"And check on Edson's status?"

He gave her a chagrined smile. "You know me too well. You okay?"

"Yeah, I'm good. Take your time." She closed her eyes.

# 18

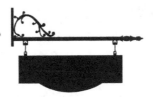

*Two days later*

"Megan! You made it!" Kate hugged her niece in the lobby. "Where's your luggage?"

"In the car. I wasn't sure where you were putting me. Mom was a little vague."

"Well, we thought we'd give you your pick of the rooms up here. Unless you'd like to take my room in the carriage house, and I'll sleep up here."

"Oh no, I don't want to put you out." Megan leaned toward her. "Besides, I've always wanted to sleep in the Galadriel Room—if it's available."

"It certainly is. Let me help you bring your bags in, and I'll take you up."

"Where's Mom?" Megan asked as they strolled out to her ten-year-old Fusion.

"I insisted she rest this morning. We only had a few guests, so I handled breakfast on my own."

Megan frowned. "You're going to have to give me the scoop

on what's been happening here. I know Mom didn't tell me everything. Is she really okay?"

"Yes, she's fine. She's got a little nick on her shoulder, but they stitched her up. She's just a little sore."

Kate waited while Megan opened the trunk of her car and then she reached in for the largest bag. "Once you're settled, you can go down to the house if you want. She's excited that you're coming today."

Megan lifted out another bag and shut the trunk. "I wasn't going to come until Saturday, but I finished my last exam this morning, and frankly, I was worried about her. I did a little Web surfing last night, and those guys were nasty!"

"They were. But Jillian's going to be fine, I promise. She can tell you all about it. And we've invited Rick and Diana and the kids over for supper tonight. We can all eat in the inn's dining room, so we'll have plenty of space."

"Yeah, that dining area in the carriage house is pretty small." Megan wheeled her suitcase to the steps and lifted it to the porch, ignoring the ramp to one side.

Kate took her inside and swiped a card to code it for Room 4, then guided Megan to the elevator. They got off on the second floor and turned left.

"Galadriel has a shared bath with the Virginian Room, but nobody's in there now," she said. "There are separate powder rooms, but the bath area has doors on each side that you can lock from inside to be sure no one comes in by mistake."

"Great."

Kate inserted the key card and pushed the door open, letting Megan enter first.

"Oh, wow. I'd forgotten how magical this room was. I haven't been in it since Grandma showed it to me once, a couple of years ago. I fell in love with it then."

"It's one of my favorites too." Kate opened the small closet and rolled the larger suitcase inside. "There's a luggage rack in here, and you can use the dresser. Coffee's there on the table, and there's a small microwave, but we hope you'll eat most of your meals with us."

"This is great. Thanks so much, Aunt Kate." Megan moved in for a hug.

"Take your time," Kate said. "I'll be down on the front desk."

———

Jillian looked down the table, thrilled to have her entire family with her. She and Rick had put aside their differences, and since Edson had attacked her, he hadn't lectured her once on letting the police handle the investigating. Diana looked gorgeous in a new sweater the color of her blue eyes, and their two children, Ashley and Joel, were on their best behavior tonight.

But Megan was the guest of honor. Kate must have cooked all afternoon, preparing Parmesan chicken, loaded baked potatoes, and salad. The delicious meal was followed by apple pie Diana had baked and ice cream. Jillian felt as though she'd just finished a Thanksgiving dinner.

"I couldn't eat another bite, but everything was delicious." She turned her appreciative gaze on Kate and Diana.

"It sure was," Megan said. "I'd say my aunts cook nearly as well as Grandma used to."

"Time for coffee?" Rick asked hopefully. He was out of uniform tonight, wearing a casual shirt and Dockers. He looked more relaxed than Jillian had seen him in weeks.

Kate jumped up. "I'll get it. Why don't you all go sit in the living room? We can clear the table later."

"I'll help you." Megan rose, and just as she reached for a serving dish, the doorbell rang.

"And I'll get that," Rick said.

"If it's reporters, get rid of them," Jillian told him. They'd had more than enough of the press over the past few days. There'd been no hiding the fact that the town's entire police force and ambulance crew had descended on them Tuesday, and they'd become quite glib at saying, "You'll have to ask Chief Clement about that."

She and Diana walked into the big living room where the windows overlooked the carriage house and the bay beyond.

"Mom, can we go up to the game room?" Ashley asked. She and her brother loved playing the old-fashioned board games that stocked the shelves there.

"Ask Aunt Jillian."

"Of course you may," Jillian said. "Just please be quiet. We do have a few guests on the third level."

"We won't be noisy," Ashley said.

Joel smirked. "Unless she cheats."

"No cheating and no yelling," Diana said firmly.

"Hey, Dad said this place has a secret room." Joel eyed his Aunt Jillian hopefully.

"This is not the time," his mother said. "Skedaddle."

As the children scurried for the curving stairway that led from the lobby up to the landing by the door to the game room, Rick came in carrying a bouquet of tulips and iris.

"Oh, lovely," Jillian said.

Kate came tromping behind her brother, her face twisted. "If those are from Coastal Family Practice, throw them away!"

"Uh-uh-uh." Rick held the flowers over his head and turned around to face her. "Don't be so feisty."

"I told those guys I'd had it! I'm going to march over there tomorrow morning and make a scene right in the waiting room. I'll tell them what I think of them—in front of everyone!"

"Easy, now." Rick lowered the bouquet and fingered the small envelope nestled among the stems. "This delivery is not for you."

"Oh." Nonplussed, Kate stepped back and said grudgingly, "Well, they're pretty. Who are they for?"

Rick looked up and grinned at his older sister. "Jillian."

"What?" Stunned, she rose and walked toward him. "Oh, they're beautiful." She gingerly took the small envelope, and a comforting thought struck her. "I'll bet Emma sent them. She's so thoughtful."

She opened the flap and slid the card out. On a creamy card from the florist's shop with a violet in the corner, the words were written in black ink. "Jillian—I hope you're feeling better. Thanks so much for all your help. Craig." Her jaw dropped.

"Well?" Kate demanded.

Rick, reading over Jillian's shoulder, grinned. "Just a little token of appreciation from the SCPD." He gave her a surreptitious wink.

Kate's brow furrowed. "The Skirmish Cove Police Department. Since when do they budget for flowers?"

"I guess you'll have to ask Sergeant Watkins about that. Jillian, where do you want these?"

"Uh ... leave them on the end table for now. I'll take them to my office later." She smiled brightly at Rick. "Didn't you want coffee?"

"I'd love some, but I'll get it." He set the vase on the table and went out to the beverage bar. A minute later, he brought several full mugs into the living room on a tray.

Megan accepted a cup and smiled at Rick. "Mom and Aunt Kate are buying ads for the inn."

"Oh yeah?" he walked over to Jillian and Diana and lowered the tray for them.

"Yes, the first ones ran today," Jillian said. "We've already had two calls, and next week we're running two more ads."

"We're bartering for them." Kate grinned and took a mug. "It was Jillian's brilliant idea. We're hoping that by Memorial Day, we're booked solid for the month of June."

"That's a bit optimistic, but yeah." Jillian sipped her coffee.

"So, Megan," Diana said, "I understand you'll be with us at least a week. What are your plans?"

Megan smiled sheepishly. "First I intend to sleep a lot. And Mom mentioned cleaning an attic."

Rick laughed and took the last mug. "Sounds like a blast."

"No, really," Jillian said. "Mom and Dad left a lot of stuff in the attic at the carriage house, and we haven't touched it yet."

"Then there's the attic here," Kate said. "It has quite a lot of old furniture and kitchen utensils. Old artwork from the guest rooms, even. We've poked around a little up there, but honestly, I think we're going to have to organize a huge yard sale."

"What fun!" Diana's eyes sparkled. "I'll help."

"Thanks," Jillian said. "It may take us a while to get ready, but I thought we'd at least make a start while Megan's here."

"I've been thinking," Kate said. "We ought to name the attic, like the other rooms are named."

"Something like Atticus Finch?" Megan said.

"No, no, we've already got Scout Finch," Jillian said in protest. If Kate and Megan kept on with this theme, things could get wild.

"Flowers in the Attic?" Kate said.

Rick scowled at her as he sat down beside Diana. "That's not a name."

"How about Uriah Heep?" Megan suggested. "With all those heaps of stuff up there."

Jillian held up both hands. "Please. No more attic names. I'm not ready for that."

"Yeah, you're supposed to be taking it easy." Rick threw her a look that reminded Jillian decidedly of her father.

"What's the word on the man who attacked Mom?" Megan asked with a sympathetic glance toward Jillian.

"Mark Edson?" Rick asked. "He'll live. His right lung was collapsed, but he's improving. I'd say he'll be out of the hospital just about in time for his arraignment."

"They won't let him loose, will they?" Jillian asked, not liking the fear that swept over her, making her hand tremble for a moment.

"Not for a good long time," Rick said. "Between Jillian's testimony and Danielle Redding's, I'd say he's going away for quite a stretch."

"That's good." Kate lifted her mug of coffee. "Here's to a peaceful and prosperous summer for the Novel Inn."

"Hear, hear," Rick said heartily.

Jillian smiled and raised her mug to her lips.

The end

# ABOUT SUSAN PAGE DAVIS

*Cliffhanger* is Susan Page Davis's one hundredth published novel. Her books include Christian novels and novellas in the historical romance, mystery, and romantic suspense genres. Her work has won several awards, including the Carol Award, two Will Rogers Medallions, and two Faith, Hope, & Love Reader's Choice Awards. She has also been a finalist in the WILLA Literary Awards and a multi-time finalist in the Carol Awards. A Maine native, Susan has lived in Oregon and now resides in western Kentucky with her husband Jim, a retired news editor. They are the parents of six and grandparents of eleven. Visit her website at: https://susanpagedavis.com.

# ALSO BY SUSAN PAGE DAVIS

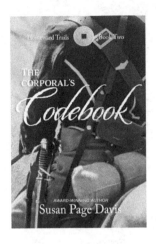

### *The Corporal's Codebook*

### Homeward Trails - Book Two

*Historical Romance*

Jack Miller stumbles through the Civil War, winding up a telegrapher and cryptographer for the army. In the field with General Sherman in Georgia, he is captured along with his precious cipher key.

His captor, Hamilton Buckley, thinks he should have been president of the Confederacy, not Jefferson Davis. Jack doubts Buckley's sanity and longs to escape. Buckley's kindhearted niece, Marilla, might help him—but only if Jack helps her achieve her own goal.

Meanwhile, a private investigator, stymied by the difficulty of travel and communication in wartime, is trying his best to locate Jack for the grandmother he longs to see again but can barely remember.

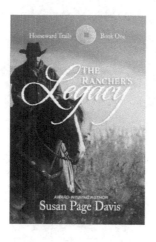

### *The Rancher's Legacy*

### Homeward Trails - Book One

*Historical Romance*

Matthew Anderson and his father try to help neighbor Bill Maxwell when his ranch is attacked. On the day his daughter Rachel is to return from school back East, outlaws target the Maxwell ranch. After Rachel's world is shattered, she won't even consider the plan her father and Matt's cooked up—to see their two children marry and combine the ranches.

Meanwhile in Maine, sea captain's widow Edith Rose hires a private investigator to locate her three missing grandchildren. The children were abandoned by their father nearly twenty years ago. They've been adopted into very different families, and they're scattered across the country. Can investigator Ryland Atkins find them all while the elderly woman still lives? His first attempt is to find the boy now called Matthew Anderson. Can Ryland survive his trip into the wild Colorado Territory and find Matt before the outlaws finish destroying a legacy?

*Blue Plate Special*

*by Susan Page Davis*

**Book One of the True Blue Mysteries Series**

Campbell McBride drives to her father's house in Murray, Kentucky, dreading telling him she's lost her job as an English professor. Her father, private investigator Bill McBride, isn't there or at his office in town. His brash young employee, Nick Emerson, says Bill hasn't come in this morning, but he did call the night before with news that he had a new case.

When her dad doesn't show up by late afternoon, Campbell and Nick decide to follow up on a phone number he'd jotted on a memo sheet. They learn who last spoke to her father, but they also find a dead body. The next day, Campbell files a missing persons report. When Bill's car is found, locked and empty in a secluded spot, she and Nick must get past their differences and work together to find him.

*Ice Cold Blue*

*by Susan Page Davis*

**Book Two of the True Blue Mysteries Series**

Campbell McBride is now working for her father Bill as a private investigator in Murray, Kentucky. Xina Harrison wants them to find out what is going on with her aunt, Katherine Tyler.

Katherine is a rich, reclusive author, and she has resisted letting Xina visit her for several years. Xina arrived unannounced, and Katherine was upset and didn't want to let her in. When Xina did gain entry, she learned Katherine fired her longtime housekeeper. She noticed that a few family heirlooms previously on display have disappeared. Xina is afraid someone is stealing from her aunt or influencing her to give them her money and valuables. True Blue accepts the case, and the investigators follow a twisting path to the truth.

# COMING SOON FROM SUSAN PAGE DAVIS

### *The Sister's Search*

### Homeward Trails - Book Three

### Coming in July 2022

*Historical Romance*

*A young woman searches for her missing brother and finds much more awaits her—if she can escape war-torn Texas.*

Molly Weaver and her widowed mother embark on an arduous journey at the end of the Civil War. They hope to join Molly's brother Andrew on his ranch in Texas. When they arrive, Andrew is missing and squatters threaten the ranch. Can they trust Joe, the stranger who claims to be Andrew's friend? Joe's offer to help may be a godsend—or a snare. And who is the man claiming to be Molly's father? If he's telling the truth, Molly's past is a sham, and she must learn where she really belongs.

———

**Persian Blue Puzzle**

**True Blue Investigations - Book Three**

**Coming in April 2022**

*Mystery*

Someone's broken into Miss Louanne's house. Campbell McBride and her father Bill have moved their home and detective business into an old Victorian house. Their new neighbors bring in unexpected cases for True Blue Investigations to unravel.

While helping Miss Louanne look for her missing cat, Campbell learns of other suspicious activities in Murray. Another neighbor tells the detectives about a stranger in town who's peddling an investment plan. They aren't sure any crimes have been committed, but they're intrigued enough for Campbell to visit a psychic along with police detective Keith Fuller's mom and to start checking up on the financier. Things heat up when a customer threatens the psychic and then she vanishes.

Scrivenings
PRESS
Quench your thirst for story.
www.ScriveningsPress.com

*Stay up-to-date on your favorite books and authors with our free e-newsletters.*

ScriveningsPress.com

9 781649 171856